Aurin M. Payson, Albert Laighton

The Poets of Portsmouth.

Aurin M. Payson, Albert Laighton

The Poets of Portsmouth.

ISBN/EAN: 9783337156312

Printed in Europe, USA, Canada, Australia, Japan

Cover: Foto ©Andreas Hilbeck / pixelio.de

More available books at **www.hansebooks.com**

THE

POETS OF PORTSMOUTH.

COMPILED BY

AURIN M. PAYSON AND ALBERT LAIGHTON.

Sweet are the memories of Home.

BOSTON:

WALKER, WISE, AND COMPANY.

PORTSMOUTH: JOS. H. FOSTER.

1865.

BOSTON:

PRINTED BY JOHN WILSON AND SON,

No. 15, Water Street.

TO THE

Sons and Daughters of Portsmouth, N.H.,

AT HOME AND ABROAD,

THIS VOLUME IS DEDICATED

BY THE COMPILERS.

PREFACE.

In offering this volume to the public, while we would put forth no extravagant claims in its behalf, we cannot deny that we regard it as indicating a high average order of taste, sentiment, culture, and poetical ability in the writers. It must be remembered, that, of the entire number, not more than four or five have placed themselves prominently before the world as candidates for fame; that most of them have made poetry their pastime, and not even one among their occupations; and that the pieces now gathered were, for the most part, literally fugitive pieces, — some written with no view to publication, others prepared only for the brief life which the weekly or daily newspaper might give them. Yet, among these last, there are not a few which the public will not let die.

It will be seen that all but two of the poets here represented belong to the present generation, and that

the greater part of them are still living. Dr. HAVEN
and JONATHAN MITCHELL SEWALL were the only
Portsmouth poets of the last century whose collected
poems have come down to us ; nor can we add to the
list, from any tradition that has reached us. But the
last half-century has been throughout a period of great
literary activity in our community. Not to speak of the
elder among our living poets, to whom we trust like
praise will be rendered at some distant day, Portsmouth was greatly indebted to NATHANIEL APPLE-
TON HAVEN for the impulse given in every direction
of high culture, and especially for the institution and
successful management of at least two literary socie-
ties, by whose exercises the habit of composition was
invited and cultivated, while, at the same time, a dis-
criminating taste received its development and educa-
tion. In later years, two chronic invalids, sufferers
beyond measure, with minds only the brighter and
clearer for the severe ordeal, — JAMES KENNARD, jun.,
and CAROLINE ELIZABETH JENNESS, — were largely
influential in creating and directing literary ambition ;
they themselves beguiling else weary months of seclu-
sion from the outward world by book and pen, and
inspiring in the numerous friends that sought their
society the desire for kindred pursuits. To others of
the departed, we would gladly offer the meed of grateful eulogy ; and we regret that we cannot, without
violating conventional propriety, express our friendly

and high appreciation of those of the living whose intimacy has been our privilege and pleasure. We send the book forth with satisfaction and pride, and can ask nothing better than that our city may be judged by its poets.

A. P. P.

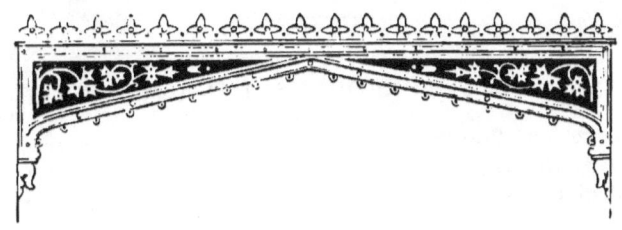

CONTENTS.

MARY CUTTS.

SAMUEL M. DEMERITT.

DANIEL A. DROWN.

JAMES T. FIELDS.

WOODBURY M. FERNALD.

SARAH H. FOSTER.

FANNIE E. FOSTER.

REV. SAMUEL HAVEN, D.D.

NATHANIEL APPLETON HAVEN.

ALBERT LAIGHTON.

BENJAMIN D. LAIGHTON.

MARY E. B. MILLER.

THOMAS P. MOSES.

JOHN N. MOSES.

JAMES R. MAY.

CATHERINE M. McCLINTOCK.

EDWARD P. NOWELL.

MRS. C. E. R. PARKER.

MRS. C. E. R. PARKER (*continued*).

MRS. ADELAIDE E. M. PARKER.

AURIN M. PAYSON.

EDWARD A. RAND.

JONATHAN M. SEWALL.

MRS. C. E. WHITON (*continued*).

MRS. JULIA VAN NESS WHIPPLE.

S. ADAMS WIGGIN.

POETS OF PORTSMOUTH.

POETS OF PORTSMOUTH.

THOMAS BAILEY ALDRICH.

PISCATAQUA RIVER.

HOU singest by the gleaming isles,
   By woods and fields of corn ;
Thou singest, and the heaven smiles
   Upon my birthday morn.

But I, within a city, — I,
   So full of vague unrest, —
Would almost give my life to lie
   An hour upon thy breast ;

To let the wherry listless go,
   And, wrapped in dreamy joy,
Dip, and surge idly to and fro,
   Like the red harbor-buoy !

1

To sit in happy indolence,
   To rest upon the oars,
And catch the heavy earthy scents
   That blow from summer shores;

To see the rounded sun go down,
   And with its parting fires
Light up the windows of the town,
   And burn the tapering spires;

And then to hear the muffled tolls
   From steeples slim and white;
And watch, among the Isles of Shoals,
   The Beacon's orange light.

O River, flowing to the main
   Through woods and fields of corn!
Hear thou my longing and my pain,
   This sunny birthday morn;

And take this song which sorrow shapes
   To music like thine own,
And sing it to the cliffs and capes
   And crags where I am known.

BEFORE THE RAIN.

We knew it would rain; for, all the morn,
   A spirit, on slender ropes of mist,
Was lowering its golden buckets down
   Into the vapory amethyst

Of marshes and swamps and dismal fens, —
   Scooping the dew that lay in the flowers,
Dipping the jewels out of the sea,
   To sprinkle them over the land in showers.

We knew it would rain; for the poplars showed
   The white of their leaves, the amber grain
Shrunk in the wind, and the lightning now
   Is tangled in tremulous skeins of rain!

THE BALLAD OF BABIE BELL.

I.

Have you not heard the poets tell
How came the dainty Babie Bell
   Into this world of ours?
The gates of heaven were left ajar:
With folded hands and dreamy eyes,
Wandering out of Paradise,
She saw this planet, like a star,
Hung in the glistening depths of even, —
Its bridges, running to and fro,
O'er which the white-winged Angels go,
Bearing the holy Dead to heaven!
She touched a bridge of flowers, — those feet,
So light they did not bend the bells
Of the celestial asphodels!
They fell like dew upon the flowers,
Then all the air grew strangely sweet!
And thus came dainty Babie Bell
   Into this world of ours.

II.

She came, and brought delicious May.
The swallows built beneath the eaves ;
Like sunlight in and out the leaves,
The robins went, the livelong day ;
The lily swung its noiseless bell,
And o'er the porch the trembling vine
Seemed bursting with its veins of wine :
How sweetly, softly, twilight fell !
Oh ! earth was full of singing-birds,
    And opening spring-tide flowers,
When the dainty Babie Bell
    Came to this world of ours.

III.

O Babie, dainty Babie Bell !
How fair she grew from day to day !
What woman-nature filled her eyes !
What poetry within them lay !
Those deep and tender twilight eyes,
So full of meaning, pure and bright
As if she yet stood in the light
Of those oped gates of Paradise !
And so we loved her more and more :
Ah ! never in our hearts before
    Was love so lovely born :
We felt we had a link between
This real world and that unseen, —
    The land beyond the morn !
And for the love of those dear eyes,
For love of her whom God led forth
(The mother's being ceased on earth
When Babie came from Paradise), —

For love of Him who smote our lives,
And woke the chords of joy and pain,
We said, *Dear Christ!* — our hearts bent down
    Like violets after rain.

IV.

And now the orchards, which were white
And red with blossoms when she came,
Were rich in autumn's mellow prime;
The clustered apples burnt like flame,
The soft-cheeked peaches blushed and fell,
The ivory chestnut burst its shell,
The grapes hung purpling in the grange;
And time wrought just as rich a change
    In little Babie Bell.
Her lissom form more perfect grew,
And in her features we could trace,
In softened curves, her mother's face!
Her angel-nature ripened too.
We thought her lovely when she came;
But she was holy, saintly now:
Around her pale angelic brow
We saw a slender ring of flame!

V.

God's hand had taken away the seal
That held the portals of her speech;
And oft she said a few strange words,
Whose meaning lay beyond our reach.
She never was a child to us;
We never held her being's key;
We could not teach her holy things:
She was Christ's self in purity.

VI.

It came upon us by degrees :
We saw its shadow ere it fell, —
The knowledge that our God had sent
His messenger for Babic Bell.
We shuddered with unlanguaged pain,
And all our hopes were changed to fears,
And all our thoughts ran into tears
    Like sunshine into rain.
We cried aloud in our belief,
" Oh, smite us gently, gently, God !
Teach us to bend, and kiss the rod,
    And perfect grow through grief."
Ah ! how we loved her, God can tell :
Her heart was folded deep in ours.
Our hearts are broken, Babie Bell !

VII.

At last he came, the messenger, —
The messenger from unseen lands :
And what did dainty Babie Bell ?
She only crossed her little hands,
She only looked more meek and fair !
We parted back her silken hair ;
We wove the roses round her brow,
White buds, the summer's drifted snow, —
Wrapped her from head to foot in flowers !
And thus went dainty Babie Bell
    Out of this world of ours !

THE CRESCENT AND THE CROSS.

KIND was my friend who, in the Eastern land,
Remembered me with such a gracious hand,
And sent this Moorish Crescent, which has been
Worn on the tawny bosom of a queen.

No more it sinks and rises in unrest
To the soft music of her heathen breast;
No barbarous chief shall bow before it more,
No turbaned slave shall envy and adore.

I place beside this relic of the Sun
A Cross of Cedar, brought from Lebanon;
Once borne, perchance, by some pale monk, who trod
The desert to Jerusalem — and his God!

Here do they lie, two symbols of two creeds,
Each meaning something to our human needs;
Both stained with blood, and sacred made by faith,
By tears and prayers, and martyrdom and death.

That for the Moslem is, but this for me!
The waning Crescent lacks divinity:
It gives me dreams of battles, and the woes
Of women shut in hushed seraglios.

But, when this Cross of simple wood I see,
The Star of Bethlehem shines again for me;
And glorious visions break upon my gloom, —
The patient Christ, and Mary at the Tomb!

LAMIA.

Go on your way, and let me pass.
 You stop a wild despair:
I would that I were turned to brass,
 Like that grim dragon there, —

Which, couchant by the postern gate,
 In weather foul or fair,
Looks down serenely desolate,
 And nothing does but stare!

Ah! what's to me the burgeoned year,
 The sad leaf or the gay!
Let Launcelot and Queen Guinevere
 Their falcons fly this day.

'Twill be as royal sport, pardie,
 As falconers have tried
At Astolat; — but let me be!
 I would that I had died.

I met a woman in the glade:
 Her hair was soft and brown,
And long bent silken lashes weighed
 Her ivory eyelids down.

I kissed her hand, I called her blest,
 I held her leal and fair:
She turned to shadow on my breast,
 And melted in the air!

And, lo! about me, fold on fold,
  A writhing serpent hung, —
An eye of jet, a skin of gold,
  A garnet for a tongue!

Oh! let the petted falcons fly
  Right merry in the sun;
But let me be! for I shall die
  Before the year is done.

PYTHAGORAS.

Above the petty passions of the crowd,
I stand in frozen marble like a god,
Inviolate, and ancient as the moon.
The thing I am, and not the thing Man is,
Fills my deep dreaming. Let him moan and die;
For he is dust that shall be laid again:
I know my own creation was divine.
Strewn on the breezy continents I see
The veinèd shells and burnished scales which once
Inwrapped my being, — husks that had their use;
I brood on all the shapes I must attain
Before I reach the Perfect, which is God,
And dream my dream, and let the rabble go:
For I am of the mountains and the sea,
The deserts, and the caverns in the earth,
The catacombs and fragments of old worlds.

I was a spirit on the mountain-tops,
A perfume in the valleys, a simoom

On arid deserts, a nomadic wind
Roaming the universe, a tireless Voice.
I was ere Romulus and Remus were ;
I was ere Nineveh and Babylon ;
I was, and am, and evermore shall be,
Progressing, never reaching to the end.

A hundred years I trembled in the grass,
The delicate trefoil that muffled warm
A slope on Ida ; for a hundred years
Moved in the purple gyre of those dark flowers
The Grecian women strew upon the dead.
Under the earth, in fragrant glooms, I dwelt ;
Then in the veins and sinews of a pine
On a lone isle, where, from the Cyclades,
A mighty wind, like a leviathan,
Ploughed through the brine, and from those solitudes
Sent Silence, frightened.   To and fro I swayed,
Drawing the sunshine from the stooping clouds.
Suns came and went, and many a mystic moon,
Orbing and waning, and fierce meteors,
Leaving their lurid ghosts to haunt the night.
I heard loud voices by the sounding shore,
The stormy sea-gods ; and from fluted conchs
Wild music, and strange shadows floated by,
Some moaning and some singing.   So the years
Clustered about me, till the hand of God
Let down the lightning from a sultry sky,
Splintered the pine, and split the iron rock ;
And from my odorous prison-house a bird,
I in its bosom, darted : so we fled,
Turning the brittle edge of one high wave,
Island and tree and sea-gods left behind !

Free as the air, from zone to zone I flew,
Far from the tumult, to the quiet gates
Of daybreak; and beneath me I beheld
Vineyards, and rivers that like silver threads
Ran through the green and gold of pasture-lands,
And here and there a hamlet, a white rose,
And here and there a city, whose slim spires
And palace-roofs and swollen domes uprose
Like scintillant stalagmites in the sun:
I saw huge navies battling with a storm
By ragged reefs along the desolate coasts,
And lazy merchantmen, that crawled, like flies,
Over the blue enamel of the sea,
To India or the icy Labradors.

A century was as a single day.
What is a day to an immortal soul?
A breath, no more. And yet I hold one hour
Beyond all price, — that hour when from the sky
I circled near and nearer to the earth,
Nearer and nearer, till I brushed my wings
Against the pointed chestnuts, where a stream,
That foamed and chattered over pebbly shoals,
Fled through the briony, and with a shout
Leaped headlong down a precipice; and there,
Gathering wild-flowers in the cool ravine,
Wandered a woman more divinely shaped
Than any of the creatures of the air,
Or river-goddesses, or restless shades
Of noble matrons marvellous in their time
For beauty and great suffering; and I sung,
I charmed her thought, I gave her dreams, and then,
Down from the dewy atmosphere, I stole,

And nestled in her bosom.   There I slept
From moon to moon, while in her eyes a thought
Grew sweet and sweeter, deepening like the dawn, —
A mystical forewarning !   When the stream,
Breaking through leafless brambles and dead leaves,
Piped shriller treble, and from chestnut boughs
The fruit dropped noiseless through the autumn night,
I gave a quick, low cry, as infants do :
We weep when we are born, not when we die !
So was it destined ; and thus came I here,
To walk the earth and wear the form of Man,
To suffer bravely as becomes my state,
One step, one grade, one cycle nearer God.

And, knowing these things, can I stoop to fret,
And lie, and haggle in the market-place,
Give dross for dross, or every thing for nought?
No ! let me sit above the crowd, and sing,
Waiting with hope for that miraculous change
Which seems like sleep ; and, though I waiting starve,
I cannot kiss the idols that are set
By every gate, in every street and park ;
I cannot fawn, I cannot soil my soul :
For I am of the mountains and the sea,
The deserts and the caverns in the earth,
The catacombs and fragments of old worlds.

THE TRAGEDY.

LA DAME AUX CAMELIAS.

THE " Dame with the Camelias," —
　　I think that was the play ;
The house was packed from pit to dome
　　With the gallant and the gay,
Who had come to see the Tragedy,
　　And while the hours away.

There was the oily Exquisite,
　　With gloves and glass sublime ;
There was the grave Historian,
　　And there the man of Rhyme,
And the surly Critic, front to front,
　　To see the play of Crime.

And there was pompous Ignorance,
　　And Vice in Honiton lace ;
Sir Crœsus and Sir Pandarus, —
　　And the music played apace :
But, of all that crowd, I only saw
　　A single, single face ! —

That of a girl whom I had known
　　In the summers long ago,
When her breath was like the new-mown hay,
　　Or the sweetest flowers that grow ;
When her heart was light, and her soul was white
　　As the winter's driven snow.

And there she sat with her great brown eyes, —
　　They wore a troubled look ;
And I read the history of her life
　　As it were an open book ;
And saw her Soul, like a slimy thing
　　In the bottom of a brook.

There she sat in her rustling silk,
　　With diamonds on her wrist,
And on her brow a trembling thread
　　Of pearl and amethyst.
" A cheat, a gilded grief ! " I said ;
　　And my eyes were filled with mist.

I could not see the players play :
　　I heard the music moan ;
It moaned like a dismal autumn wind,
　　That dies in the woods alone ;
And, when it stopped, I heard it still, —
　　The mournful monotone !

What if the Count were true or false ?
　　I did not care, not I ;
What if Camille for Armand died ?
　　I did not see her die.
There sat a woman opposite
　　Who held me with her eye !

The great green curtain fell on all, —
　　On laugh and wine and woe, —
Just as death some day will fall
　　'Twixt us and life, I know !
The play was done, the bitter play ;
　　And the people turned to go.

And did they see the Tragedy?
　　They saw the painted scene;
They saw Armand, the jealous fool,
　　And the sick Parisian quean:
But they did not see the Tragedy, —
　　The one I saw, I mean!

They did not see that cold-cut face,
　　Those braids of golden hair;
Or, seeing her jewels, only said,
　　" The lady's rich and fair."
But I tell you, 'twas the Play of Life,
　　And that woman played Despair!

PALABRAS CARIÑOSAS.

Spanish Air.

GOOD-NIGHT! I have to say good night
To such a host of peerless things!
Good-night unto that fragile hand
All queenly with its weight of rings;
Good-night to fond, uplifted eyes;
Good-night to chestnut braids of hair;
Good-night unto the perfect mouth,
And all the sweetness nestled there. —
　　The snowy hand detains me, then
　　I'll have to say Good-night again!

But there will come a time, my love,
When, if I read our stars aright,
I shall not linger by this porch
With my adieus.　Till then, good night!

You wish the time were now?   And I.
You do. not blush to wish it so?
You would have blushed yourself to death
To own so much a year ago. —
   What, both these snowy hands! ah, then,
   I'll have to say Good-night again!

———

THE LUNCH.

. A GOTHIC window, where a damask curtain
Made the blank daylight shadowy and uncertain ;
A slab of agate on four eagle-talons
Held trimly up and neatly taught to balance ;
A porcelain dish, o'er which in many a cluster
Plump grapes hung down, dead-ripe and without lus-
A melon cut in thin delicious slices ;   [tre ;
A cake that seemed mosaic-work in spices ;
Two China cups with golden tulips sunny,
And rich inside with chocolate like honey ;
And she and I the banquet-scene completing
With dreamy words — and very pleasant eating !

REV. J. G. ADAMS.

STRIVE TO MAKE THE WORLD BETTER.

" Take the world as it is! — there are good and bad in it,
And good and bad will be from now to the end;
And they who expect to make saints in a minute
Are in danger of marring more hearts than they mend.
If ye wish to be happy, ne'er seek for the faults,
Or you're sure to find something or other amiss :
'Mid much that debases, and much that exalts,
The world's not a bad one, if left as it is ! "
CHARLES SWAIN.

STRIVE to make the world better ! — this, this
    is the duty
    Proclaimed to each mortal in truth every
    hour ;
Call not its wrong, right, — its deformity, beauty :
  In the midst of its weakness, remember God's
    power.
And, though in a minute no wrong can be righted,
  Think not of contentment with just what you see :
The world needs repentance, where souls are so
    blighted ;
  And what it is now is not what it must be !

" Take the world as it is ! " To be sure, if such taking
  Will win you the heart of a brother, or lend
A soft word or kind look that shall, haply, be making
  Some ruin-bound pilgrim his life-ways amend.

2

If to praise it shall call thee, or suffering or prayer,
    To discipline such as may strengthen thy heart, —
Be thankful for this, every way, but beware
    Lest thy world-taking lesson be learned but in part !

" Take the world as it is ! "   So the world's honored
    sages
    Of many a clime have consented and taught ;
So walked with mankind the true Guide of all ages ;
    So lived his apostles, and labored and wrought, —
Yet not to be easy with present attainments,
    Assenting to evil in lullaby song,
But, rather, to startle, with Truth's strong arraign-
    ments,
    The victims of sin, and the lovers of wrong !

" Take the world as it is ! "   How the slothful and
    sleeping
Have ever consented these words to obey !
Conservator dolts still their sluggish steps keeping,
    And fearing the angel Reform in their way !
The selfish observer of manners and men.
    Who would never offend by his arrant fault-finding,
Provided his own ends are answered — and then,
    All the world is but good, and its faults not worth
    minding !

Strive to make the world better !   How true to this
    aim
    Have the heroes of Right kept their way in the
    past :
'Mid the world's accusations, through dungeon and
    flame,
    Abroad have the seeds of their greatness been cast !

And we have the harvest, — their word have we, too,
  That the seed-time for us is to-day! Let it be
That the world we now have, though so goodly to view,
  Is not that improved one to-morrow shall see!

SABBATH EVENING BY THE SEA-SIDE.

ALONE, my God, alone with thee,
  At this bright sabbath evening hour,
Where the strong voices of the sea
  Declare thy greatness and thy power!
I have been in thy courts to-day,
  Where mortals meet, thy name to bless;
And where, with one accord, they pay
  Their homage to thy holiness.
Now to these outer courts I come,
  Alone at this rock-altar, Lord,
Beneath this ample evening dome,
  To hear thee speak thy wondrous word.
That word the waves are uttering clear
  In their full accents at my feet,
While notes of woodland warblers near
  Are with thy glorious name replete.
On sunlit spire and roof and shore,
  And sail that stains the dark-blue sea,
And red horizon spread out o'er
  That emblem of eternity, —
I read thy brightness, God of love,
  And, in this matchless temple, raise
Anew my feeble thought above,
  In silent evening prayer and praise.

Thy mercies to my soul extend,
   Whose strength is nought without thy power;
Loved ones and dear from ill defend,
   And draw to thee, at this blest hour;
To friend and foe thy peace be given;
   The weak make strong, the simple wise;
Be to the poorest, wealth of heaven;
   To lameness, strength; to blindness, eyes.
As sheds this sun its rays divine
   O'er hill, and shore, and widening sea,
So may thy truth in mercy shine,
   Wherever man on earth may be!
As flow these everlasting waves,
   Bearers of life, from shore to shore,
So may that grace, which seeks and saves,
   Flow full and free the wide world o'er,
Till in this temple, all thine own,
   No soul shall false or faithless be,
But man's heart-worship at thy throne
   Complete the world's great harmony!

THE LAST PATCH OF SNOW.

Tiny memento of the winter's reign,
Reposing in the shadow of the wall,
Ere thou hast left us, ne'er to come again,
Past scenes and seasons let thy face recall, —

Days, when that robe of which thou art a shred
Lay everywhere the hills and valleys o'er;
When winter's hosts were to the war-field led, —
Her drifting squadrons 'mid the north wind's roar;

When lake, and mountain-stream, and river wide,
The frost-king's potent hand had gilded bright
With silver covering o'er the glassy tide,
That gleamed in day's full blaze, or moon-lit night.

By drifts beleagured in the sheltering home,
How blest the peace and comfort there enjoyed!
Where the rude blast intrusive cannot come,
And love's best sympathies are well employed.

And yet, again, I think of want and woe,
O'er which that fading winter garb was spread,
Unpitied suffering, or where Mercy's glow
Relights the hearth-fire, wakes to life the dead.

Soon, wintry visitant, and thou art gone:
These April rays will give thee flight ere noon,
And in thy sleeping-place shall there be born
The healthful buds and beauteous flowers of June.

Death's winter thus with man must have its reign,
Its cold shroud wrap this perishable clay;
But heavenly spring-time shall appear again,
And its last lingering vestige melt away.

TO MY SLEEPING BOY.

Loved sleeping one! " 'tis passing strange "
　　That pen and wakened minstrelsy,
In their incessant toil and range,
　　Have uttered no sweet song for thee.
Why this? I surely cannot tell,
And herewith break the mystic spell.

A parent's welcome greets thee, boy,
　　With heart and eye upraised to heaven
In thanks of gratitude and joy,
　　That thou in goodness hast been given
To cheer life's way, and recompense
Our toil with thy glad innocence.

Yet as my soul, in gratitude
　　That thou wert born, goes up to God,
Emotions sadder far intrude. —
　　The Future, child, thou hast not trod,
That way before thee ; — what will be
Thy late or early destiny?

Is it that thou hast come to bless
　　Our nightly pillow with thy breath,
Our day-dreams with thy loveliness, —
　　Then to depart in early death?
Loved boy, is this — is this thy doom, —
An infant's bier, an infant's tomb?

Ah! now I know what sympathies
　　Flow ever round the parent's heart:
Affection's deepest fount will rise,
　　And warmest tears unbidden start ; —
That innocent and gladsome face
For ever paled in death's embrace!

Or if thou shouldst not early die,
　　And longer life to thee be given,
If manhood and old age now lie
　　Along thy path from earth to heaven, —
What words of truth do they declare
Of thee, — the sorrowful or fair?

For well I know, that in this world
   Just entered. pilgrim boy, by thee,
Sin's blood-stained banner is unfurled
   Where thy light footsteps soon may be ;
And multitudes will seek to lure
Thee to destruction swift and sure.

And, when temptation's hour shall come,
   A father's voice, a mother's care,
May not forewarn ; or, if thy home
   Their earthly presence still may share,
Perchance e'en their unsleeping love
A shield from danger may not prove.

I've known so many bright joys dimmed,
   Such ruin made of hopes high-flushed,
Hearts drugged with woe when almost brimmed
   With bliss, and strongest virtues crushed,
That I do tremble as I see
Thy future coming thus to me.

Then will I give thee up to Him
   Whose eye in heaven's own light doth run
From highest rank of seraphim
   To lowest grade beneath the sun ;
Whose name is Love, whose watchful care
The feeblest of his children share.

If, from this infant home of thine,
   It please him early to remove
Thy young soul hence, to dwell and shine
   Among the purified above ;
And, if thy little voice no more
Should greet us on this pilgrim shore, —

A parent's trusting heart will know,
   That he who gave and takes away,
Can joy impart for keenest woe,
   And strength all equal to our day ;
And that, amid our tears for thee,
Shall shine thine immortality !

Or, if long life to thee be given
   Rather than ease or wealth or fame,
For thee, my child, I ask of Heaven
   A Christian's life, — a Christian's name ;
A soul made strong in Virtue's might,
And ever toiling for the Right.

This sure, I bid solicitude
   For thee depart : why should I not ?
If thou art numbered with the good,
   Thine are the blessings of their lot,
Brighter through all thy future way,
To cloudless, endless, perfect day.

CHRISTIAN TOIL.

In the field or work-shop, brother,
   In the mart or on the sea,
Wheresoe'er thy life's allotment,
   Toil, nor mourn thy destiny.

In thy quiet home, fond mother,
   Where thy loves and cares abound,
Labor on, though often weary :
   Strengthening angels thee surround !

Statesman, for thy nation toiling,
  Where the world thy name shall see ;
Lowliest minister of mercy,
  Who at misery's bed would be, —

All, of every grade and honor, —
  Know the work your hands should do :
" Go, and labor in my vineyard,"
  Is God's present word to you.

Thus we read our Christian duty :
  Work for daily bread alone
Is not all of life's great mission,
  As the Master's word hath shown.

" Labor for the meat enduring : "
  This the mandate from above,
Enter thou the Spirit-conflict ;
  Labor in the Life of Love.

Much to do behold before ye !
  Error, meanness, sin, and shame,
All await their destination, —
  The Reformer's axe and flame !

Nerve thy heart and hand to action ;
  Be thy soul within aright ;
Then God's blessing shall attend thee
  In the labor and the fight !

DEATH OF N. P. ROGERS.

A LIGHT in Freedom's temple dimmed!
　A star gone from our northern sky!
A requiem for the noble, hymned
　In Love's deep harmony!

No little earthly king is dead;
　No warrior in blood-contest slain;
But one whose hero-soul was wed
　To Truth's great strife and gain;

Who not with zeal for sect or clan
　In stinted words his message brought;
But, in deep love for suffering man,
　Dared, uttered, lived, and wrought.

He scorned what others might allow,
　To ask what Church or State would say,
When Wrong was bold;—the Right! and now
　Let's follow and obey!

Though small the day when first he gave
　True heart and hand in manhood's cause,
Yet, in his love of duty, brave,
　He could not quail or pause.

By silver lake and winding stream,
   And up where mountain cloud-wreaths hung,
In busy mart and hermit's dream,
   His pealing trump-notes rung.

They waked the echoes far and near,
   Called many a true-born witness forth;
Life-soldier in this new career
   Of Freedom in the North.

Brave spirit! more like thee we need
   In this our world's great conflict-hour,
To sow, with trusting hand, Truth's seed,
   And wait her ripening power.

REV. CHARLES BURROUGHS, D.D.

———◆———

LAKE GEORGE.

Written on board the Steamer " Caldwell," on Lake George,
July 2, 1845.

WIFT o'er thy waters, Horicon,
  Our gallant bark most gayly glides,
  While isles and mountains, verdure clad,
  Are passing swiftly at our sides.

All seems a pageant of romance,
A living, brilliant fairy tale,
As if the spirits from above
Peopled this lake, each hill and vale.

Green and translucent are thy waves,
And pure as sacramental font
Which would baptize with holy love
All who a heavenly spirit want.

Come, all who would the world renounce,
Come here, your hands and temples lave ;
Some bright Archangel spans the lake
To bless with sacred hands each wave.

Rise then, renewed, and look around
On all that meets the enchanted eye ;
For Nature here with glorious love
Has mixed her choicest scenery.

Miss not one scene of Horicon,
Lose not one virtue of this spot ;
For this is earth's sweet Paradise,
The foretaste of a heavenly lot.

No wonder that warm Christian zeal
To God's dear Church thy stream has sent,
And named thee. to the world's delight,
Lake of the Holy Sacrament.

For if, with holy feelings now
O'er thy pure breast we peaceful glide,
Each spot will seem with glory filled,
And God through life will be our guide.

Blessed be the day that made me know
Thy brilliant scenes and mighty fame ;
For peace will ever fill my soul
At mention of thy sacred name.

AN INDIAN LAMENT.

On the Death of the Sachem Mogg, who perished in Battle at
Black-Point Garrison, May 16th, 1677.

REST, Warrior, rest ; thy work is now done :
   Our cause thou hast nobly defended ;
Thy soul has away to the Great Spirit gone ;
   And we mourn that thy warfare is ended.

Not a bolder in war ever faced a fierce foe ;
    And none in the chase did exceed him :
Always true in his aim, always swift as the doe,
    Nor mountain nor stream could impede him.

His genius was lofty. above all his tribes ;
    He was born for dread war's wild commotion ;
His name on her temple Fame boldly inscribes,
    For his conflicts on earth and on ocean.

Our brother is gone, and our spirits now quail ;
    There is none to exceed him in glory :
Our tribes must all cease, for our red men will fail
    To make themselves famous in story.

We groaned, as our sachem received his death-blow
    From the white man, that cruelly hates us :
Our chase and our lands we must all now forego ;
    But a vengeance more dreadful awaits us.

Wrap our chief in his shroud ; lay his corse in the
        grave ;
    Let his gun and his pipe be placed near him ;
And, when he'll awake o'er the far western wave,
    He'll find game and green fields there to cheer him.

Let us speed to our home ere the close of this day, .
    And repeat to our children our sorrow ;
And ask the Great Spirit to take us away,
    Ere we wake on the woes of to-morrow.

Our chief now we leave on his last field of fame :
    But no monument need we raise o'er him ;
For he leaves on the earth an illustrious name,
    And the brave will for ever deplore him.

NIAGARA FALLS.

Composed there, August 10, 1846.

HARK! what sounds of mighty thunders!
    O'er those cliffs an ocean pours!
Mark its foaming furious surges,
    Booming on the rocky shores.

Why is all this awful tempest
    Of Niagara's flood so vast?
Why these hurricanes of waters,
    Seeming like destruction's blast?

Hear the story of these wonders;
    This decree did God proclaim:
" Let the waters here be gathered
    To adore my glorious name."

Lakes immense, and icebergs melted
    From the stormy northern pole,
Babbling brooks, and countless rivers,
    To Niagara's temple roll.

To that glorious altar move they:
    Not with slow, reluctant pace,
But with eager speed and transport
    Rush they to that sacred place.

All their garments beam with splendor;
    Some are whiter than the snow:
These display a crimson lustre;
    Those like brightest emeralds glow.

Some are graced with tints of azure ;
  Those with amber, these with green ;
Boundless wreaths of glittering diamonds
  O'er Niagara's robes are seen.

Thus the stream, all clothed with glory,
  To its God with rapture sings,
And the heavenly vaults re-echo
  With its awful thunderings.

Then ascend thick clouds of incense,
  Which is borne on angels' wings,
And o'er earth the richest blessings
  With unbounded mercy flings.

Then did Christ our blessed Saviour,
  For those harmonies so loud,
Paint the rainbow's radiant beauties
  On the fleecy incense-cloud.

There I saw the bow of promise
  As it came from God's right hand ;
And it spread its arch transcendent
  On our own and Britain's land.

Here a Church has Christ erected ;
  All these sounds are praise to him ;
All this stream's a font baptismal,
  And its drops are seraphim.

These grand cliffs are altars sacred
  To that God who reigns above ;
All this rush and deafening roaring
  Are but songs of holy love.

All these foaming crystal surges
    Hath a Saviour's mercy hurled
O'er those craggy heights, to christen
    And redeem a fallen world.

It is wise that erring mortals
    Should frequent these wondrous scenes,
Here to see the God of Nature,
    And to learn what worship means.

'Tis not strange that red men always
    View this spot as God's dread home,
And their pipes and beaded wampums
    Humbly offer on the foam.

'Tis not strange that unbelievers
    Here betray remorse and shame,
And confess our Lord's dominion
    Over cataract and flame.

'Tis not strange that Christian pilgrims
    Here the richest blessings know ;
Here's the hem of Christ's bright garment,
    Which, when touched, will grace bestow.

These dread scenes portend the judgment,
    When in triumph Christ shall come,
With a voice, like mighty waters,
    To pronounce earth's endless doom.

Then, O God ! in mercy save me
    From thine everlasting frown,
That in bliss my ears may hear thee,
    And my eyes behold thy crown.

MOUNT WASHINGTON.

Written on the Summit of Mount Washington, Wednesday noon, July 9, 1845.

ILLUSTRIOUS Mountain! thou dost stand alone,
The loftiest sentinel that guards our land;
The glorious image of the Eternal One;
The work sublime of his Almighty hand.

On every side, what boundless prospects rise!
What oceans vast of mountain scenery!
What dread magnificence of earth and skies!
What regions of unrolled immensity!

Now, raised above earth's cares and toil and din,
I sit serene, to holy musings given;
To soar in bliss above this world of sin,
And hold communion with the hosts of heaven.

Right well thy granite pile baptized has been,
In name of one whose virtues none assail;
Who towered in glory o'er his fellow-men,
Like thy proud summit o'er the humble vale.

Thy rocks, unhurt, have felt the tempest's power,
And lightnings harmless have played round thy form;
So, too, our Washington in war's fierce hour
Did breast each shock, and triumph o'er each storm.

Our Nation's boast! Mount of eternal stone!
In freedom, truth, and virtue may we stand,
Exalted like thyself and Washington,
The pride and honor of our blessed land!

A MORNING PRAYER.

As from my couch I now arise,
And grateful view the earth and skies,
Grant me, in all things, Lord, I pray,
Thy glory to consult this day.

At meals, at prayer, where'er I wend,
What hours in cares or joys I spend,
Be it my highest joy and fame
To glorify thy blessed name.

Should dangerous snares my soul assault,
And tempt me to a sin or fault,
Oh, keep me pure in act and word,
Ever to honor thee, my Lord!

Should any sufferer I may see
Need offices of love from me,
Oh, may I gladly show such love,
To glorify my God above!

Should sickness, sorrows, trials, woes,
Befall me, ere this day shall close,
With patience may I bear each ill,
And bow submissive to thy will!

Dear Lord, may all my labors be
Begun, continued, closed in thee,
And all bring glory to thy name,
And give me endless life and fame!

Then, when her pall Night o'er me throws,
And on my couch I seek repose,
I'll bless thee that I still do live
New glories to thy name to give.

DAILY DUTIES.

*Version of a Paper written in French, and given by a French
Priest to an humble Female Peasant of Savoy, who allowed
a Traveller to take a Copy of it.*

Now remember what I say,
Christian, that you have to-day
Glory to your God to pay ;
Christ to copy and obey ;
Love for angels to display ;
A soul to save, that's gone astray ;
All the body's lusts to slay ;
To God for every grace to pray ;
Grief for every sin betray ;
To Paradise to find the way ;
To hell's dark borders ne'er to stray ;
Dread eternity to weigh ;
Time's precious value to survey ;
Nought, but what is good, essay ;
Penitence no more to stay ;
Love to neighbors to convey ;
A world to fear, where dangers lay ;
Fiends to meet in fierce affray ;
All your passions well to sway ;
And perhaps to drop this clay,
And be judged without delay.

MEDITATIONS,

*While sick in bed, Communion Sunday Morning, May 3, 1846:
suggested by my unexpected confinement there, and the con-
sequent closing of my Church.*

Not in thy Temple, O my God!
   Bend I this day my knee;
Nor lead my people in the prayers
   Of our blest Liturgy;

Nor break to them the Bread of Life;
   Nor pour the sacred wine;
Nor. in the glorious chants and hymns,
   With them in transport join.

Like sheep without a shepherd's care,
   To pastures strange they roam;
As if some awful destiny '
   Had visited their home.

All other streams of healing power
   Their souls will ne'er compare
With that which flows from Zion's hill,
   Their favorite place of prayer.

But I, thy sinful servant, Lord!
   Denied thy courts of praise,
Within my chamber's quiet walls,
   To thee my soul would raise.

Stretched on my couch by thy wise will,
   This sacred spot I'll view,
As pulpit, altar, and as desk,
   To bring each offering due.

Here, as a Priest, I'll worship Christ,
   My Saviour, Guide, and Rock ;
And make my couch a church, to bring
   Grace on myself and flock.

Teach us submission to thy hand,
   And greater love for thee,
Thy courts, thy day, and thy dear Son,
   That Heaven our Church may be ;

Where " none shall say that he is sick ; "
   Where tears shall never flow ;
Where all shall join the nuptial song,
   And endless raptures know.

MICHAEL W. BECK.

BORN, NOV. 29, 1815; DIED, MARCH 9, 1843.

THE WORLD AS IT IS.

THIS world is not so bad a world
   As some would wish to make it;
Though whether good, or whether bad,
   Depends on how we take it.
For if we scold and fret all day,
   From dewy morn till even,
This world will ne'er afford to man
   A foretaste here of heaven.

This world in truth's as good a world
   As e'er was known to any
Who have not seen another yet
   (And these are very many);
And if the men and women too
   Have plenty of employment,
Those surely must be hard to please,
   Who cannot find enjoyment.

This world is quite a clever world
   In rain, or pleasant weather,
If people would but learn to live
   In harmony together;

Nor seek to break the kindly bond
  By love and peace cemented,
And learn that best of lessons yet,
  To always be contented.

Then were the world a pleasant world,
  And pleasant folks were in it:
The day would pass most pleasantly
  To those who thus begin it;
And all the nameless grievances
  Brought on by borrowed troubles
Would prove, as certainly they are,
  A mass of empty bubbles!

THE SOUL.

WHENCE came the intellectual ray
  That lights the eye with fire,
That earthward will not bide its stay,
  But heavenward bids aspire?
Is it a spark from God's high throne,
  Given with our earliest breath?
And will he claim it as his own,
  When we are chilled in death?

Oh, precious faith! cling to my breast,
  A hallowed pilgrim there:
When to my bosom thou art pressed,
  How free am I from care!
Let sickness rage, let pain invade
  My vitals for its food,
No doubt my faith shall make afraid,
  Nor aught be mine but good.

Through death's dark valley I must tread,
    Ere youth's fair sun is set:
Calmly resigned, I bow my head,
    And earth's vain joys forget.
The spark that gleams, the jewelled soul,
    The casket thrown away,
Shall mingle with that perfect whole
    That forms God's brightest day!

THE INDIAN SUMMER.

It comes, it comes with golden sheaf,
In the time of the sear and yellow leaf;
It flings the fruit from the bending tree,
And scatters it round in reckless glee:
It plays on the brow of the maiden fair,
And parts, with its fingers, her raven hair.

It comes, it comes; and its minstrel's wing
O'er the glassy lake is quivering
With music soft as the mellow strain
Of zephyrs over the swelling main:
It gladdens the vales as it floats along,
And stream and mountain re-echo the song.

It comes, it comes like a fairy sprite
Arrayed in robes of gossamer white;
And the carpet of leaves on the ground is spread;
And the flowers yield 'neath its conquering tread:
For it strides along its kingly way,
Like shadows that flit at the close of day.

It comes, it comes ; and the ripened grain
Is weaving crowns for its golden reign ;
And the bright eye sparkles with liquid light,
Like the star enthroned on the brow of night ;
And the teeming fields their offering bring
At the sainted shrine of the Autumn king.

TO A SNOW-BIRD.

In what far region is thy home,
    Fair lady of the snow-white breast,
That far away thou need'st to roam,
    And wander from thine own soft nest?
Is it within some fairy bower
    Where one unfading summer's smile,
And flashing brook, and fragrant flower,
    The wanderer's golden hours beguile?

Or is it where the icebergs float
    'Mid frozen regions far away,
Where no sweet bird with minstrel note
    Pours forth its melancholy lay?
Is this thy summer wandering,
    Fair pilgrim, from that ice-bound coast?
Alas ! a weary journeying
    Repays thee for thy labor lost.

Ah ! cold methinks that heart must be
    Within that bosom fluttering ;
And yet thy tones right merrily
    A strain of gladness seem to fling.

What though the Spirit of the Snow
    Her mantle spreads o'er vale and hill?
Thy pleasant song imparts a glow
    That mingles in the bosom's thrill.

Where'er thy home, a welcoming
    From many a heart is given thee:
'Tis thine, the humble offering,
    Through months that linger wearily;
And when the joyous notes of spring,
    And richer strains than thine are heard,
Then fondly will thy visit cling
    Around our memory, winter bird.

THE SUMMER WIND.

The summer wind of a summer night!
The moon is up; the stars shine bright;
The voice of music is floating by,
Filling the air with its melody;
The grass bends low 'neath the grateful blast,
And whispers praise as it rushes past.

The summer wind of a summer night!
Swelling and swelling with all its might, —
How it stoops to kiss the lowly rose,
And wafts its fragrance where'er it goes!
How it bathes its brow in the silvery stream,
And awakens to life the wild bird's scream!

The summer wind of a summer night!
Earth seems glad at the sound and sight;

And Nature's children — *all* are hers —
Are thronging her courts as worshippers,
And join in the anthem of praise ascending
From the votaries now at her altar bending.

The summer wind of a summer night!
Away from the world the thoughts take flight:
On airy pinions they soar away,
Where the fountains of pleasure ever play,
Where the waters of bliss, as onward they roll,
Display to the vision *the home of the soul.*

THE FIRST BIRD OF SPRING.

I.

THERE's music on the breeze!
Gently it steals o'er vale and moss-crowned hill,
And sweetly murmurs o'er the mountain rill,
   And through the leafless trees.

II.

Hail, harbinger of Spring!
Let gladsome voices in the olden wood,
And elfin shouts 'mid Nature's solitude,
   Their pleasant welcome ring.

III.

Pour forth thy minstrelsy,
While streamlets, from their icy fetters free,
And joyful sound of waters' sportive glee,
   Attest thy ministry!

IV.

'Tis good to linger here,
And listen to this minister of love,
Whose thrilling tones of sweetness from the grove
    Fall softly on the ear.

V.

There's magic in thy voice!
And echoing earth her thousand vales among,
And sea and air, repeat thy simple song, —
    And all things there rejoice,

MY OLD YELLOW VEST.

I LOVE it of all my old relics the best;
Most dearly I cherish my yellow vest;
I've worn it at parties, at routs and balls;
I've worn it at morning and evening calls;
I've worn it when threading the mazy dance,
Midst the blithesome step and flashing glance, —
Alas! not an eye nor a step do I see,
Of the friends of my youthful revelry.

I wore it that night 'neath the trysting-tree,
When the stars shone out most brilliantly,
And I my burning passion confessed
To the blushing maid I clasped to my breast:
Ah me, alas! she hath long lain low
'Neath the summer rain and the winter snow;
And I never can gaze on that yellow vest,
But on the fair vision mine eyes seem to rest.

Old vest, old vest! my eye-sight grows dim;
And age hath touched with its frost each limb;
And I totter on in an old man's way,
Impressed with the finger of Time's decay;
But ye 'mind me of days when my step was light,
And the star of my destiny glimmered bright;
And I feel that full soon I shall go to my rest,
And leave thee behind me, my old loved vest!

And will they scorn thee, and fling thee by,
As a faded thing kept uselessly?
Alas! they know not the comfort thou art,
Old friend I have worn long near to my heart;
The link that unites in memory's chain
With the past, and makes me young again:
'Tis an old man's fancy, — oh! grant his behest,
And place in his coffin that old yellow vest.

THE SOLILOQUY, — YES OR NO?

By all the vows he made to me,
　His earnest suit so urgent pressing;
By all his tortured agony
　Of love, which seemed indeed distressing;
By all the passion's ebb and flow, —
He seeks an answer, *yes* or *no.*

By all the dew-drops of the Spring,
　And notes of music, joyous thrilling;
By every bird upon the wing,
　And every note of gladness trilling, —
By all above and all below,
I dare not answer *yes* or *no.*

No! how it chills the soul to speak
  This word, the very blood congealing!
And this poor bosom's far too weak
  To cherish such a want of feeling;
For thoughts of bitter grief and woe
Will mingle with that sad word, *no.*

Yes! there is rapture in the sound;
  It breathes of joy, of mirth and gladness,
Of merry voices whispering round,
  And nought of cold and dreary sadness;
And pleasant thoughts to fond hearts press,
And gather round that glad word, *yes.*

Yes! I am thine, and wholly thine;
  The word in bliss and truth is spoken;
And wilt thou give a heart for mine, —
  Thy heart, — a maiden's dearest token?
Say, wilt thou thine on me bestow?
I'm sure you cannot answer, *no!*

ESTHER W. BARNES.

THE OCEAN.

Sabbath Musings on the Seashore.

NONE of thy works, great Father! speak to me
As speaks the Ocean in its majesty.
Boundless, immense, it rolls from shore to
shore,
And I, thy child, here "tremble and adore,"
While it uplifts its crested waves on high,
And rolls its anthem through the deep-blue sky.
Others to-day in social worship bend;
But here, alone, to thee my thoughts ascend;
And in thy presence, humbled by thy power,
My spirit worships at this hallowed hour,
And a meet homage offers at thy shrine,
God of the restless Seas! — a homage all divine.

Ocean! I've loved thee from my earliest years,
With that deep love which only speaks in tears:
Upon thy shores I've watched the surging sea,
And felt my soul allied to heaven through thee;
And, while thy white foam brought me ocean-flowers,
I've dreamed of beauty in thy sea-girt bowers.

Whether thy waves tumultuous bound and roar,
Or in light ripples break upon the shore ;
Whether the storm upon thy bosom ride,
Or broken sunbeams o'er thy mirror glide ;
In every mood, thou ever-changing Sea !
I feel, and hear in thee, the voice of Deity.

Thou sleep'st within the hollow of His hand,
By whose dear love the universe is spanned ;
And o'er thee bends the soft and cloudless heaven,
Vast as his mercy shown to man forgiven :
Alone with thee, and " by the world forgot,"
" The world forgetting," could I now but blot,
From out life's page, its cares, transgressions, fears,
And come, all bathed with penitential tears,
To yield my heart *for ever* to his power, —
This were indeed to me a consecrated hour !

But, Ocean ! I shall turn from thee away ;
Back to the world must I reluctant stray,
Mingle in changing scenes, and feel the power
Of human weakness to my latest hour :
Yet in my heart an echo will I bear
Of thy wild music, mingling with my prayer ;
And its sweet memory through my life shall glide,
As the warm gulf-stream through the ocean's tide ;
While, in my " heart of hearts," the love of thee
Shall never cease to blend with that of Deity.

4

THE SEA-SHELL.

Oh! there is music at my heart,
  If thou wilt bend thine ear,
And listen to the plaintive tone
  That is to me so dear:
'Tis the echo of my mother's voice;
  And I bore it thence with me
When they tore me from her heaving breast, —
  The bosom of the sea.

Now ye may bear me whereso'er
  Your wandering steps may roam;
But the music of my mother's voice
  Shall tell me of my home.
Ye may bear me o'er the mountain-peak,
  ·Ye may bear me where ye will;
But ye cannot tear it from my heart:
  'Twill be my solace still.

Ye may not bid it die away
  Upon the passing breeze;
For 'tis treasured, like the diver's pearls, —
  Aye, dearer far than these, —
Within the heart which ye must break,
  Ere the sound will cease to be
Of my mother's voice, the ocean's voice,
  The murmur of the sea.

SEA-MOSSES.

WHENCE came ye, beauteous gems of the sea !
  With your golden and Tyrian dyes?
As gorgeous as if ye had borrowed your tints
  From the bright Italian skies.

Perchance, when sunset its hues hath flung
  On the breast of the bounding sea,
Ye have come from your ocean-haunts awhile,
  In its glorious light to be ;

And then, entranced with the varied tints,
  Ye have bathed in the gorgeous dyes,
And borne unto Neptune's halls again
  The hues of the rainbow skies.

But now, cast abroad on the dreary waste,
  On the treacherous ocean's foam,
Ye have come, as many an exile hath,
  To find in our land a home.

Ye have battled long with powerful foes ;
  Ye have struggled with adverse tides ;
Ye have fought the waves : on their plumèd crest,
  Each, now as a conqueror, rides.

For " the God of storms," with his mighty arm,
  Led you on o'er the trackless foam ;
And gems of beauty ye still will be,
  Though torn from your ocean-home.

THE BARK AND THE BLADE OF GRASS.

Some years since, a small party visited a romantic spot in the neighborhood of Boston. While there, a gentleman, having cut a slip of bark from a tree, presented it sportively to a lady, who *tied a blade of grass* around it, and offered it to the writer as a beautiful subject for a poem. To that lady the following is dedicated, with the hope that she will read its moral, and never again connect beauty and freshness with age and deformity.

She cut the bark from off the tree ;
    And, with the grass, *she* bound it :
This bark man's emblem is, thought she,
    And woman's love is round it !

Now the bark was scar and sapless grown,
    For the lapse of time had scathed it ;
But the grass was green as the emerald-stone,
    And bright, for the dew had bathed it.

A woman's love is the prettiest vine,
    When, unchilled by time or weather,
It clings to the youthful oak, and both
    On the spot grow old together ;

When it doth its own sweet fetters fling
    On the thing it loves most dearly ;
And is taught by age and by ills to cling
    To the constant stem more nearly :

But, when the hand of another hath bound
    The green to the bough that's faded,   .
Oh ! who shall say it will there be found,
    When by clouds and woe 'tis shaded ?

A tie more firm than the " Gordian knot "
  Should then be bound about it ;
For, when youth unto age *thus* binds its lot,
  Love ne'er will stay without it.

OH! VISIT ME IN DREAMS.

OFT in my day-dreams, Brother ! do I see
Thy face so loved : it gently smiles on me
In the glad sunbeam of the glowing day,
And in the pensive moonbeam's milder ray.
Thy voice, it greets me in each mirthful tone
That Nature's wild harp breathes ; and, in the moan
Of Autumn's requiem o'er her dying flowers,
I hear thy sigh o'er by-gone, happy hours.
I see thee, and I feel that thou art near,
When music's sweetness falls upon mine ear ;
And, in the rippling of the summer's rill,
Thy glad laugh weaves its gladness round me still !

Would that my visions of the night were blest,
And thy dear spirit hovered o'er my rest !
Would that in dreams, when darkness has unfurled
Her star-lit banner o'er a slumbering world,
Thou, with the shadowy train of loved ones dear,
Would hold communion with my spirit here !
May I not call you from your far-off home ?
And will ye not, beloved ones ! hither come ?
Oh ! hover now about my couch of rest ;
Blend with my dreams the thought that ye are blest ;
Tell me of those pure joys that hidden lie
'Neath the dark curtain of futurity ;

Speak of our blest re-union in that land
Where love shall bind us once more, hand in hand;
Oh, hover o'er me! spread your angel wings;
Bear me in dreams, at least, from earth's frail things;
Whisper of heaven; enraptured sing its bliss,
And on my brow impress the angels' kiss.
Oh, if the grave *must* shut ye from my sight,
Return, return in visions of the night!

My Brother! on my hand thy ring I see,
The talisman of *hope* and *memory:*
Hope for the hour when falls the captive's chain,
And thou'lt enfold me to thy heart again;
And *memory* of the love that bound us here,—
A love that made e'en this bright world more dear.
'Twas on the day that gave to me my birth
(And thou wert passing then away from earth).
Thou bad'st them bear to me the precious token
Of thy dear love, whose bond *is yet unbroken!*
The wreath affection twines, death cannot sever:
It bloometh still in heaven, fadeless, for ever!
No canker blights its amaranthine leaves,
No cruel reaper binds it 'mid his sheaves.

Yes, thou wert passing to thy *home* away:
But I a little longer here shall stay;
A little longer linger on the shore;
Then clasp thee, Brother! in my arms once more.
There *all* shall meet,—beholding face to face,
"No wanderer lost,"—meet in one long embrace;
Heart unto heart, and hand to hand, we'll be
United closely through eternity!
The broken links a bond shall form in heaven;
To broken hearts shall healing then be given;

Affection twine us with its deathless chain,
And bid us breathe no parting sigh again.
Oh! then, most welcome shall be that blest hour
When Death unites, and Love asserts its power!

THE MOONBEAM.

I HAVE trod with silver footprint
    On the white wave's foaming crest;
And I've seen my mirrored beauty
    In the glassy lake at rest.
I have played amid the foliage
    Of the blossom-laden tree;
And I've rested on the white wings
    Of the Argosy at sea.

I have slept upon the summit
    Of the snow-crowned Alpine heights,
Where the north wind's icy breathing
    Every little floweret blights.
I have trod where chilling glaciers
    Lift their pointed spires to heaven,
And, within Chamouni's valley,
    Bathed in perfumed dews at even.

On Niagara's mist-wreaths resting,
    I have thrown my lunar light;
Spanning them, with bow of promise,
    Like a halo pure and bright.
I have played within the fountain,
    Sparkling as in fairy dream;
And I've smiled upon the spray-drops
    As they sought to quench my beam.

I have nestled oft at midnight
   In the music-breathing pine,
Lulled to slumber calm and holy
   By its melody divine;
And I've crept within the petals
   Of the lily pure and white;
And, from out the crystal chalice,
   Sipped the dew-drop sparkling bright.

But, alas! some hours of sadness
   E'en the moonbeam's lot must share;
And on scenes of human anguish,
   Heart-bereavement, and despair,
Must I smile with seeming lightness, —
   Coldly smile as oft they deem;
While my heart with grief is breaking, —
   Grief they neither know nor dream.

I must gaze upon the death-bed
   Of the young, the good, the fair;
I must see life's glowing taper
   Quenched in darkness and despair.
When the silver cord is loosened,
   Broken is the golden bowl,
I must calmly gaze, nor tremble,
   E'en though anguish rend my soul.

But let not the moonbeam murmur,
   Whispereth an inward voice:
It can breathe in soothing accents,
   Bid the mourner's heart rejoice;
It can whisper *peace*, which calmeth
   All the stricken soul's unrest;
It can whisper of that heaven
   Where the suffering shall be blest.

It can light the storm-tossed wanderer
  On the trackless, heaving main ;
And, to God, the reckless sceptic
  It can bring with hope again.
Who, beneath the moonbeam smiling,
  And its glory poured o'er earth,
Can forget His love whose mandate
  Gave unto the light its birth ?

Who can doubt He ever liveth,
  Who from chaos formed this world ;
Set the stars ; the moon's soft radiance
  Like a silver flag unfurled ?
Cease then, gentle beam ! to murmur :
  Sweet thy task to tell of Him
From whose throne the glory beaming
  Maketh sun and stars grow dim.

MRS. SARAH ROBERTS BOYLE.

THE VOICE OF THE GRASS.

HERE I come creeping, creeping everywhere:
 By the dusty roadside,
 On the sunny hillside,
 Close by the noisy brook,
 In every shady nook,
I come creeping, creeping everywhere.

Here I come creeping, smiling everywhere:
 All round the open door,
 Where sit the aged poor,
 Here, where the children play
 In the bright and merry May,
I come creeping, creeping everywhere.

Here I come creeping, creeping everywhere:
 In the noisy city street
 My pleasant face you'll meet,
 Cheering the sick at heart,
 Toiling his busy part;
Silently creeping, creeping everywhere.

Here I come creeping, creeping everywhere :
    You cannot see me coming,
    Nor hear my low sweet humming ;
    For in the starry night,
    And the glad morning light,
I come quietly creeping everywhere.

Here I come creeping, creeping everywhere :
    More welcome than the flowers
    In summer's pleasant hours :
    The gentle cow is glad,
    And the merry bird not sad,
To see me creeping, creeping everywhere.

Here I come creeping, creeping everywhere :
    When you're numbered with the dead
    In your still and narrow bed,
    In the happy spring I'll come,
    And deck your silent home ;
Creeping, silently creeping everywhere.

Here I come creeping, creeping everywhere :
    My humble song of praise,
    Most gratefully I raise
    To Him at whose command
    I beautify the land ;
Creeping, silently creeping everywhere.

THE DESERTED NURSERY.

The little crib is empty,
    Where oft I've seen thee lie
So beautiful in thy deep sleep,
    Emblem of purity.
And, oh! how silent is the place
    Where late I heard thy voice
In gleeful shout or merry laugh,
    Making my heart rejoice!

In vain I look around me,
    Thy cherub form to see:
Art thou not hiding, baby?
    Is this reality?
God's sunshine streameth in the room,
    But midnight's in my heart:
I never dreamed such agony,
    Baby, that we could part.

Thy playthings lie around me,
    The silent rattle here,
Gay toys and picture-books are there:
    Ah! sure thou must be near.
Thy tiny pair of half-worn shoes,
    Thy life-like frock of red,
Thy whistle, hat, and favorite whip, —
    Sweet baby, art thou dead?

My trembling hand encloses
　Thy bright and clustering curls;
Millions of gold can't buy them,
　Nor India's gems or pearls:
'Tis all that's left to mortal sight,
　Of thee, sweet baby, now.
O Holy Father! teach my soul
　Submissively to bow.

Last night, in troubled slumber,
　I thought I heard thy cry,
And started quick to soothe thee, dear;
　But, oh, what agony!
The dimpled hand was not in mine,
　Nor sweet lips pressed my cheek;
The lisping voice, it called me not:
　What could I do but weep?

Father! forgive my anguish,
　Thy ways are ever just;
Speak comfort to our broken hearts,
　For thou art all our trust:
With thee the spirit liveth,
　So cherished and so dear,
Sent to us for a little while,
　Our earthly home to cheer.
Now the Good Shepherd leadeth him
　Through pastures green and fair:
Onward and upward be our aim,
　To meet our loved one there.

THE CITY ROSE TO THE WILD ROSE.

THE wild bee brought your message
  Just at the peep of day,
Tapping, buzzing at my window;
  Then gayly flew away.
I thank you, fair young sister;
  But t'would break my heart to roam,
So many, many love me
  In my dusty city home.

You tell of fresh green meadows;
  Of upland, hill, and glade;
Of the many merry sisters,
  And the still and pleasant shade;
Of fragrant flowers around you;
  Of a laughing, noisy brook
Tripping gayly at your feet all day,
  Reflecting every look.

You say you'll have sweet music
  With the early morning light;
That the nightingale will cheer us
  Through all the summer night;
That the humming-bird and bee
  Shall do my bidding every day,
Bring all the city news to me
  From friends so far away.

You say I must be lonely ;
    That you tremble for my health ;
That the fresh and fragrant breezes
    Are worth the city's wealth.
But, could you see the fair young girl
    That ministers to me,
You'd say how happy was my lot,
    Cherished so tenderly.

There are but few to love her,
    And why? for she is poor ;
And toiling, toiling all the day,
    She loveth me the more.
She smiles to see my beauty ;
    She'll weep when I am dead :
Wild sister, who will weep for you,
    When winter bows your head?

She opes the window early
    To give me air and sun,
Then sitteth sadly at my side
    To toil till day is done ;
And when she rests her weary hands,
    And drops a tear on me,
My sweetest fragrance I impart,
    And cheer her gratefully.

The children poor and wretched
    Smile as they gaze on me,
And often stop in passing,
    And praise me timidly.

So I cannot leave my noisy home,
    Though brighter are your hours :
I have the love of many hearts, —
    You've but the love of flowers.

My gentle mistress seemeth ill :
    I sometimes think she'll die.
Then send the robin and the thrush
    To bear me where she'll lie ;
And come to me, sweet sister,
    Where sombre willows wave,
And side by side we'll weep and watch
    Over her early grave.

THE BLIND MAN TO HIS WIFE.

I NEVER saw you, Bertha,
    Though you're my own sweet wife ;
And fondly, dearly do I love
    The sunshine of my life.
For midnight brooded o'er my soul,
    And midnight was my day,
Till your kind voice and gleesome laugh
    Made e'en the blind man gay.

Young maidens jeered you, Bertha,
    When you became my bride ;
And wealth and titles bowed to you,
    To lure you from my side.

My form, they said, was noble,
　That godlike was my mind,
My brow told thought and intellect:
　Alas! but I was blind.

My eyes indeed are clouded;
　But visions bright and fair
Of Nature's thousand beauties
　My mind sees everywhere.
Dearest of all, sweet Bertha mine,
　Is thy loved image bright:
I would not lose its impress there,
　To see God's blessèd light.

They ofttimes speak of beauty,
　And then I think of thee;
Gay-tinted flowers and sunset clouds,
　And still I think of thee;
The starry heavens, the sparkling brook,
　Faces most fair to see:
But my fond heart earth's loveliness
　Embodies all in thee.

Thy voice to me, dear Bertha,
　Is sweeter than the birds;
Nor harp nor lute so sweet to me
　As thine own gentle words:
At thy light footfall on the stair,
　My heart beats high with joy;
And, though ten wedded years have passed,
　I love as when a boy.

God bless thee, dearest Bertha,
　For all thou'st been to me,
For light and joy and sunshine poured
　On my sad destiny!
Oh! when the scales fall from these eyes,
　In the land where all can see,
Next to my God, sweet wife of mine,
　My gaze shall fall on thee.

"I HEARD A VOICE SAYING UNTO ME, COME UP HITHER."—Revelation.

There ever are around me
　Sweet voices in the air:
When friends are near, or when alone,
　They're ever with me there.
In the bright and gladsome morning,
　Or the silent time of eve,
They fill the air with melody,
　And this little song they weave,
　　" Come up hither."

There ever are around me
　Bright forms I love to see,
Invisible to human eye,
　But beautiful to me.
With mind's keen eye I see them;
　I feel their fanning wing;
With mind's keen ear I ever hear
　This solemn song they sing,
　　" Come up hither."

As night's dark pinion o'er me,
   They hover round my bed :
In sorrow, pain, or loneliness,
   They hold my weary head.
'Tis sweet to lean on angels,
   To feel they're ever near ;
'Tis sweet to hear their plaintive song
   For ever in mine ear,
      " Come up hither."

Why flit ye so around me,
   Ye bright angelic ones?
Why ever sound ye in mine ear
   Those sweet and solemn tones?
" We have a message, mortal,
   Our Father bade us bring ;
And we do his gracious bidding,
   When our solemn song we sing,
      ' Come up hither.'

" Oh! ever upward be thine aim,
   And upward be thine eye ;
The path of duty meekly tread,
   With heart and hope on high.
Ye've no abiding city here,
   Ye're creatures of a day ;
Then listen, listen, mortal,
   And hear our solemn lay,
      ' Come up hither.' "

Be ever, ever near me,
   Bright forms I love to see !
Oh! let me ever, ever hear
   Those tones of melody.

When on my death-bed lying,
   And eternity is near,
Oh! hover, hover o'er me,
   And those sweet tones let me hear,
      "Come up hither."

OUR REST.

" The sufferings of this present time are not worthy to be com-
pared to the glory that shall be revealed in us."

My feet are worn and weary with the march
   Over rough roads and up the steep hill-side:
O city of our God! I fain would see
   Thy pastures green, where peaceful waters glide.

My hands are weary, laboring, toiling on,
   Day after day, for perishable meat:
O city of our God! I fain would rest;
   I sigh to gain thy glorious mercy-seat.

My garments, travel-worn, and stained with dust,
   Oft rent by briars and thorns that crowd my way,
Would fain be made, O Lord my righteousness!
   Spotless and white in heaven's unclouded ray.

My eyes are weary looking at the sin,
   Impiety, and scorn upon the earth:
O city of our God! within thy walls,
   All, all are clothed upon with the new birth.

My heart is weary of its own deep sin, —
  Sinning, repenting, sinning still alway:
When shall my soul thy glorious presence feel,
  And find its guilt, dear Saviour, washed away?

Patience, poor soul! the Saviour's feet were worn,
  The Saviour's heart and hands were weary too,
His garments stained and travel-worn and old,
  His sacred eyes blinded with tears for you.

Love thou the path of sorrow that he trod;
  Toil on, and wait in patience for thy rest:
O city of our God! we soon shall see
  Thy glorious walls, home of the loved and blest.

CHARLES W. BREWSTER.

---◆---

THE VANE OF THE OLD NORTH CHURCH.

The vane of the old North Church bore the date of 1732, when it was put up. It was not gilded until 1796. When destined to come down, in 1854, the vane is thus personified, to enable it to tell its story.

 CAN'T come down ! I can't come down !
    Call loudly as you may !
    A century and a third I've stood ;
    Another I must stay.

Long have I watched the changing scene,
    As every point I've faced ;
And witnessed generations rise,
    Which others have displaced.

The points of steel which o'er me rise
    Have branched since I perched here ;
For Franklin then was but a boy,
    Who gave the lightning gear.

The day when Cook exploring sailed,
    I faced the eastern breeze ;
Stationed at home, I turned my head
    To the far western seas.

I've stood while isles of savage men
　Grew harmless as the dove ;
And spears and battle-axes turned
　To purposes of love.

I looked on when those noble elms
　Upon my east first sprung,
And heard, where now a factory stands,
　The ship-yard's busy hum.

When tumult filled the anxious throng,
　I found on every side
The constant breezes fanned a flame,
　And Freedom's fire supplied.

William and Mary's fort I've oft,
　Through storms, kept full in view ;
Queen's Chapel in the snow-squalls faced ;
　And, west, looked *King Street* through.

Fort Constitution now takes place,
　To meet my south-east glance ;
The shrill north-easters from *St. John's*
　Up *Congress Street* advance.

In peace I once felt truly vain ;
　For 'neath my shadow stood
The man whom all the people loved, —
　George Washington the good !

But why recount the sights I've seen ?
　You'll say I'm getting old :
I'll quit my tale, long though it be,
　And leave it half untold.

The fame of Rogers, Fitch, and Stiles,
    And Buckminster, — all true ;
And later men, whom all do know,
    Come passing in review.

Their sainted souls, and hearers too —
    Your fathers — where are they ?
The temple of their love still stands, —
    Its memories cheer your way.

Till that old oak, among whose boughs
    The sun my first shade cast,
Lays low in dust his vigorous form,
    A respite I may ask.

This little boon I now must crave, —
    (Time's peltings I will scorn,) —
Till, coward like, I turn my head,
    Let me still face the storm.

THE INFANT TWINS.

Parental Dedication.

YES, lovely ones, ye are the gift of Heaven !
From God's own hand ye were directly given !
And, though but mortal charms do meet the eye,
Within your bosoms immortality
A spark has kindled, which may burn more bright
Than brilliant noonday sun, — when sable night
Her reign resigns to one unceasing day,
And seraph vestments take the place of clay.

Sublime the thought, — it will not, *cannot* die,
Through years infinite an infinity!
May hope support through this short vale of tears:
There's *Balm in Gilead* for all anxious fears.

That trials here surround we do not sorrow:
　Without a cross no crown can e'er be borne:
But joy that from your Saviour ye can borrow
　That perfect armor which himself has worn.

O God! this trust of thine to thee we give;
To be for ever thine, teach them to live!
Oh! teach them early, by thy Spirit's aid,
That life, at best, is but a fleeting shade;
Teach them to venerate thy holy name, —
To know their Saviour, and his love proclaim;
Spirits of love within their bosoms bind,
And to each act and thought be close entwined.
From thine own hand oh teach them they are fed!
Thy hand their pillow, and thine arm their bed.
To thee for strength, whene'er temptations rise,
Raised be their voice, and thou wilt hear their cries.

Then, gracious God! before thy holy shrine,
　When the vast portals of the skies are riven,
May we with joy our offspring there resign:
　Here are we, Lord, and those whom thou hast given.

HISTORY OF NEWS.—BIRTH OF THE PRESS.

Lo! when the Eternal planned his wise design,
Created earth, and, like his smile benign,
With splendor, beauty, mildness, decked the skies,—
Waked from eternal sleep, with wondering eyes
Man viewed the scene, and gave to News its rise.

New of himself, to Adam all was new,—
The concave canopy, the landscape's view;
The murmuring rivulet, and the zephyr's sound;
The songster's carol, and the deer's light bound;
The fruit luxuriant, where no brier sprung;
No weary toil, from morn to setting sun;
But every gale sweet odors wafted on,
His joys to freshen.   Though he yet was lone,
This news was good indeed: such riches given,
Enough almost to make of earth a heaven.
But better news by far did Adam hear,
When woman's voice first hailed his raptured ear,—
News which, in later days, full well we know
Lightens life's load of many a heavy woe.

But scarce our common parent rose from earth,
Inhaled the breath of life, and Eve had birth,
When twined the monster round the fatal tree,—
Dispelled their joy, content, and purity:
Then agonizing Nature brought to view
Ills which in Eden's bowers they never knew;
Then, at that hour accursed, that hour forlorn,
Bad news—the demon's first bequest—was born.

But, though ignobly born, to seek we're prone
The bad as well as good, and make our own
The knowledge of the griefs and woes of all
On whom the withering frowns of fortune fall.

Bad news abundant since has filled our world :
War's bloody garments oft have been unfurled, —
The kindly parent oft been called to yield
His earthly hope to dye the ensanguined field ;
Disease oft torn our dearest hopes away,
Tyrannic princes borne despotic sway ; ·
And every day the reckless bearer's been
Of evil tidings to the sons of men.

But change this picture of a darkened hue ;
Let scenes more bright now open to the view :
Though things may change with ever-varying flow,
They do not bring to all unmingled woe.
Do millions mourn a kingdom's fallen state?
A Cæsar hails the news with joy elate.
Does drought or frost destroy the planter's hope,
And climes more genial yield a fruitful crop?
Enhanced by contrast, these delight the more
In the good tidings of their bounteous store.
Does " the insatiate archer " claim a prize?
The weeping friend, the heir with tearless eyes,
Show joy is oft the associate of grief,
And pain to some, to others is relief.

Full many ages, centuries, rolled along,
Ere news a record found, the press a tongue.
From sire to son, tradition's tale was told,
Or musty parchment spoke the days of old ;

No minor incidents of passing time
Ere filled a page or occupied a rhyme ;
No wars of politics on paper fought,
And few the favored ones by science taught.
Minerva saw the dreary waste below,
And urged the gods their bounties to bestow,
The mind of man to chaste refinement bring,
And ope to all the pure Pierian spring.
The gods convened ; but still Minerva frowned :
Not one of all their gifts her wishes crowned,
Till Vulcan thus, — and simple the address, —
" My richest gifts behold, — the TYPES and PRESS ! "
The goddess smiled, and swiftly Mercury flies
To bear to earth the god's most favored prize.
Auspicious hour ! hail, morn of brighter day !
Ages of darkness, close ! to light give way !

The morn is past, the splendid sun is high !
The mist dispelled, and all beneath the sky
Feel its kind influence ; and its cheering ray
Enlivens all, and shines in brilliant day.
The sacred writ, which once was scarcely known
To teachers, now (almost a dream !) is thrown
Into a book, — all, in one little hour,
Alike in king's and lowest menial's power ;
And bounteous given — scarce is felt the task —
In every work which use or fancy ask.
Thousands of years a dreary night had been,
Ere Vulcan's art surpassed the tedious pen, —
Ere down from heaven this precious gift was brought,
To lend the speed of lightning unto thought.

THE LOCOMOTIVE AND THE SNOW-FLAKES.

ARMED with a giant's mighty strength, —
My feeblest nerves all brass, —
My sinews, in their devious length,
Strong iron muscles grasp.

I breathe, — and lightnings fiercely glare ;
I step, — and thunders roll :
What length of train can ever dare
Impede me from my goal?

Quick as the speedy thought I fly :
What earthly power can dare
In rapid flight with me to vie,
Or tithe of burden bear?

I glory in unequalled might, —
Of strength, where rests such power?
I dare earth's legions to a fight !
I'd scorn all, in that hour !
.   .   .   .   .   .

His wide-spread nostrils, highly steamed,
A vapor slight did bear ;
In modest cloud a moment gleamed,
Then disappeared in air.

Unheeded in its upward flight,
The pearl-drops floated high,
Till in new robes of downy white
They marshalled in the sky.
.   .   . .

" Didst hear our generator's boast?"
  A snow-flake, whispering, said ;
" Come, let us, though a puny host,
  Attack the mighty steed!"

" I'm nothing mere," a flake replied ;
  " And can I dare contemn
That mighty power which has defied
  The strength, the skill, of men?"

"We need your influence, one and all!"
  Was now the stirring cry ;
" Our union is the despot's fall!"
  The puny flakes reply.

The flakes then dropped in order down,
  So small and feathery light,
They raised not e'en suspicion's frown,
  O'er carpet spread so white.

The steam is raised, — the courser raves,
  For flakes his feet have bound!
He strains each nerve ; in vain he braves :
  A match at last is found!

In voice of wisdom snow-flakes speak :
  " May man this semblance see, —
United effort nerves the weak,
  And gives the victory."

MARY CUTTS.

SEA-SHELLS.

BRIGHT, radiant shells from foreign climes,
   How beautiful ye are,
Decked with the roseate tints ye bring
   From native shore afar !

I love your colors and your shine,
   Stray ones from other shores ;
But yet a deeper grace ye have,
   A dearer charm is yours.

Ye bring the mighty ocean's roar
   Within your little space,
As if no change, no new abode,
   Its memory could efface.

Ah ! others praise your glowing hues :
   More wonderful to me
Than even the most gorgeous tints,
   These whispers of the sea.

They seem to speak of hidden power :
   And yet it is not so :
Strange, strange it is that ye should bring
   The raging water's flow !

Ah ! it is strange that what we love
　In joyous, early day,
Should never, never from the soul,
　The spirit, fade away !

Then sing, sweet shells, sing on, and tell
　Of the old ocean's roar :
It was your first love, and aught else
　Shall vanish that before.

When first created, weak and frail,
　The mighty sound ye heard ;
And now no music of the land,
　No zephyr, song of bird,

Will e'er efface it.　Be it so.
　Sing on : ye bring to me
The dashing bound, the foaming spray,
　The glory of the sea !

I seem to view the curling wave,
　I hear the whizzing gush,
As bright and clear, as swift and bold,
　The sparkling waters rush.

Then ever breathe the song to me
　That tells of native shore :
I love your beauty ; for this charm,
　Bright ones, I love you more.

SONG.

I KNEW a hearth where bright eyes met :
  Why is my spirit sad?
For round that hearth there only thronged
  The sweet, the pure, the glad.

Alas! how much is in the word,
  That simple word, I knew!
Yet can we ever cease to love
  The beautiful and true?

Ah! 'mid the varied scenes of life,
  Its hour of woe or mirth,
How oft my heart will wander back
  To that beloved hearth ;

And trust, though years may desolate
  That once so cherished spot,
There may remain one gentle heart
  That will forget me not!

I knew a hearth where bright eyes met :
  Why is my spirit sad?
For round that hearth there only thronged
  The sweet, the pure, the glad.

THE FATED.

I saw a picture once, or had a dream, —
I know not which; but oft there comes a gleam
Across my mind of what it did portray.
It was a stormy, wild, tempestuous day;
And a poor sailor on a rock is cast,
With nought to shield him from the angry blast.
Alone he stands; and, far as eye can reach,
There is no sign of ship or isle or beach:
Nought seen but ocean, — ocean all around,
With its tumultuous heaves, — no other sound:
No form but his, no human arm to save,
As wave on wave came tumbling over wave.
The ocean roared and beat and splashed and fumed;
Still on his craggy rock stood firm the doomed.
I heard it rave — oh! terrible the sound!
Darker and darker grew the clouds around;
Not yet the fated from his rock is riven:
Yet is he there, — there, with his eye on heaven.

SAMUEL M. DEMERITT.

———◆———

FORGIVENESS.

HE virtues met in summer-time
　　Beneath an aged tree,
To see each other, and to hold
　　A converse kind and free.

They also had a prize to give
　　To one among them there ;
And who the worthy one should be
　　They *all* were to declare.

The fair ones, meekly joining hands,
　　Their mutual honor plight,
And seek, with truly honest zeal,
　　To recompense the right.

When all had thought, it was agreed
　　(A judgment ne'er more wise !)
By all as one, with heart and voice,
　　" FORGIVENESS takes the prize."

TO ——.

WERE I to twine a beauteous wreath
    Thy tranquil brow to bind,
I would not take from Flora's hand
    Her flowers of choicest kind.

I would not seek for pearls, or gold,
    Or diamonds bright and rare :
I'd cull from virtue's garden rich,
    Adornments far more fair.

I'd make a crown of modesty,
    And deck it o'er with truth ;
With cheerfulness I'd have it shine,
    Like buoyant hopes of youth.

Sincerity, and friendship true,
    And kindness, should be there ;
And, more than all, thy brow the gem
    Of *piety* should wear.

GOD AND OUR NEIGHBOR.

ALTHOUGH our duties are in number great,
Of vast proportions and of wondrous weight ;
Yet all, when rightly seen and understood,
Tend toward ourselves, our neighbor, and our God.

Our neighbor, who ? Our duty to him, what ?
In palace dwells he, or in humble cot ?
Where'er he dwells, 'tis he, we must confess,
Whom we can aid : our duty is to bless.

DANIEL A. DROWN.

—◆—

SPRING IS COMING.

GENIAL Spring once more is coming,
And the bees will soon be humming
　　Round the scented thyme ;
Now, amid the mosses sleeping,
Purple eyes will soon be peeping
　　In their beauteous prime.

All along the meadows teeming,
Like bright stars in valleys gleaming,
　　Golden flowers shall bloom,
Welcoming each sunny ray,
Which around their leaves shall play,
　　And their crowns illume.

Birdlings from the Southern clime,
Glad to hail this pleasant time,
　　Now in crowds appear ;
And in all the forest bowers,
Charming all the morning hours,
　　Carol sweet and clear.

Flowers fair in meads reposing,
As the wintry months are closing,
    Long once more to bloom ;
With the dew-drops on them lying,
While the northern breeze is sighing
    No more o'er their tomb.

Petals from green nests emerging
Shall, on wavy branches surging,
    Sport like doves on high ;
Fluttering, when the vernal breeze
Whispers softly through the trees,
    With its plaintive sigh.

Streamlets through green valleys flowing,
All their joy and beauty showing,
    Sparkling clear and bright,
Dance along, where banks of flowers
Soon shall bless the summer hours,
    In the warm sunlight.

Fragrance through the soft air stealing,
Unseen treasures fast revealing
    From the blooming trees,
Soon shall charm the rosy morning,
Beautified with fresh adorning,
    Lading every breeze.

Let all, in these pleasant hours,
Wander in the woodland bowers,
    In the morning light,
Seeking health and strength and pleasure,
Thanking GOD for every treasure
    That can cheer the sight.

MAY.

Once more the fragrant breath of Spring
  Speaks kindly unto me,
Though emerald twigs and opening buds
  No more with joy I see;
But well I know a snowy cloud
  Of blossoms decks the trees,
Inviting with mellifluous sweets
  Gay birds and honey-bees.

The dimpled brooks, long held in chains
  By Winter's icy hand,
Now speak their joy with native grace,
  Which we may not withstand;
And flowers nod upon the banks,
  Kissed by the laughing stream,
As if to greet upon its face
  Each golden sunny beam.

A choral anthem floats along,
  O'er meadow, field, and wood,
Enlivening with melodious strains
  The deepest solitude,
Where violets profusely bloom
  Within each mossy dell,
And woo warm sunshine through the leaves,
  And speak their praises well.

I love to think of the new life
  Which decks the stately trees,
And list the song they ever sing,
  Fanned by the vernal breeze;

I love to read upon each leaf
    This sacred, precious truth, —
Though we must die, there yet remains
    A blest eternal youth.

A genial glow our pulses thrills
    While musing on the scene,
A holy charm pervades our hearts,
    Of purest thoughts serene ;
For, in each leaf and opening bud,
    A higher life we trace :
Our drooping forms shall be revived
    And crowned with heavenly grace.

HE, who now dots the landscape o'er
    With flowers pure and fair,
Smiles ever on his children here,
    And makes us all his care ;
And when our mission is fulfilled,
    Each earthly fetter riven,
For us within the pearly gates
    Shall bloom a Spring in heaven.

———————

MUSINGS ON THE CLOSE OF THE YEAR.

How swiftly ebb the waves of time
    Along life's broken shore,
Revealing scenes of joy and pain,
    Which charmed and grieved before !
For memory wakes at twilight hour,
    While musing on the past,
Recalling bright and sunny days,
    By shadows overcast.

Upon the tide of hope we sail
    Adown the flowing stream,
Inspired by warm and earnest zeal,
    And many a thoughtful dream.
We see the goal towards which we haste,
    Beaming with golden light,
Nor fear the unknown depths which hide
    The dangers of the night.

Life's voyage bids us fearless roam
    O'er many a stormy sea,
With boisterous winds still urging on,
    And breakers on the lea ;
But, trusting to our chart and guide,
    We press unwearied on,
Nor rest till in the haven sure
    The welcome prize is won.

But, ere we reach that " open sea,"
    Beyond this earthly veil,
How many a toilsome course we make,
    Where untried storms prevail !
But cherished hopes are often hid
    Beneath a threatening sky ;
And many a weary day must pass,
    Ere light will beam on high.

Blest be the hope which cheers our heart,
    'Mid darkness, fears, and pain ;
There yet remains a welcome rest, —
    An everlasting gain.
Beyond the ever-changing scene
    Of life's tempestuous tide,
A home is found, where purest joys
    Eternally abide.

DEW ON THE GRASS.

How beautiful at morning light,
  When summer winds are sighing,
To view the sparkling dew-drops bright
  Upon the green turf lying,
With myriad rainbows circling round
  These crystal forms reposing
So humbly near the thirsty ground,
  As night's moist wings are closing!

So pure and fresh the gorgeous scene,
  They seem a diamond sea,
With isles of amethyst between,
  And emerald shores to lea ;
O'er whose bright waters blue-birds skim,
  As o'er a crystal cup,
To sweetly pour their morning hymn,
  And pick the jewels up.

As silently as dews distil,
  For Nature kindly given,
So may Thy grace my bosom fill
  With choicest gifts from Heaven :
E'en though I lie recumbent, far
  Down in a suffering vale,
Let my dark night know one bright star,
  Nor let my courage fail.

Within this valley, let me feel
  The dews which round me fall,
Which o'er my life so quiet steal
  In blessings large and small ;

Let me behold in sorrow's night
    The jewels which descend,
Which yet shall sparkle in the light,
    When life's short day shall end.

———

"PAX VOBISCUM."

As sweet music in a valley
    Floats through shady aisles along,
Where the tinkling ripplets' murmur
    Only joins the wavy song;
So, amid my own deep silence,
    Floated near, one stilly night,
Silvery strains, whose pleasant echoes
    Filled my heart with cheering light.

Clear the voice, and pure the accents,
    Which surprised my patient ear,·
Ever listening, 'mid the stillness,
    Some good angel's wings to hear;
And they stirred within my bosom
    Thoughts of loved ones far away,
Who might send, with heavenly blessing,
    Perfumed words to light my way.

When the heart is pained and weary,
    Sad in its own solitude,
Is it not to sweetest memories
    By some soothing accents wooed?
Then the faintest loving echo
    Which the soul has ever heard
Vibrates, with a lengthened cadence,
    In each kindly spoken word.

In the silent midnight hours,
  When I watch, all still and lone,
I would claim this benison, —
  " Peace be with you ! " — for my own :
As if it were by angels spoken,
  I would feel its sacred power,
Welcome, as to withering flowers
  Comes the cool, refreshing shower.

When life's storm shall gather fierceness,
  And its clouds shall grow more dark ;
When the foamed-capped billows threaten
  To ingulf my trembling bark ;
Then, amid the angry waters,
  When my strength is wholly vain,
May strong faith " beyond the river "
  See the smiles of " Love " again.

May that blessed peace sustain me
  In the darkest, saddest hour,
Which a Father's love bestoweth,
  When the clouds of sorrow lower !
Let my heart, still loving, trusting,
  Safe repose in His own will, —
Knowing, in each fiery trial,
  His *great heart but loves me still.*

JAMES T. FIELDS.

BALLAD OF THE TEMPEST.

E were crowded in the cabin;
    Not a soul would dare to sleep:
It was midnight on the waters,
    And a storm was on the deep.

'Tis a fearful thing in winter
    To be shattered in the blast,
And to hear the rattling trumpet
    Thunder, " Cut away the mast!"

So we shuddered there in silence;
    For the stoutest held his breath,
While the hungry sea was roaring,
    And the breakers talked with Death.

As thus we sat in darkness,
    Each one busy in his prayers,
" We are lost!" the captain shouted,
    As he staggered down the stairs.

But his little daughter whispered,
   As she took his icy hand,
" Isn't God upon the ocean,
   Just the same as on the land? "

Then we kissed the little maiden,
   And we spoke in better cheer;
And we anchored safe in harbor,
   When the morn was shining clear.

TO T. S. K.

Go with a manly heart,
Where courage leads the brave ;
High thoughts, not years, have stamped their part,
Who shunned the coward's grave.

Clear, to the eye of youth,
Their record stands enrolled,
Who held aloft the flag of Truth,
Nor slept beneath its fold.

They heard the trumpet sound
Where hosts to battle trod,
And marched along that burning ground :
Fear not ! they rest with God.

Like them, advance in love,
And upward bend thy sight ;
Win Faith through Prayer : He rules above
Who still protects the right.

ON A BOOK OF SEA-MOSSES,

Sent to an Eminent English Poet.

To him who sang of Venice, and revealed
How Wealth and Glory clustered in her streets,
And poised her marble domes with wondrous skill,
We send these tributes, plundered from the sea.
These many-colored, variegated forms
Sail to our rougher shores, and rise and fall
To the deep music of the Atlantic wave.
Such spoils we capture where the rainbows drop,
Melting in ocean. Here are broideries strange,
Wrought by the sea-nymphs from their golden hair,
And wove by moonlight. Gently turn the leaf.
From narrow cells, scooped in the rocks, we take
These fairy textures, lightly moored at morn.
Down sunny slopes, outstretching to the deep,
We roam at noon, and gather shapes like these.
Note now the painted webs from verdurous isles,
Festooned and spangled in sea-caves, and say
What hues of land can rival tints like those,
Torn from the scarfs and gonfalons of kings
Who dwell beneath the waters.
                                        Such our Gift,
Culled from a margin of the Western World,
And offered unto Genius, in the Old.

WORDSWORTH.

1847.

THE grass hung wet on Rydal banks,
The golden day with pearls adorning,
When side by side with him we walked,
To meet midway the summer morning.

The west-wind took a softer breath,
The sun himself seemed brighter shining,
As through the porch the minstrel stepped,
His eye sweet Nature's look enshrining.

He passed along the dewy sward,
The linnet sang aloft, " Good morrow ! "
He plucked a bud ; the flower awoke,
And smiled without one pang of sorrow.

He spoke of all that graced the scene
In tones that fell like music round us :
We felt the charm descend, nor strove
To break the rapturous spell that bound us.

We listened with mysterious awe,
Strange feelings mingling with our pleasure ;
We heard that day prophetic words, —
High thoughts the heart must always treasure.

Great Nature's Priest ! thy calm career
With that sweet morn on earth has ended ;
But who shall say thy mission died,
When, winged for heaven, thy soul ascended?

"THE STORMY PETREL."

WHERE the gray crags beat back the northern main,
And all around, the ever restless waves,
Like white sea-wolves, howl on the lonely sands,
Clings a low roof, close by the sounding surge.
If, in your summer rambles by the shore,
His spray-tost cottage you may chance espy,
Enter and greet the blind old mariner.

Full sixty winters he has watched beside
The turbulent ocean, with one purpose warmed :
To rescue drowning men. And round the coast —
For so his comrades named him in his youth —
They know him as " The Stormy Petrel " still.

Once he was lightning-swift, and strong ; his eyes
Peered through the dark, and far discerned the wreck
Plunged on the reef. Then with bold speed he flew,
The life-boat launched, and dared the smiting rocks.

'Tis said by those long dwelling near his door,
That hundreds have been storm-saved by his arm ;
That never was he known to sleep, or lag
In-doors, when danger swept the seas. His life
Was given to toil, his strength to perilous blasts.
In freezing floods when tempests hurled the deep,
And battling winds clashed in their icy caves,
Scared housewives, waking, thought of him, and said,
" ' The Stormy Petrel ' is abroad to-night,
And watches from the cliffs."

He could not rest
When shipwrecked forms might gasp amid the waves,
And not a cry be answered from the shore.

Now Heaven has quenched his sight ; but when he hears
By his lone hearth the sullen sea-winds clang,
Or listens, in the mad, wild, drowning night,
As younger footsteps hurry o'er the beach
To pluck the sailor from his sharp-fanged death, —
The old man starts, with generous impulse thrilled,
And, with the natural habit of his heart,
Calls to his neighbors in a cheery tone,
Tells them he'll pilot toward the signal guns,
And then, remembering all his weight of years,
Sinks on his couch, and weeps that he is blind.

AN INVITATION.

THE warm wide hills are muffled thick with green,
And fluttering swallows fill the air with song.
Come to our cottage-home.   Lowly it stands,
Set in a vale of flowers, deep fringed with grass.
The sweetbrier (noiseless herald of the place)
Flies with its odor, meeting all who roam
With welcome footsteps to our small abode.
No splendid cares live here, — no barren shows ; —
The bee makes harbor at our perfumed door,
And hums all day his breezy note of joy.

Come, O my friend ! and share our festal month,
And while the west-wind walks the leafy woods,

While orchard-blooms are white in all the lanes,
And brooks make music in the deep, cool dells,
Enjoy the golden moments as they pass,
And gain new strength for days that are to come.

SPRING, AMONG THE HILLS.

SIT and talk with the mountain streams
  In the beautiful spring of the year,
When the violet gleams through the golden sunbeams,
  And whispers, "Come look for me here," —
  In the beautiful spring of the year.

I will show you a glorious nook,
  Where the censers of morning are swung;
Nature will lend you her bell and her book,
  Where the chimes of the forest are hung, —
  And the censers of morning are swung.

Come and breathe in this heaven-sent air
  The breeze that the wild-bird inhales,
Come and forget that life has a care,
  In these exquisite mountain-gales, —
  The breeze that the wild-bird inhales.

Oh wonders of God! oh bounteous and good!
  We feel that thy presence is here, —
That thine audible voice is abroad in this wood,
  ·In the beautiful spring of the year, —
  And we know that *our Father* is here.

ON A PAIR OF ANTLERS BROUGHT FROM GERMANY.

GIFT from the land of song and wine,
　Can I forget the enchanted day,
When first along the glorious Rhine
　I heard the huntsman's bugle play,
And marked the early star that dwells
　Among the cliffs of Drachenfels!

Again the isles of beauty rise;
　Again the crumbling tower appears,
That stands, defying stormy skies,
　With memories of a thousand years;
And dark old forests wave again,
　And shadows crowd the dusky plain.

They brought the gift, that I might hear　.
　The music of the roaring pine, —
To fill again my charmèd ear
　With echoes of the Rodenstein, —
With echoes of the silver horn, —
　Across the wailing waters borne.

Trophies of spoil! henceforth your place
　Is in this quiet home of mine:
Farewell the busy, bloody chase,
　Mute emblems now of " auld lang syne,"
When Youth and Hope went hand in hand
　To roam the dear old German land.

RELICS.

You ask me why with such a jealous care
I hoard these rings, this chain of silken hair,
This cross of pearl, this simple key of gold,
And all these trifles which my hands enfold.
I'll tell you, friend, why all these things become
My blest companions when remote from home ;
Why, when I sleep, these first secured I see,
With wakeful eye and guarded constancy.
Each little token, each familiar toy,
My mother gave her once too happy boy ;
Her kiss went with them ; — chide me, then, no more,
That thus I count my treasures o'er and o'er.
Alas ! she sleeps beneath the dust of years,
And these few flowers I water with my tears !

SONG IN A DREAM.

Winter rose-leaves, silver-white,
    Drifting o'er our darling's bed, —
He's asleep, withdrawn from sight, —
    All his little prayers are said,
    And he droops his shining head.

Winter rose-leaves, falling still,
    Go and waken his sad eyes,
Touch his pillowed rest, until
    He shall start with glad surprise,
    And from slumber sweet arise !

M. W. B.

THEY tell me thou art laid to rest,
    Companion of my happiest years!
That thou hast joined the loved and blest,
    Whose early graves are wet with tears;
That I shall never hear again
    The voice that charmed my boyhood's ear,
Nor meet among the haunts of men
    Thy honest grasp of love sincere.

Friend of my youth! my buried friend!
    Thy step was gayest in the ring;
My thoughts far back through childhood wend,
    And can I now thy requiem sing?
Alas! I feel 'tis all in vain, —
    Before such grief my spirits bow:
Farewell! I cannot trace the pain
    That weighs upon my heart-strings now.

THE FLIGHT OF ANGELS.

Two pilgrims to the Holy Land
    Passed through our open door, —
Two sinless Angels, hand in hand,
    Have reached the promised shore.

We saw them take their heavenward flight
    Through floods of drowning tears,
And felt, in woe's bewildering night,
    The agony of years.

But now we watch the golden path
　Their blessèd feet have trod,
And know that voice was not in wrath
　Which called them both to God.

COMMON SENSE.

SHE came among the gathering crowd,
A maiden fair, without pretence ;
And when they asked her humble name,
She whispered mildly, " Common Sense."

Her modest garb drew every eye,
Her ample cloak, her shoes of leather ;
And, when they sneered, she simply said,
" I dress according to the weather."

They argued long, and reasoned loud,
In dubious Hindoo phrase mysterious,
While she, poor child, could not divine
Why girls so young should be so serious.

They knew the length of Plato's beard,
And how the scholars wrote in Saturn ;
She studied authors not so deep,
And took the Bible for her pattern.

And so she said, " Excuse me, friends,
I find all have their proper places ;
And *Common Sense* should stay at home
With cheerful hearts and smiling faces."

TO MY LITTLE FRIEND AT THE SOUTH END.

DEAR CHILD ! what thought or word of mine
Is worthy thy first Valentine?
Those sweet blue eyes, thy witching smile,
(That angel hearts might well beguile,)
Have claims to win from deeper chords
A strain beyond my simple words.

What shall I wish thee, Baby, fair?
All choicest gifts? — Heaven's kindly care?
Beauty thou hast : a world of love,
Pure as the purest born above,
Lies sleeping in that little face,
In mild repose, in infant grace.

Ah ! dearest child ! we'll pray that thou
Mayst always smile on us as now ;
That years may bring thee added charms ;
That love may shield thy path from harms ;
And all that's best and bright below
Around thy life-long journey flow.

So take, Therese, the song I bring ;
And when thou'rt old enough to sing,
And pass me by, on some spring day,
When all my locks are dangling gray,
(If haply, far away, my head
Is not then pillowed with the dead,)
Forget not him whose lips to thine
Were pledged to write this Valentine !

MARIAN IN HER CELL.

'After the Murder.

You looked across the meadows
  At the red sun in the west,
And the wood was full of shadows;
  But my head lay on your breast,
And your words were low and sweet,
And our hearts in music beat.

You spoke, — I only listened, —
  (Blest hours without alloy !)
You sang, — my tear-drops glistened, —
  I was dumb and blind with joy.
Could I hear your bridal bell —
You in Heaven, and I in Hell !

Could I stop the cursèd blade,
  At your throat so warm and white ;
Where my loving fingers played
  With the moonlight through the night ?
Could I *think*, and hold the steel !
Could I *pause*, and *live* to feel !

By the hallowed word of God
  There is Murder on your soul !
As I knelt upon the sod
  Where the death-black waters roll,
I could hear the angry flood
Calling, hoarsely, " *Blood for Blood !* "

LOT SKINNER'S ELEGY.

Lot Skinner was the meanest man
  That ever saved his neck ;
He grudged the very breath he drew,
  As if it were a check.

When he was in the grocer line,
  And turning fruit to gold,
He'd bite a raisin straight in halves
  To make the weight he sold.

Day in and out, through heat and cold,
  For thirty years or more,
He well observed the copper-mean,
  And — something blessed his store.

He never gave a dime away,
  He never lost a pin ;
A ninepence saved rejoiced him more
  Than taking ninepence in.

Of counterfeited bills he used
  The best of every kind,
Which in the way of trade he kept,
  To swap off on the blind.

The poor came round his counter's edge,
  And raised a feeble cry :
" Don't speak so loud," the rogue exclaimed,
  " For I am always nigh."

" ''Tis little things that make a pile," —
  (This maxim he could trust.)
So, when he sawed his pile of wood,
  He always saved the dust.

He had but one book in the house,
  And *that* he never read !
'Twas called " Economy of Life," —
  And did him good, he said.   .

He welcomed in the rising moon, —
  'Twas such a cheerful sight ;
For then he'd blow the candle out,
  And use the gratis light.

He liked in other people's pews
  To settle meekly down,
And steal his preaching, here and there,
  By sneaking round the town.

Sometimes we saw a greenish smile
  Coil up his bony face :
'Twas when the parson chose a theme
  That spoke of saving grace.

At last it cost so much to live, —
  (Per day some twenty cents,)
" I won't stand this ! " he inly groaned,
  And died to save expense.

Now, having gone where all his means
  Are shut up in a box,
He cannot lift that heavy lid
  The careful sexton locks.

Adieu! thou scrap of lifeless clay!
Thou pale-ink human blot!
This line shall be thine epitaph, —
"*An unproductive Lot!*"

THE OLD YEAR.

THE white dawn glimmered, and he said, "'Tis day!"
The east was reddening, and he sighed, "Farewell!"
The herald Sun came forth, and he was dead.

Life was in all his veins but yestermorn,
And ruddy health seemed laughing on his lips;
Now he is dust, and will not breathe again!

Give him a place to lay his regal head,
Give him a tomb beside his brothers gone,
Give him a tablet for his deeds and name!

Hear the new voice that claims the vacant throne,
Take the new hand outstretched to meet thy kiss,
But give the Past — 'tis all thou canst — thy tears!

WOODBURY M. FERNALD.

—◆—

TRIBUTE OF AFFECTION TO THE LATE REV. THOMAS STARR KING.

TAR of the West! thy rising and thy setting,
 Like a fair planet in the evening sky, —
How brief the space! but, ah, how past for-
  getting
 The glory of that fleeting brilliancy!

Sweet soul of love! I've watched thy early dawning,
 E'en from thy childhood's innocence and play,
When first the glow and beauty of life's morning
 Gave promise of the glory of the day.

Fair day to us! a time of cheerful gladness,
 Continual summer, and a genial sky:
Oh, could some genius, without shade or sadness,
 View but *thy* nature with thy practised eye!

What scenes of flowing and of radiant beauty! —
 Fair fields of verdure; silver rolling streams;
Mountains of grandeur, stern and bold as duty,
 O'er which the sunlight of the spirit gleams;

An inner world, — a world of pure emotion,
  With fruit and foliage, rich with golden store ;
And broad expanse of sky and air and ocean,
  With waves still breaking on that mystic shore.

Ah ! 'twas *such* nature, genial friend and brother,
  That from thy spirit looked so truly out,
In rapt responses, to behold another,
  To lift the soul, and banish every doubt.

But thou art risen, — gone to be transfigured
  In that high world where angels hold their seat,
And where diviner scenes, to souls delivered,
  Thy wondering vision shall in glory greet.

Farewell, farewell ! but not as gone for ever
  E'en from the earth thou so delightedst in ;
For nought can such an intimacy sever
  With the sweet soul of all things so akin.

And long as Nature wears her wondrous beauty ;
  Long as the mountains tower in heights sublime ;
Or, in the higher walks of Christian duty,
  Great Heaven hath need of earnestness like thine ;

While patriot Truth may wake a slumbering nation ;
  And gaunt Rebellion strike fair Freedom's form :
So long thine influence, like a sweet oblation,
  Shall blend with ours, and face the threatening storm.

Not gone from us ! for, like the trembling wire
  That flashed afar the tidings of thy death,
So thy quick spirit hath but to desire,
  And thou art here, — we feel thy quickening breath.

And thus, dear Starr, for ever shall we cherish
  Thyself, thy virtues, all thy kindling love ;
Passed from our sight, but, nevermore to perish,
  Rising and shining in new light above.

BEAUTY OF CHARACTER.

" All the angels are forms of their own affections."—SWEDENBORG.

LADY, there is one truth, and one alone,
Which to the lover of the beautiful,
In person or in manners, stands supreme.
It is that good alone, in its fair form,
Is Beauty. All else perishes. The eye
Of light, with its bewitching fire ; the brow,
The cheek, the lip, the graceful form ; all the
Fair symmetry that's held so dear, in man
Or woman, must, by the eternal law
Of the Creator's power, which moulds and shapes
All outward forms from inward essences,
At last be made to correspond to the
Indwelling spirit. Then one only thing —
When outward forms have crumbled into dust,
And nature's indistinguishable earth
Holds all that hath so charmed us — one thing then,
Of all we had admired, shall have the power
To assume this mystic grace. Remember, lady,
It is CHARACTER !
  When virtue's plastic spirit hath inwrought,
And love, sweet sympathy, and tenderness,
And melting charity for others' woes,
And patience, gentleness, and humble trust,

Have all conspired to fix the angelic form —
To shape the countenance, to light the eye,
To give the curve and all the lineament
To this immortal and this living sculpture
Of heaven's divinest work — oh ! that shall last.
When sun and moon and stars decay, and time
Itself expires, and sin alone takes on,
In the dark regions of eternity,
The shape and hue of dread deformity,
This shall for ever freshen and delight.
'Tis virtue's own and high prerogative ; —
The very *essence* of divinest beauty,
Such as pure angels love, and God himself
In holiness admires.

MY SOUL AND ME.

Written on the Island of Nantucket, Jan. 2, 1858.

O God ! a sense of loneliness to-day
Comes over me, as I am far away
    From wife and home ;
    Sadly I roam
O'er this dear island of the deep blue sea, —
Engulfing waters round, — my soul and me.

Ah yes, 'tis this, — this mystic, double me ;
This sense of something which I cannot see ;
    So near, so far,
    No midnight star
More distant seems, or nearer shines more bright,
When, as to-day, dark clouds blend with the light.

Ah me! that very nearness 'tis which makes
An island of my soul, and almost shakes
      The solid land,
      The mind's firm stand,
Girt round with waters far more deep and drear
Than all old ocean has to offer here.

This double self — what is it? I have met,
Here in this Island Home where I am set,
      Fair beauty's form,
      And welcomes warm,
From eyes and voices thrilling with delight,
That grace the homes by day, the halls by night; —

I've listened to the melodies of sense,
Such as melodious souls alone dispense;
      The voice of song,
      The fancy throng
Of sun-bright memories waked from classic heart,
With wit, refinement, eloquence, and art.

But still this mystic being drooped and fell;
No wit could liven, and no charm dispel;
      Lonely, my soul,
      Thou art not whole,
For that which now is felt most near to me
Leaves me a mateless wanderer by the sea.

    .   .   .   .   .

Oh Heaven, I see! — 'Tis but *my Soul and Me*
That thus communes with solitude so free:
      Fast by my side,
      Immortal Bride,
Thou walkest with me wheresoe'er I go,
And 'tis my blindness that afflicts me so.

I want but sight.   She's all my soul desired.
The great ideal — beauty, love inspired,
    Came from her heart,
    With gentlest art,
And all that clouds the heaven of my mind
Is that my other self I cannot find.

Joy! Joy! and welcome to this heart of thine,
For wheresoe'er thou art, thou still art mine;
    In earth or heaven,
    To me thou'rt given,
To cheer my lonely hours and make me glad,
And be most near me when I am most sad.

A VISION OF THE ETERNAL GLORY.

O God of glory! when with eye uplifted,
    Eye of the soul in visioned wonder clear;
And when by thine eternal Spirit gifted,
    What deep revealings to the soul appear!

Nature recedes; and in the expanse eternal,
    Spreading and opening to my raptured sight,
I see the hosts of God, the heights supernal,
    The church triumphant crowned in heaven's own
        light.

Ah! there are they who, once among the lowly,
    Erst trod the paths of patient virtue here;
And there are they who, in thy presence holy,
    Trembled for sin, but knew no other fear:

Prophets, reformers, — they who, God revering,
   Battled with hoary wrong and ancient might ;
Behold them now in triumph re-appearing
   On all the hills of God, in glory bright !

In deepening vision, flames a light before them,
   Where a long train of *martyrs* rise to view ;
And, lo ! a central figure bending o'er them, —
   The dear Redeemer crowning them anew.

Victors and heroes all, I see them waving
   Triumphant palms, in robes of purest white :
No more the terrors of the conflict braving,
   Peace is their lot, and heaven their high delight.

LONELINESS.

I AM lonely ; I am lonely !
   O my Father ! 'tis not only
That I feel no presence with me, drawing near my
      weary soul ;
   But it is that very presence,
   With its quick and subtle essence,
Touching all the floods of feeling that in anguish o'er
      me roll.

O my Father ! could my spirit,
   Mounting upward, thus inherit
Joys of sympathetic nature from a true, accordant
      sphere,

Oh how swiftly, oh how freely,
Would I flee from all beneath me,
Soaring to the far-off regions and from all that trou-
bleth here !

In that high and deep revealing,
Touching all the secret feeling
Of my soul's imprisoned nature, here in darkness and
in grief,
Should I chance to find the greeting,
In a true and spirit meeting,
Of but *one* who truly knows me, 'twere a sweet and
blest relief.

One there must be.   And the others, —
Friends, companions, sisters, brothers, —
Small the circle, if congenial, that sufficeth for my
peace :
Farewell, then, this earth's confusion,
Social mockeries, heart's delusion ;
Come the sweet and satisfying soul's communion and
release.

Son of God, too, shall I call thee ?
Lo ! the sin that doth inthrall me,
Still inviting, still attracting demons foul about my
way ;
Ah ! no solitude so dreary,
And no company so weary ;
Break this bondage, blest Redeemer ! and I rise to
cheerful day.

Not then lonely; lo! above me,
Where the dear ones are that love me,
Gleams athwart my raptured vision, from a bright and
blissful shore,
Shadowy forms that hover o'er me,
Lights that glimmer now before me,
Waking in my lonely bosom life and joy for evermore.

Hail, my soul! the blest presentment;
Learn from it the sweet contentment
Of a life so large and noble, spreading forth from
sphere to sphere,
That, when earthly joys forsake thee,
Heaven to its embrace may take thee,
In a grand and high communion, free from all that
troubleth here.

THE AMERICAN FLAG.

A Song.

HAIL! glorious ensign of the free,
Token of gladdening hope to me,
   My country, and the world;
Ten thousand pealing cheers be given,
And million souls be touched of heaven,
   Where'er thou art unfurled.
      For thee the patriot braveth
         The soldier's fearless death;
      And where it proudly waveth,
         He yields his willing breath.

Flow on, broad banner ; every fold
Some great idea shall uphold,
    And waft it round the earth :
Each wind of heaven, evermore,
Shall blow it forth from shore to shore,
    Flag of a Nation's birth !
        O'er every hill and valley,
            From East to Western coast,
        Around it all shall rally —
            A brave and mighty host.

Its flaming beams of holy light,
Its martyr red, its truthful white,
    Its starry heaven of blue, —
In flowing beauty on the air,
Its kindling message shall declare,
    With glories ever new.
        On every noble river,
            On every mountain height,
        It calls us to deliver
            The land from Slavery's blight.

Ye sons of Freedom, bear it on ! —
It has in thousand victories shone,
    March boldly to the last :
For lo ! the Star of Destiny
Now brightly gleams in Freedom's sky,
    Above war's stormy blast !
        Wave ! then, o'er land and ocean,
            From spire and dome and tree,
        Flag of our heart's devotion,
            Till all the bond are free !

Then to the lands beyond the seas,
Where tyrants write their stern decrees,
  And old oppression reigns ;
Be thou the hope of future years,
Banner that every despot fears,
  Symbol of falling chains !
    To every land and nation
      Beneath the circling sun,
    Wave ! flag of our salvation,
      Till Freedom's work is done.

SARAH H. FOSTER.

AUGUST, 1864.

I.

THEY ask, where are my songs for thee,
  Thrice dear and cherished land!
They know not that the trembling heart
  Unnerves the tuneful hand;
They know not that the troubled soul
  Bids all sweet fancies fly,
As Summer's minstrels mutely cower
  Beneath a stormy sky.

II.

Ask one who loves, to part in song
  From friends of early years;
The song would faint beneath its theme,
  And tremble into tears.
The harmony of life is drawn
  By gentle touch alone:
The deepest note, when struck, gives back
  Not music, but a moan.

III.

A stronger voice than mine must ring
  The clarion note of war ;
A higher flight than mine must scan
  The morning from afar ;
The flowers I fain would pluck for thee,
  With woful drops are wet ;
The cloud too closely o'er us lowers
  To see the morning yet.

IV.

The lurid smoke of battlefields
  Obscures the blessèd light ;
The stars of promise faintly shine
  To cheer the lengthened night ;
The wail from out thy thousand homes
  Hath hushed the angels' strain ;
Glory to God ! we still can hear, —
  Oh ! when the " PEACE " again ?

V.

When God hath cleansed away thy curse,
  And speaks thy penance done ;
When all thy children join to hail
  The rise of Freedom's sun :
Then will the sons of God again
  The unbroken anthem raise,
Nor will earth's humblest lyre refuse
  To echo back the praise.

ST. PAUL AT ROME.

2 Tim. iv. 6–8.

Thou stately Empress, with disdainful foot
Upon the neck of the submissive world,
Fair, marble-towered Rome! not earth alone
Bends her attentive eyes upon thee now:
Heaven's angel hosts on their celestial cars
Above thee pause.   Watch they your lordly dome,
Where throned caprice plays with a nation's fate?
Your laurelled band that Fame herself hath crowned?
Thy proud patricians, or thy martial pomp,
Self-conscious city?   A neglected guest
Within thee stands, before whose glorious light
The judgment-day shall see thine own go out;
Whose name Eternity has written down
Higher than thine!   Beside his lowly door
True victory stands, whose shadow thou hast chased
O'er Egypt's fatal sands, and Scythia's snows!
The good fight he has fought, the course has won:
Above his humble roof, a wingèd guard
Wait his approach, with chariot of fire,
And pomp of escort, to the King of kings.
The hour of his departure is at hand:
Yea, soon shall he depart, and be with Christ.
Oh, glorious hope that lights that upward eye!
Oh, faith made sight, that sees in heaven's ark
The crown of righteousness laid up for him!
Through the bright courts his trancèd spirit flies, —
The boundless riches man conceiveth not, —
And sees one chief, one best, to be with Christ!

That form benign whose footstep, scarce effaced,
Earth thrilled to bear ; whose glory, since revealed,
Hath blazed conviction on his blinded sense ;
Whose name his watchword and his power hath
    been, —
The Christ he lived, — will make it gain to die !
Fly, fly, rapt soul ! to meet the expected smile
To whose reward all else was counted dross,
Dust on the balances : why turnest thou
From heaven's expanded gate, and bend'st again
Thy lofty eye to earth?   One message more
To thy loved brethren, soon forlorn of thee ;
One pleading of His name, one girding-up
Thy spirit to its final strife, and then
Thanks be to God who giveth thee the victory !

THE CROWN OF THORNS.

Hath earth no other diadem for thee,
O Christ, anointed King of Majesty !
No crown but one of thorns to suit thy royalty?

Her wide-spread empires, and her treasures stored,
No pomp of sovereignty can they afford?
No wreath of glorious light to lay before her Lord?

Bring forth the wreath by conquering heroes worn :
Alas, how many brows that wreath has torn !
What is the Victor's crown but one of thorns?

Let Mammon's hand his coronet present,
Lo ! gilded care, and jewelled discontent ! —
Small rest for weary heads beneath such burden bent !

Where is thy laurel fit for high renown?
Envy has seared it, hate hath torn it down:
Ah, pale-browed sons of fame, ye wear a thorny crown!

The flowery wreath of sweet affection bring:
But, lo! among the flowers a piercing sting, —
The heart that loveth best must sharpest sorrows wring.

Aye, lay thy crown of thorns before His feet:
'Tis thy best guerdon, thy reward most meet, —
More fit such open woe than bitter hid in sweet.

Refuse the offering not, O Prince divine!
Upon thy brow it will transfigured shine:
Wear thou our crown, that so our souls may rise to
　　thine.

No more the thorn a sign of curse shall be;
Henceforth a trophy of thy victory:
Pain, sorrow, loss, are blest since they are shared by
　　thee.

THE CRICKET.

I.

In the fading Summer's stillness,
　　Through the pallid light,
Comes the crickets' chirping, chirping,
　　With the sinking night:
No other sound beneath the twilight sky, —
The ceaseless monotone of that low cry.

II.

Rising from the shady meadows,
　　From the dusky lea,
Call it not a sound of gladness :
　　'Tis a dirge to me, —
'Tis beauty's passing bell, in sadness rung ;
'Tis her own requiem, by Summer sung.

III.

Glowing flowers, the gifts of Autumn,
　　Crown her dying state :
Laughing in the sunny noontide,
　　She forgets her fate ;
But, with the evening, sadder thoughts arise :
She sings herself to sleep with tearful eyes, —

IV.

Sadder thoughts than day can cherish,
　　Full of fond regret ;
Thoughts of early hopes defeated,
　　Early glories set ;
Spring's joyous promise, ah, how unfulfilled ! —
Her roses perished, and her minstrels stilled.

V.

Cease thy chirping, pensive insect !
　　Summoned by thy note,
Thronging images unbidden
　　Through the fancy float :
Mem'ry counts up her cherished stores again,
And finds her choicest treasures turned to pain.

VI.

Echoes of familiar voices,
     Ah, the voices gone!
Shadows of belovèd faces,
     Shadows now alone!
Sweet homelike scenes portrayed in childhood's years,
Drawn by the sunshine, now baptized in tears.

VII.

Weeping Mem'ry clasps her jewels,
     Changed, but dearer yet!
Weeping with the sad foreboding
     That she may forget:
Will not these echoes cease, these shadows fly?
O mournful, mournful cricket! cease thy cry.

THE CHANT OF OCEAN.

'Tis the hush of early twilight;
     And calmly the western gray,
With voiceless gesture arising,
     Hath motioned the night away.

Over the western landscape
     The obedient night hath gone,
As, with a foot of silence,
     Comes in the winter morn.

No hum from the whitened meadow;
     No chorus from the tree;
No sound in the frosty stillness,
     But the roar of the distant sea!

The Earth lies listening mutely
  To the deep, mysterious strain,
That, all night long, with her visions
  Has mingled its low refrain.

All night o'er the snow-hushed forest,
  And over the mountain's steep,
That music has swelled and fallen, —
  The anthem of the deep !

As monks in the old cathedral
  Their midnight masses chant,
Till the lights on the holy altar
  In the morning splendors faint ;

So chants the solemn ocean,
  Till the torches of the night
Are quenched on the arch of heaven,
  At the signal of the light.

Dawn on the whitened meadow ;
  Dawn on the snowy lea ;
No sound in the frosty stillness,
  But the chant of the distant sea.

FANNIE E. FOSTER.

THE POET'S GRAVE.

WEET Spring approached with fairy feet,
   And gladsome smiles she wore ;
But why comes not her poet forth
   To greet her as of yore?

She sought him in the fields and groves,
   Along the murmuring rills ;
And sent her birds with sweetest songs
   To lure him to the hills ;

Then strewed around her fairest flowers,
   And bid the perfumed breeze
Awake sweet melody for him
   In all the forest-trees.

The winding brooks ran here and there,
   In every calm retreat,
To see if they a trace could find
   Of their lost poet's feet.

At length a wandering zephyr caught
   The loved, familiar sound
Of music, hovering just above
   A sweet, low, grassy mound.

Its tones were so refined and pure,
  That mortals scarce might hear;
And told, that, with the poet now,
  'Twas spring-time all the year.

Then gentle Spring, with showers of tears,
  The sweet, low mound did lave;
And dear forget-me-nots sprang up
  All o'er the poet's grave.

THE BLIND MAN'S CRY.

A CROWD to Jericho approached;
  And, lo! as on they sped,
A blind man sat beside the way,
  And asked his daily bread.

He heard the sound of many feet,
  And sought the reason why;
And learned that Jesus, David's son,
  Of Nazareth, passed by.

His heart for joy within him leaped;
  For well he knew 'twas he
Who healed the sick, and raised the dead,
  And made the blind to see.

And loudly now on him he calls;
  And still his tones increase,
As voices from the crowd he hears,
  Bidding him hold his peace.

9

But One, on whom none calls in vain,
　　Had also heard his cry,
And stopped to hear the sufferer's prayer,
　　As he was passing by.

He hears that kind and gentle voice
　　Ask what his wish may be:
He had but one in the wide world, —
　　That was, — that he might see.

But who the blind man's joy can tell,
　　When broke upon his night
The heavenly radiance of His face,
　　Who said, " Receive thy sight"?

O sick of soul, and blind of heart!
　　Why lift ye not your cry?
Since IIe, who hath all power to save,
　　To-day is passing by.

I WILL NOT FEAR TO DIE.

I will not fear to die,
　　Since this at last I know, —
I cannot from God's thought fade out,
　　From his dear presence go.

Death does not abrogate his care;
　　And so, henceforward, I,
Rejoicing still in him to live,
　　Will fear no more to die.

REV. SAMUEL HAVEN, D. D.

BORN 1727; DIED 1806.

—◆—

ON RESIGNATION AND HOPE IN GOD UNDER TROUBLES.

E still my heart, be mute my tongue;
Thou ne'er, as yet, hast suffered wrong:
A Father's love inflicts the rod,
To bring thee nearer to thy God.

Do thunders roar and billows roll?
Do tempests beat upon thy soul?
They are directed by his hand,
To drive thee to the promised land.

Great Lord of all! thy will is just:
We rest secure; we firmly trust,
That what thy will approves as good
Results alike from all of God.

Thy wisdom, power, and grace combine
To prove the whole an act divine:
E'en justice here unites with grace,
And shines with lustre in thy face.

Shall mortals then contend on earth?
Shall they forget their humble birth,
And quarrel with the Power above,
Or dare dispute that God is love?

Hush, murmuring thoughts! my tongue be still,
My heart resign to Heaven's high will;
Trust all to him, — he can't deceive:
The humble soul shall surely live.

ON EVIL SURMISINGS.

ALAS! the eye perverse,
    Which never looks within;
But, ever eager, looks aside
    To spy another's sin.

Alas! the heart deceived,
    Which swells with cursèd pride,
Crying, " I'm free from every sin:
    Let others stand aside."

My soul! thou know'st enough
    To keep thee humble still;
For, oh! how often do thy sins
    Prevail against thy will!

Grant, Heaven, that I may ne'er
    Invade thy awful throne;
And, e'er I search for others' faults,
    Oh, cleanse me from my own!

THE PRAISE OF ANGELS.

Ps. ciii. 20: " Bless the Lord, ye his angels, that excel in strength ; that do his commandments, hearkening unto the voice of his word."

LET cherub and let cherubim
Clap their blest wings in praise of Him ;
And all their powers in rapture raise,
While their great object is his praise.

He formed their nature like his own,
And placed their ranks around his throne ;
But conscious distance veiled their face :
They bowed, adoring wondrous grace.

Ye first-born sons of early day,
Sing to his praise, his will obey ;
And while you fly from pole to pole,
And other systems round you roll,

You'll aid his praise, till all at last,
When ages yet unborn are passed,
Centre in one, — in one great throng,
In perfect unison their song.

Angels and men their voice shall raise
In sweetest concert to his praise :
The great MESSIAH then shall shine,
Arrayed in glories all divine, —
The head of angels and of men,
Uniting all to God again.

ON THE QUESTION BEING ASKED, — WHAT TITLE
SHALL BE GIVEN TO PRESIDENT WASHINGTON,
ON HIS VISIT TO PORTSMOUTH?

FAME spread her wings, and with her trumpet blew,
Great WASHINGTON is near ! — what praise his due?
What *title* shall he have?   She paused, and said,
Not one, — *his Name alone* strikes every title *dead.*

NATHANIEL APPLETON HAVEN.

BORN 1790; DIED 1826.

———◆———

A FRAGMENT.

LOW sweeps the northern blast
    Along the dreary way,
    While from the ice-bound streams
    The chilling moonbeams play;
Yet still I love to linger here,
While sad Remembrance claims a tear
For joys, which youthful Fancy brought,
When Pleasure stamped each glowing thought.

Ah! then what scenes arose!
What pleasure thrilled the breast!
How beamed the distant world,
In dazzling splendor dressed!
    Ambition waked each dormant power,
    While Fancy lured me to her bower;
    Hope's day star beamed; the flattering ray
    Presaged a bright, a prosperous day.

But *now* the scene how changed!
What clouds of darkness roll!
Cold each aspiring thought, —
The winter of the soul!
    No more my bosom swells with joy,
    No flattering scenes my thoughts employ;
    But hopes once fondly cherished seem
    The phantoms of a feverish dream.

Thou God of all, whose power
The elements obey,
Save me from Passion's rage,
From Pleasure's maddening sway!
    Thou seest my heart with rapture glow,
    Thou seest my life-blood swiftly flow,
    When Fancy, Pleasure, Passion, fire
    Reason too weak to rule desire.
Ah! when, from all illusion free,
Shall every hope be placed in thee?

PSALM CXXX.

De profundis clamavi.

From sin's dark depths, my God, to thee
    I pour in tears my faltering prayer:
Oh, hear my cry of agony!
    Oh, save me, save me from despair!

For, if thy justice should pursue
    Whate'er of guilt thine eye hath known,
Oh! who could bear thy piercing view,
    Or stand before thy awful throne?

But thou canst burst the twofold chain
   That binds me still to sin and woe ;
And thou canst cleanse the earthly stain
   That tells my fall before my foe.

Oh ! free me, cleanse me, bid me live ;
   And bondage, guilt, and death remove :
And, while I tremble, still forgive ;
   For thou art mercy, thou art love.

Then by thy mercy reconciled,
   Boundless, unmerited, and free,
Saviour ! receive thy long-lost child,
   His life, his hope, his all in thee.

LINES ON AUTUMN.

I LOVE the dews of night,
   I love the howling wind,
I love to hear the tempest sweep
O'er the billows of the deep ;
For Nature's saddest scenes delight
   The melancholy mind.

Autumn ! I love thy bower
   With faded garlands dressed :
How sweet alone to linger there,
When tempests ride the midnight air !
To snatch from mirth a fleeting hour, —
   The sabbath of the breast !

Autumn! I love thee well,
Though bleak thy breezes blow:
I love to see the vapors rise,
And clouds roll wildly round the skies,
Where from the plain the mountains swell,
And foaming torrents flow.

Autumn! thy fading flowers
Droop but to bloom again;
So man, though doomed to grief awhile,
To hang on fortune's fickle smile,
Shall glow in heaven with nobler powers,
Nor sigh for peace in vain.

THE PURSE OF CHARITY.

This little purse, of silver thread
And silken cord entwined,
Was given to ease the painful bed,
And soothe the anxious mind.

The maker's secret bounty flows
To bid the poor rejoice;
And many a child of sorrow knows
The music of *her* voice.

The little purse her hands have wrought
Should bear her image still;
And, with her generous feelings fraught,
Her liberal plans fulfil.

Its glittering thread should never daunt
  The humble child of woe ;
But well the asking eye of want
  Its silver spring should know.

While age or youth with misery dwell,
  To cold neglect consigned,
No useless treasures e'er should swell
  The purse with silver twined.

HYMN FOR THE FOURTH OF JULY, 1813.

FATHER, again before thy throne,
  Thy suppliant children humbly pray ;
With grateful hearts thy mercy own,
  That crowns once more their natal day.

Though War our fertile valleys stain,
  Though Slaughter bare his gory hand,
Though Famine lead her ghastly train,
  We glory in our native land.

Yes : 'tis our own, our fathers' home, —
  Their ashes rest beneath the sod :
The fields that now our children roam,
  Their footsteps once as gladly trod.

Our hardy sons, who till the earth,
  Undaunted still will danger face :
The land that gave our fathers birth
  Will never bear a coward race.

The gallant few, who plough the deep,
   Can sternly meet the raging storm ;
And o'er the swelling ocean sweep,
   Unmoved at Danger's giant form.

But braver hearts have shrunk from fight,
   When kindred blood must dye the steel :
The boldest to contend for right
   The ties of nature strongest feel.

Father, once more " good-will " proclaim,
   And bid conflicting passions cease ;
Repress each proud, ambitious aim,
   And give thy suppliant children " peace."

STANZAS.

" Après ma mort, quand toutes mes parties
  Par la corruption sont anéanties,
  Par un même destin il ne pensera plus ! "
               FRÉDÉRIC LE GRAND.

ARE these the dictates of eternal truth ?—
These the glad news your boasted reason brings?
Can these control the restless fire of youth,
The craft of statesmen, or the pride of kings?

Whence is the throb that swells my rising breast?
What lofty hopes my beating heart inspire?
Why do I proudly spurn inglorious rest,
The pomp of wealth, the tumult of desire?

Is it to swell the brazen trump of fame,
To bind the laurel round an aching head,
To hear for once a people's loud acclaim,
Then lie for ever with the nameless dead?

Oh, no ! far nobler hopes my life control,
Presenting scenes of splendor yet to be :
Great God, thy word directs the lofty soul
To live for glory, not from man, but thee.

CAROLINE ELIZABETH JENNESS.

BORN 1824; DIED 1858.

---◆---

THE FLOWERS OF MY GARDEN.

FAIR Flowers in my garden grow;
No fairer Flowers this earth can show:
Each one, a miracle of art,
Hath won how many a poet's heart!
And, though misnamed, how many still
Recall the poet's mystic skill!
O Flowers! affection's sweetest token,
The pledge of faith and troth unbroken!
O fairest, frailest Flowers! ye can
No labor do for toiling man,
But bloom, returning love for love, —
Meek messengers of heaven above.
How many sorrows ye have soothed!
How many doubting fears removed!
First, with the Spring, children of love,
The Hyacinths my care approve;
For love I rather see than woe
On Hyacinthus' floweret grow,

Which sprang all bleeding from the sods,
Red with his frolic with the gods:
O feeblest love, which could not save,
Even when immortal, from the grave!
But, sweetest Crocus! wast thou born
Of Hermes' grief for one alone?
Or, youth too loving, hath some power
Immortalized love in a flower?
And here are Pansies freaked with jet;
And here the sombre Violet;
While close the Cowslips hide in green,
The pensioners of the Fairy Queen.
And low the nodding blossoms wave
Which grew on fond Narcissus' grave,
Who loved his shadow on the stream,
And died of love; for none, I ween,
Not even the Nereids, were so fair, —
Fairer than Scylla, fairest there;
While famed St. Edward's royal flower,
The brown Imperial, rules the hour;
Later, Spring Tulips, passion-fired;
And Honeysuckles well attired;
And Pinks and Larkspurs blue and dark,
Like birds imprisoned on the stalk;
Canterbury's Cathedral Bell,
Whose notes with swaying breezes swell,
By golden tongues, with rise and falls,
Swinging in amethystine walls;
And sweeter Bells, with azure dyes,
Which caught their color from the skies;
And here the great White Lily springs,
Rarest of all rare blossomings, —
Born of that milk which gave, sweet shower!
A god to heaven, to earth a flower,

Second to none which Summer brings,
" Lilies," perchance the Mantuan sings,
" The sylvan gods bore in their hands ; "
Or sweeter song, in Christian lands,
Says that it blossoms on the days
Sacred unto the Virgin's praise.
But, Fleur de Lis ! mysterious flower
Carved on the Sphinx in Egypt's power, —
An emblem, would fond Fancy ask,
Of the great Hebrew and his task.
O wondrous flower, Fleur de Lis !
Old and new France will blazon thee !
Drawn by an angel's pen at night
    Upon the banner of her host,
The heavens glowing with strange light,
    Strange echoes startling all the coast,
Oft folded o'er the Indian's rest,
And Canada's ungenial breast, —
O proudest Lily, none like thee
Have spread their wings o'er land and sea !
Here Marigolds their florets spread,
Like glories round the Virgin's head ;
And red Nasturtiums, rich and rare,
Sparkle to greet the evening air,
Which once, on some triumphal gate,
Added fresh glory to the State ;
Whose leaves are shields that heroes bear,
Its flowers the helmets heroes wear.
And here the Heliotrope's soft dyes
Turn to the sun, like Clyte's eyes ;
And, underneath the wall and thorn,
Grow flowers of Mintha, maid forlorn,
The prey of Proserpine's proud scorn, —
Mintha, whose crushèd leaves distil

The comfort she could never feel.
And here the gaudy flower appears
Which sprang from Helen's flowing tears, —
Bold flower, not half so sweetly glowing
As those fair buds, which, dew bestowing,
Wakened by Phyllis' mournful doom,
Blushed into life and sweet perfume.
These could I number, more than these ;
Nor once would gather Daphne's leaves,
Who with ambitious laurels strove
To soothe Apollo's ardent love.
But, fairest flower ! thou Queen of Flowers !
I watch thee most in sun and showers,
Who hast the nightingale's warm heart,
Thy perfumes of his song a part ;
For Fable says, that Flora, straying
Through summer woods, and oft delaying,
Found in a covert still and dark
A Dryad maiden cold and stark, —
So pale, alas ! — dear gods defend
All maidens from so sad an end !
And Flora, mourning o'er her loss,
Made of her essence, free from dross,
A Rose as lovely as her face ;
And every god did add some grace, —
A Rose all blanched like her own beauty ;
But Cupid, missing of his duty,
O'erturned some nectar on the flower,
Which crimson grew beneath the shower,
And, in love's warm and tender flush,
Rivalled her beauty's living blush.
O Rose of Love ! what flower like this, —
The type of sorrow, type of bliss ?

In dewy garlands, freshly made,
I wore thee once upon my head;
Now, hid in silence on my heart,
Part of my love and grief a part:
O Rose! my love, though dead, still blooms;
Faded like thee, still breathes perfumes.

REPOSE.

On downy pillows lain, she prays:
    Her soft eyes ope and close again;
And, unto her unfinished prayer,
    The angels say the glad " Amen;"
While, half-unclasped her languid hands,
    She sleeps with such a gentle art,
That scarce her heaving limbs betray
    The quiet heaving of her heart:
So quick asleep, not hidden quite,
Her lovely limbs peep to the light
The envious down would hide from sight.

Her golden hair curls round her cap;
    And, as her rosy lips unclose,
The easy breathings falter forth
    Like perfumes loath to leave a rose;
And, dimly bright, the lashes seem
    To steal light from her eyes in mirth,
Or as some homesick beams, returned
    Unto the suns that gave them birth;
While, gathered in her snowy breast,
Life and the Loves together rest:
How could they leave so sweet a nest?

The air is sweet; for dying flowers
  Send their last breath to scenes like this;
And, sighing, blows the love-sick wind,
  Trembling to meet her with a kiss:
While, with a faint and dreamy light,
  The lamp half shows, half hides her face,
As night were, by itself illumed,
  Burning to see her lovely face;
And worthless Fancy flieth thence,
Where she lies sleeping, with shut sense,
Like the child-goddess, Innocence.

FEAR NOT.

I WILL not fear, I will not fear;
  For He is by my side:
In pastures fair he leadeth me,
  In pastures green and wide,
And by the rivers calm and clear,
  And where bright waters roll:
I will not fear, I will not fear;
  His strength is in my soul.

He watcheth me amid the storm,
  And on the raging sea;
His guidance is my steadfast hope,
  When earthly hopes may flee.
I weep no more for grief or woe,
  And I will fear no ill:
He loveth me, he feedeth me:
  My God is with me still.

LOVE FLIES.

Love flies, Love flies!
Round his throat is floating all his golden hair;
On each dimpled shoulder snowy wings there are:
While his empty quiver down his back is hung,
On his arm he beareth forth his bow unstrung;
While he looketh backward, laughing from his eyes,
      " Love flies, Love flies!"

All the flowers are drooping, birds in silence fly,
And the brutes, neglected, raise a piteous cry;
While the winds of Autumn o'er the meadows mourn,
And the gathering darkness shows the coming storm;
And lone Echo answers, — answers and replies, —
      " Love flies, Love flies!"

Idly falls the hammer, idly turns the wheel;
And the careless spinner often drops her reel;
Hushed the song and whistle, hushed the joking strain;
Hymen, pale and fainting, fans a flickering flame;
While sad Faith, attending, languishes, and sighs,
      " Love flies, Love flies!"

" Hush!" cries Love, half pouting, " if I fly before,
I would wait you, mortals, on a better shore:
Always ye reproach me, — now I will return,
All re-armed, to plague you till your planet burn:
Last to leave, oh! gladly then you'll raise your cries,
      " Love flies, Love flies!"

EPITAPH.

HERE, within this silent dell,
  Where the moss is old and hoary,
Where the turf is green the latest,
And the Fall leaves fade the fairest,
  Lies a maid of humble story.
She had loved — ah, common lesson!
Tenderly, and was forgotten;
And when, weeping, sleep o'ercame her,
Angels suffered none to wake her.
Oft the brightly dawning morning,
  Oft the birds upon the ground,
Singing softly, seem to call her
  To the happy life around:
But the Eve, with dewy fingers,
  Decks her mould with fragrant sighs;
And kind Pity, leaning o'er her,
  Drops a requiem from her eyes;
While the violets, blooming, dying,
  Lay their leaves upon her breast,
As if their true love could bring her
  Healing for a heart distressed.
Wandering here, perchance, kind stranger,
Where the Zephyrs, glad to linger,
  Balmy sweetness borrow;
Where e'en Grief loops up her tresses, —
Do not sigh or breathe kind wishes,
  That she could share thy morrow,
But sing dirges softly o'er her,
Lest unpitying Love disturb her
  With a dream of sorrow.

CHRISTMAS HYMN.

THERE came no pealing trumpet;
  No banner borne on high ;
No clanging drum or cymbal,
  That stirred the air and sky.

They strewed no palms by the wayside ;
  There was no listening throng
To sing glad songs of triumph,
  With voices deep and strong.

No censer there was wreathing,
  With dim and perfumed shrouds,
Around the holy Stranger,
  In soft and purple clouds.

And kings still bore the sceptre,
  Yet bowed not lowly down
Before the holy Son of God,
  With his immortal crown.

In lowliness, forgotten,
  A manger for his bed,
On his young mother's bosom
  The Saviour laid his head.

And save the thrilling music
  Of harp-strings struck above,
By the cherubim of heaven,
  Around the throne of Love ;

And save the starry beacon
   That shone in light on high, —
There was no word to welcome him,
   The Son of earth and sky.

Thou Star of glory! lead us;
   Thou Music deep and sweet,
Lead us unto the manger;
   Lead us to Jesus' feet!

THE FOUNTAIN OF YOUTH.

The first discoverers of America believed that there was a fountain in Florida, which
possessed the miraculous power of restoring youth to the aged.

WE are travelling on to the Fountain of Youth;
   Yet, brothers, stay awhile,
And dream once more of our sunny land,
   Where the laughing vineyards smile:
Then our steps we'll speed, though weary and faint,
   To the dim and distant shore,
Where we deem that the clouds of sorrow and grief
   Will darken our eyes no more.

For they tell us, that there, in that radiant land,
   That beautiful land of dreams,
The summer and sunshine do never pass
   From the blue and silvery streams;
And a dim and strange mysterious strength
   On the sparkling rills has lain;
For the spirit of God has breathed on the waves,
   And they bring us our youth again.

Then speed, let us speed, to the glorious strand
  Where the gems lie thick like dew;
And bathe in the fount and the murmuring rills
  That bring us our youth anew:
For our life is a cold and weary thing
  In this mansion-house of woe;
But pain will flee on the emerald banks,
  Where the lulling waters flow.

But they never found the Fountain of Youth
  On that lonely and lovely shore,
And their wasted joys and their rifled gems
  Came back to their souls no more:
Yet they found a stream of enduring strength,
  Whose beauty can never fade,
More bright than the rivers of light that flow
  In the wilderness' gloom and shade.

For their faith grew firm, and their trust more deep,
  In the spirit of God above;
And their hearts were filled with a holier hope,
  .A higher and purer love.
Their souls were strong, for they knew that their tears
  Had not been given in vain;
And they found the Fountain of Youth on high,
  In the Eden land again.

THE PLOUGHMAN'S DAUGHTER.

" THE ploughman's merry daughter, —
 What hair hath she, I pray?"
I asked two sturdy farmers,
 Who lingered by the way.
" Ah! brown," one answered gayly,
 " And soft as fleece e'er spun."
" Nay, golden," sighed the other;
 " For I've seen it in the sun."

" What eyes hath she, good people?"
 One answered, " Tender blue,
And softer than the iris
 When wet with morning dew."
" Nay, sharper," cried the other,
 When scarce the first had done,
" Than my sickle in the meadow
 " Beneath an August sun."

" And speaks she fair, good people?"
 " Oh! sweet," the elder said,
" Like soft winds o'er the clover;"
 But low the younger plead,
" Nay, say her cold voice ringeth
 Clear as the evening bell
That oft misleads the stranger
 In yonder echoing dell.

Perplexed, and wanting wisdom,
 I sought beyond the moor,
Where the ploughman's merry daughter
 Was spinning by the door;

Nor knew, 'twixt light and shadow,
  If her hair were brown or gold,
Nor 'mid the rose and lily
  The faithful color told.

Too long her eyes I pondered,
  Where true love seemed to lie ;
Too loud I praised her, hearing
  Her sweet song floating by :
When quick, in mocking laughter,
  Out rang her merry voice ;
And, weeping, to the farmers
  I turned, and made no choice.

MINISTRY OF GRIEF.

O Love ! Ambition ! watchwords of man's zeal I hear ;
And I in vain would answer from my house of clay,
Tired of my tedious bondage many a troubled year ;
And still I question, sadly question, night and day,
Why was I born to weary out love's self with grief,
To waste in idleness, or struggles for relief ?
So, grieving, half distraught, I saw the birds at dawn
Beating against the winds in their careering flight ;
And those same winds, 'gainst which they struggled
    in the morn,
Bore their light wings, o'erwearied, gently home at
    night.
And so, dear friend, these very trials, bravely borne,
May bear *my* heart at last to its own brighter Home !

HARRIET McEWEN KIMBALL.

—◆—

THE TWO CITIES.

N the dusky shores of evening, stretched in
shining peace it lies, —
City built of clouds and sunshine, wonder of
the western skies !

While I watch, and long for pinions thitherward to
take my flight,
Slowly the aërial city fades and vanishes from sight.

Ruby dome and silver temple, circling wall of amethyst,
Fall in silence, leaving only purple ruin hung with
mist.

Darkness gathers eastward, westward ; stronger wax-
eth my desire,
Reaching through celestial spaces, glittering as with
rain of fire,

To the City set in jasper, having twelve foundations
fair,
Flashing from their jewelled splendor every color soft
and rare.

Twelve in number are its gateways, — numbered by
   the Seer of old, —
Every gate a pearl most lustrous; and its streets are
   paved with gold.

In the midst, in dazzling whiteness, lightens the Eternal Throne;
From it flows the Living Water, round it gleams an
   emerald zone.

Luscious fruits and balmy odors, healing leaves and
   cooling shade,
Either side the Life-tree sheddeth, by sweet storms of
   music swayed.

O thou grand, untempled City! seen by John in visions
   bright,
Glory-flooded, needing neither sun by day nor moon
   by night,

Filled for ever and for ever by the shining light of
   Him
Who redeemed the world, and sitteth throned between
   the seraphim, —

Through thy lovely gates the nations of the saved in
   triumph stream,
Chanting praise above all praises; love of love their
   holy theme.

They no more shall thirst or hunger; they no more
   with heat shall faint:
Christ for tears will give them gladness, — blissful rest
   for sore complaint.

Blessed they who do his bidding ! cries the angel, day
and night ;
They shall find abundant entrance, they shall walk
with him in white !

———

DAY LILIES.

O SUMMER day,
Delay ! delay !
One waving of thy brooding wing,
One stirring of thy hazy wing,
And noontide light and heat
Will find my dewy shadow-lair,
And burn the coolness from the grasses
That swathe my feet
In rank and billowy masses ;
And to this claustral twilight bring
The sun's profanest glare.

O summer day,
Delay ! delay !
Let naked hill and bare brown field
Parch in thy torrid ray,
So this dim nook be unrevealed,
Where I,
Deliciously concealed,
Among the Lilies lie.
The delicate Day Lilies !
The white and wonderful Lilies !
My dark green haunt so still is,
The wildest birdling dare not sing ;

Nor insect beat a gossamer wing ;
Nor zephyr lift the lightest thing, —
        Here, where the lustrous Lilies,
        The clear, resplendent Lilies,
Pour out their heavenly sweet perfume,
        And with their snowiness,
In clusters chaste, illume
        This dusk recess.

Soft-footed Silence, royal nun !
        In this thy humid, emerald cell
        For ever dwell !
These flowers supernal ever shine,
Pure-flamed, before thy virgin shrine !
Here, one by one,
        Tell o'er thy glistering, roral beads, —
        A rosary strung on tangled weeds
        And blades and stems that intertwist.
The breath of Lilies be thy prayers !
Sweet-odored, wafted unawares
Up through the morning's lucent airs
        And evening's pallid mist.
The glittering stars shall o'er thee pass,
Deep-pillowed in the heavy grass ;
        These broad, smooth lily-leaves shall be
        A glossy coverlet for thee :
            Thy prayers and penance done,
            O royal nun !
        By day or night,
        In dark or light,
Thy fragrant shrine shall be the same ;
        These slender tapers lambent still,
        Nor blazing sun, nor mildew chill,
Shall quench their alabaster flame.

A gleam, as of a crystal wand!
 And Day peers in with curious face ;
  The jealous sunshine, stealing round,
 Doth warily chase
  The cool, dank shadows on the ground.
The cloister-walls no longer stand :
 A garish glory fills the space,
And lights the lush grass, loose and long ;
While, startled by the wild-bird's song,
 Soft-footed Silence flees apace ;
But still serene the Lilies shine,
Pure-flamed, before her ruined shrine! .

THE LAST APPEAL.

THE room is swept and garnished for thy sake ;
 The table spread with love's most liberal cheer ;
The fire is blazing brightly on the hearth ;
 Faith lingers yet to give thee welcome here.
   When wilt thou come?

Daily I weave the airy web of hope,
 Frail as the spider's wrought with beads of dew,—
That, like Penelope's, each night undone,
 Each morn in patience I begin anew.
   When wilt thou come?

Not yet? To-morrow Faith will take her flight,
 The fire die out, the banquet disappear ;
For ever will these fingers drop the web,
 And only desolation wait thee here.
   Oh, come to-day!

GOOD NEWS.

A bee flew in at my window,
   And circled around my head:
He came like a herald of summer-time,
   And what do you think he said?

" As sure as the roses shall blossom," —
   These are the words he said, —
" As sure as the gardens shall laugh in pride,
   And the meadows blush clover-red;

" As sure as the golden robin
   Shall build her a swinging nest,
And the captured sunbeam lie fast-locked
   In the marigold's burning breast;

" As sure as the water-lilies
   Shall float like a fairy-fleet;
As sure as the torrent shall leap the rocks,
   With foamy, fantastic feet;

"As sure as the bobolink's carol,
   And the plaint of the whippoorwill,
Shall gladden the morning, and sadden the night,
   And the crickets pipe loud and shrill:

" So sure, to the heart of the maiden
   Who hath loved and sorrowed long,
Glad tidings shall bring the summer of joy
   With bursting of blossom and song."

A seer as well as a herald !
For, while I sat weeping to-day,
The tenderest, cheeriest letter came
From Lionel far away.

Good news ! O little bee-prophet !
Your words I will never forget :
It may be foolish, — that dear, old sign, —
But Lionel's true to me yet !

———

W O M A N.

1862.

As though no shade of human wrong fell darkly on
their beauty,
And all men walked in brotherhood the shining ways
of duty,
The blessèd summer days glide by in calm and sweet
succession ;
God writes on Nature's palace-walls no curse against
oppression.

The strong man arms him for the fight ; he hears the
bugle calling ;
And, while between the patriot shouts her tears have
time for falling,
Pale woman plies the threaded steel, nor shapes her
lips to singing,
But still, with every stitch she draws, the pearls of
prayer is stringing.

11

She thinks of those whose wounds are fresh; of those
    in death-sleep lying,
Whose brows of youth and manhood won their bright-
    est crowns in dying;
She thinks of others brave and true, hid in the smoke
    of battle,
Where bayonets gleam, and cannon roar, and bullets
    hiss and rattle.

She shudders while the words of fate along the wires
    are chasing,
Or, trembling, waits the hurried line some comrade
    may be tracing;
Her head grows faint; she lifts her hands in anguished
    imploration:
" God save my Soldier! " first she prays; and then,
    " God save the Nation ! "

And when she moans, " The very thought of loss doth
    overcome me ! "
Crying, " If it be possible, oh, let this cup pass from
    me ! "
God chides her not, .if, choked with sobs, she adds to
    her petition
But brokenly Christ's after-words of meekness and
    submission.

He saw her pale with victory in the dark hour of trial,
When Self lay slain, and sorrowing Love was fettered
    with denial;
And the Divine One, who alone can clearly read the
    human,
Traces the Hero's autograph through tear-blots of the
    Woman.

TRUST.

To Him who hears, I whisper all ;
    And, softlier than the dews of heaven,
The tears of Christ's compassion fall :
        I know I am forgiven !

Wrapt in the peace that follows prayer,
    I fold my hands in perfect trust,
Forgetful of the cross I bear
        Through noonday heat and dust.

No more life's mysteries vex my thought ;
    No cruel doubts disturb my breast ;
My heavy-laden spirit sought
        And found the promised rest.

ALL'S WELL.

The day is ended. Ere I sink to sleep,
    My weary spirit seeks repose in thine :
Father ! forgive my trespasses, and keep
        This little life of mine.

With loving-kindness curtain thou my bed,
    And cool in rest my burning pilgrim feet ;
Thy pardon be the pillow for my head !
        So shall my sleep be sweet.

At peace with all the world, dear Lord, and thee,
    No fears my soul's unwavering faith can shake :
All's well, whichever side the grave for me
        The morning light may break !

MY WISH.

THE wish I wished was dream-fulfilled ;
 And, when I woke, I could not bear
To find the fantasy of sleep
 Had vanished in the morning air.

I rose, and slew it with a vow :
 " Vain wish, I'll cherish thee no more ! "
I flung it in Oblivion's stream,
 And saw it drifting from the shore.

Still the dark waves that rolled away
 Tossed back its plaintive moan to me,
As up from Hebrus rose the wail, —
 " Eurydice ! Eurydice ! "

THE SINGER.

SHE sits, and sings, in the room below,
A tender ballad of love and woe,
Wedded to music plaintive and slow.

And who would dream that her heart is gay,
While she singeth so sad a lay, —
Seeming to pour her soul away?

Why not? She doeth her heart no wrong :
Lips joy-laden the whole day long
Well can afford to sorrow in song !

So keep her, Heaven ! nor let her know
Other sighings than those that flow,
Rhythmic, through ballads of love and woe.

THE GUEST.

" Behold, I stand at the door, and knock: if any man hear my voice, and open the door, I will come in to him, and will sup with him, and he with me." — REV. iii. 20.

SPEECHLESS Sorrow sat with me ;
I was sighing wearily :
Lamp and fire were out, the rain
Wildly beat the window-pane.
In the dark we heard a knock ;
And a hand was on the lock ;
One in waiting spake to me,
     Saying sweetly,
" *I am come to sup with thee !* "

All my room was dark and damp :
" Sorrow ! " said I, " trim the lamp ;
Light the fire, and cheer thy face ;
Set the guest-chair in its place."
And again I heard the knock ;
In the dark I found the lock :
" Enter ! I have turned the key ! —
     Enter, Stranger !
Who art come to sup with me."

Opening wide the door, he came,
But I could not speak his name ;
In the guest-chair took his place,
But I could not see his face.
When my cheerful fire was beaming,
When my little lamp was gleaming,
And the feast was spread for three,
     Lo ! my MASTER
Was the Guest that supped with me !

THE OLD YEAR OF THE NATION.

1863.

CLOSED is the book whose crimsoned-lettered pages
  Are blurred and blotted by a Nation's grief;
Sealed up with all the ponderous tomes of ages
  By Him who turned for us its darkest leaf.

Not ours that volume to revise, erasing
  The lines that tell what deeds of shame were done;
Nor fold the page down where, with victory blazing,
  Stands the proud record of the fields we won.

Many the chapters dark with fear and failing,
  Or bright with hope of conquests yet to be;
There wrote we how the land was rent with wailing,
  Blent with the exultant sounds of jubilee.

The lists we lingered o'er with reverent sorrow,
  Filled full as heaven of stars with hero-names,
A deathless light from Freedom's triumphs borrow,
  Kindling their laurel-wreaths to martyr flames.

Round the red chronicles, on every border,
  Illuminations done by Mercy's hand
Show fair, amid fierce battling and disorder,
  Her white tents gleaming up and down the land.

The book is closed, and in His holy keeping
  Who, smiting, heals a Nation free and brave;
Who careth for the widow lowly weeping,
  Rebukes the traitor, and redeems the slave.

Despite its glooms, the grand heroic story
  We need not blush to ponder o'er again :
For Freedom on the titlepage wrote " Glory ; "
  And on the last, with firmer pen, " Amen ! "

JAMES KENNARD, JUN.

BORN 1815; DIED 1847.

MIDNIGHT MUSINGS.

N at the open window shine
  The far-off solemn stars of heaven:
With sleepless eyelids, I recline
  Upon my couch, to musing given.

A holy silence fills the air;
  In sleep repose earth's sons and daughters;
One voice alone is heard afar, —
  The rushing "sound of many waters."

Piscataqua! I know full well
  Thine old familiar tone, dear river!
To thee, as by a mighty spell,
  Mine inmost heart is bound for ever.

In boyhood, while life's morning dew
  Still moistened hope's delusive blossom;
In sail-boat, or in light canoe,
  I loved to sport upon thy bosom.

And when the summer sun sank down
  At eve among his gorgeous pillows,
Far from the hot and dusty town,
  I've bathed amid thy cooling billows.

Full many a river may, I fear,
    In point of length, be ranked before thee ;
But thou art broad and deep and clear,
    And blue as are the heavens o'er thee.

Of Mississippi they may speak
    Who find to explore him time and season ;
But I have pierced thine every creek,
    And love thee for that very reason.

No mighty common sewer art thou,
    To do the drainage of the nation ;
But thy pure waters ebb and flow
    With ocean's every heart-pulsation.

Oft sound the echoes on thy side
    With music, song, and laughter hearty,
As o'er thy breast, at eventide,
    Floats the returning water-party.

And oft, as now, when summer night
    The harsher din of daylight hushes,
I listen to thy voice of might,
    As seaward thy strong current rushes.

Anon, above thy solemn bass,
    A sound like Fate's dread step approaches,
As o'er thy bridge, at hurrying pace,
    Come tramping steeds and rumbling coaches.

That midnight train hath come and gone,
    From silence sprung, in silence ended ;
But further, nought to me is known,
    Or whence it came, or whither tended.

From voiceless gloom thus suddenly
   Emerges man, — a solemn marvel!
From mystery to mystery,
   Thus o'er the bridge of Life we travel.

Oh, what a bitter mockery
   Were this brief span to mortals given,
Had we, O God! no faith in thee,
   No staff on earth, no hope of heaven!

Oh, no! there lies beyond the tomb
   No "silent land," awaiting mortals:
A land of melody and bloom
   Spreads out behind death's gloomy portals.

Then bravely bide the doom that waits;
   Bear all of earth for all of heaven;
Step like a conqueror through those gates, —
   Not like a captive chained and driven.

O river! rushing to the sea
   With eager and impetuous motion,
Soon thy pent waters shall be free
   To roam the deep and boundless ocean.

Then, while thou murmurest in mine ear,
   Let me accept the lesson given:
Dost *thou* pant for a wider sphere?
   So should my spirit long for heaven.

Though, in the silence of the night,
   I thus discourse with thee, dear river!
Though flowing almost in my sight,
   Loved stream! we meet no more for ever!

For ever?   When the ties which chain
　My soul to clay, kind Death shall sever,
Free as the wind, I'll roam again
　Along thy banks, delightful river !

A SAIL ON THE PISCATAQUA.

O'ER the dear Piscataqua
　Gayly is our light boat dancing ;
Brightly on its crystal waves,
　Lo ! the morning sun is glancing.

Portsmouth Bridge is left behind ;
　Now we're past the " Pulpit " * pressing :
Lift your hat, and bend your head,
　To the Parson for his blessing.

Stationed on the rocky bank,
　From his Pulpit, as we near him,
Through the pine-trees, whispers he
　Solemn words, would we but hear him.

Thus sweet Nature everywhere
　Truth reveals to all who need it ;
Thus on life's tumultuous tide
　Borne along, we lightly heed it.

Far and near, on either hand,
　See the trees like giants striding
Past each other, up and down,
　With a ghostly motion gliding.

---

* " The Pulpit," a pine-clad cliff so called, on the south-
west bank of the river, before which it is customary to make
obeisance in passing.

From the rocky pass emerged,
  Sinking cliffs and shelving beaches,
Far receding, usher us
  To the loveliest of reaches.

Stretching wide, a beauteous lake
  To the raptured eye is given:
Far beyond, the blue hills melt
  In the clearer blue of heaven.

Rustic dwellings, clumps of trees,
  Upland swells, and verdant meadows,
Lie around; and over all
  Flit the summer lights and shadows.

O'er the river's broad expanse
  Here and there a boat is darting,
Swelling sails and foaming bows
  Life unto the scene imparting.

Humble market-wherry there
  Lags along with lazy oar:
Here, the lordly packet-boat
  Dashes by with rushing roar.

Comrades, look! the west-wind lulls;
  Flags the sail; the waves grow stilly:
Rouse old Æolus from his sleep!
  Whistle, whistle, whistle shrilly!

See, obedient to the call,
  O'er the beach the breeze approaching!
Now our little bark careens,
  Leeward gunwale nearly touching.

Luff a little! ease the sheet!
  On each side the bright foam flashes:
In her mouth she holds a bone,
  O'er her bow the salt spray dashes.

To and fro, long tack and short,
  Rapidly we work up river:
Comrades, seems it not to you
  That we thus could sail for ever?

WHAT SHALL I ASK IN PRAYER?

WHAT shall I ask in prayer? Have I not all
That fortune can bestow of earthly gifts, —
Health, riches, friends?
                  What shall I ask in prayer?
That God continue to pour out on me
Thus bountifully all earth's choicest blessings?
Shall I kneel down, and pray that he will still
Preserve my health inviolate, sustain
In all its robust strength this wondrous frame?
That he will still pour wealth into my coffers,
Nor leave a single wish ungratified
Which luxury can prompt? Or shall I ask
That friends may yet be true; that time may not
Estrange their hearts from me, nor death destroy?
Shall I pray thus? No! let me rather bend
In fearful, trembling meekness at the shrine:
Father in heaven! oh, give me strength to use
Aright those talents which in wisdom thou
Committedst to my care! I am thy steward;
And, when the final day of reckoning comes,
May I then render in a good account!

I pray not that thou wouldst continue all
These earthly blessings; for thou knowest what
Is best for me.   Should sickness, sorrow, want,
E'er come upon me, all I ask, O God!
Is *resignation to thy holy will.*

What shall I ask in prayer?   Misfortune sweeps
Resistless over all my earthly hopes.
Storm after storm has beat upon my head;
Broken and scattered to the winds the fabric
Of all my worldly greatness.   One by one
My plans have failed; and striving to regain
The ground which I had lost, and seat myself
Again on Fortune's highest pinnacle,
I have but overwhelmed myself the more,
And made my fall the greater.   All is gone!
Riches have fled; and deep, corroding care
Has preyed upon my very life; this frame,
Erect in health and manly vigor once,
Which scarcely knew what illness was, is bowed
By sickness, — tottering and feeble now
The once elastic step.   Pale is the cheek
Which once did wear the ruddy glow of health,
And dim the eye which shone with joy and hope.
One comfort only yet remains to me, —
A gentle friend, true as in former days,
More kind and more affectionate than ever.
She watches by my bed, and soothes my pain,
And droops not, though my spirit sinks within me.
Adversity's thine element, O woman! —
What shall I ask in prayer?   Shall I send up
To heaven's gate complaining notes of woe,
And supplicate Jehovah to give back
The riches and the health of former days?

Doth not the Lord know what is best for me?
Father, above! I bow beneath the rod:
Amid the desolation of my hopes,
I ask but *resignation to thy will.*

What shall I ask in prayer?   I have no friend!
Misfortune robbed me of my wealth; and then
I saw, alas! the ties which bound my *friends*
To me were golden strings; they snapped in twain;
My riches fled; and *friendship* was no more!
Death snatched away my last, true, only friend.
She died! and I am left alone to drag
In misery the burden of my life along.
Grim famine stares; and sickness eats into
My very vitals, nor permits repose.
Poor, friendless, sick, — I raise my thoughts to heaven.

What shall I ask in prayer?   Shall I besiege
God's throne with lamentations?   Shall I pray
That he restore to me health, riches, friends?
Then would my sorrows have been all in vain.
Health makes us thoughtless that a time will come
When " dust returns to dust; " and riches are
Too prone to keep our thoughts from higher things;
And friends do often fill the heart so wholly,
That not one thought of God can gain admittance.
" 'Tis good for me that I have been afflicted."
I thank thee, God! and, should there be in store
Yet further trials, strengthen me, I pray,
And give me spiritual health, and let
My riches be laid up in heaven above!
My everlasting Friend, thou God of mercy!
In earthly troubles, Lord! I only ask
For *resignation to thy holy will.*

THE BALLAD OF JACK RINGBOLT.*

JACK RINGBOLT lay at the Seaman's Home ;
　And sorely afraid was he,
Lest he should end upon the land
　A life spent on the sea.

He was born upon the ocean ;
　And, with her dying groan,
His mother gave him being,
　Then left him all alone, —

Alone upon the desert sea,
　With not a female hand
To nourish him and cherish him,
　Like infants on the land !

The storm-king held a festival
　Upon the deep that night :
His voice was thundering overhead,
　His eye was flashing bright.

The billows tossed their caps aloft,
　And shouted in their glee ;
But, oh ! it was for mortal men
　An awful night to see !

Among the shrouds and spars aloft,
　A host of fiends were shrieking ;
And the pump-brake's dismal clank on deck
　Told that the ship was leaking.

---

* Published in the " Knickerbocker " for December, 1846.

The ship was lying to the wind,
  Her helm was lashed a-lee ;
And, at every mighty roller,
  She was boarded by a sea.

The doom-struck vessel trembled,
  As the waves swept o'er her deck :
She rolled among the billows
  An unmanageable wreck.

To their boats they took for safety, —
  The captain and his men ;
And the helpless new-born infant
  Was not forgotten then.

A rough, hard-featured countenance
  The storm-tossed captain wore ;
But his heart for tender innocence
  With love was flowing o'er.

" He shall not perish here alone,
  Upon the ocean wild ;
But only God can nourish him,
  The motherless young child ! "

But all in vain his kindness,
  Had they not, at break of day, —
Glad sight ! — beheld before them
  A vessel on her way.

They were rescued ; and on board of her,
  As the passengers drew round,
In woman's arms the orphan boy
  The needed succor found.

He lived ; but to his inmost soul
 His birth-night gave its tone :
The spirits of the stormy deep
 Had marked him for their own.

He lived and grew to manhood
 Amid the ocean's roar :
His heaven was on the surging sea,
 His hell was on the shore !

He joyed amid the tempest,
 When spars and sails were riven,
And when the din of battle drowned
 The artillery of heaven.

He often breathed a homely prayer,
 That, when life's cruise was o'er,
His battered hulk might sink at sea,
 A thousand miles from shore.

And now, to lie up, high and dry,
 A wreck upon the sand !
To leave his weary bones at last
 Upon the hated land !

The thought was worse than death to him ;
 It shook his noble soul :
Strange sight ! adown his hollow cheek
 A tear was seen to roll.

" Could I but float my bark once more !
 'Twould be a joy to me,
Amid the howling tempest,
 To sink into the sea ! "

Then, turning to the window,
  He gazed into the sky :
The scud was flying overhead,
  The gale was piping high.

And in the fitful pauses
  Was heard old Ocean's roar,
As in vain his marshalled forces
  Rushed foaming on the shore.

Look now ! his cheek is flushing,
  And a light is in his eye, —
" Throw up the window ! let me hear
  That voice before I die !

They're hailing me, the crested waves,
  A brave and countless band,
As rank on rank, to rescue me,
  They leap upon the land.

'Tis all in vain, bold comrades !
  And yet, and yet so near !
Ye are but one short league away, —
  Must I — die — here ?

No ! the ship that brought me hither
  Is at the pier-head lying ;
And, ere to-morrow night, she'll be
  Before a norther flying.

Now, bless ye, brother sailors !
  If ye grant my wish," he cried ;
" But curse ye, if—— " He spake no more,
  Fell back, and gasped, and died.

PART SECOND.

THEY sewed him in his hammock,
  With a forty-two-pound shot
Beneath his feet, to sink him
  Into some ocean-grot.

Adown the swift Piscataqua
  They rowed with muffled oar,
And out upon the ocean,
  A league away from shore.

'Twas at the hour of twilight,
  On a chill November day,
When, on their gloomy errand,
  They held their dreary way.

The burial-service over,
  He was launched into the wave:
Now rest in peace, Jack Ringbolt!
  Thou hast found an ocean-grave.

Down went the corpse into the sea,
  As though it were of lead;
But it sank not twenty fathoms,
  Ere it touched the ocean's bed.

Then up it shot, and floated
  Half-length above the tide:
A lurid flame played round the head,
  The canvas opened wide.

No motion of the livid lips
 Or ghastly face was seen ;
But a hollow voice thrilled through their ears,
 " Quarter less nineteen ! "

Then eastward sped the awful dead,
 While, o'er the darkened sea,
Upon the billows rose and fell
 The corpse-light fitfully.

They gazed in fearful wonderment,
 Their hearts with horror rife ;
Then, panic-stricken, seized their oars,
 And rowed as if for life.

Their eyes were fixed with stony stare
 Upon the spectral light ;
They rowed like corpses galvanized,
 So silent and so white.

They darted by " The Sisters ; "
 They went rushing past " Whale's Back ; "
With tireless arms they forced the boat
 Along her foamy track :

But not a single face was flushed,
 Not one long breath they drew,
Until Fort Constitution
 Hid the ocean from their view.

PART THIRD.

'TWAS midnight on mid-ocean,
  The winds forgot to blow ;
The clouds hung pitchy black above,
  The sea rolled black below ;
On the quarter-deck of the " Glendoveer "
  The mate paced to and fro.

There was no sound upon the deep
  To wake the slumbering gales,
But the creaking of the swaying masts,
  And the flapping of the sails,
As the vessel climbed the ocean-hills,
  Or sank into the vales.

The mate looked over the starboard rail,
  And saw a light abeam :
The lantern of a ship, mayhap,
  A faint and flickering gleam :
Was it bearing down on the " Glendoveer,"
  Or did the mate but dream ?

A phantom-ship, on a breezeless night,
  To sail ten knots an hour !
Now on the beam, now quartering,
  Now close astern it bore :
All silent as the dead it moved,
  A light, — and nothing more !

No creaking block, no rumbling rope,
  Was heard, nor shivering sail ;

But, luffing on the larboard beam,
  A voice was heard to hail,
That made the hearts of the Glendoveers
  Within their bosoms quail.

It broke upon the still night-air,
  A hoarse, sepulchral sound, —
" What ship is that?" A moment,
  And the mate his breath has found :
The ' Glendoveer,' of Portsmouth,
  From Cadiz, homeward bound ! "

A livid glare, a ghastly face,
  A voice, — and all was o'er :
" Report Jack Ringbolt, sunk at sea,
  A thousand miles from shore ! "
Silence and darkness on the deep
  Resumed their sway once more.

TO —— ——.

How beautiful, how beautiful,
  Thy clear cerulean eye !
I gaze upon it as I gaze
  Upon the azure sky :
And as unto my longing look,
  At some rapt hour is given,
Far in those bright, ethereal depths,
  By faith, a glimpse of heaven ;
So, as into those orbs of blue
  My ardent glances dart,
Far in their liquid depths I read
  The heaven of thy heart.

But as the Peri mourned the fate
Which closed on her the crystal gate
  Of Paradise for ever,
Yet, while bewailing her sad lot,
Still hovered near the sacred spot
  Which she might enter never ;
So, while I look upon thy face,
And in its every feature trace
The guilelessness and matchless grace
  Of the pure heart within,
How ardently my soul aspires
  That glorious heart to win !
But soon in darkness hope expires.

It may not be ; it may not be ;
And yet I linger near to thee,
  And nourish passion's fires
By gazing at those azure eyes,
Which, like the gates of Paradise,
Half-opened, show the heaven within,
All-glorious and free from sin.

O lady ! is there not for me,
  As for the Peri, still a hope,
As she won heaven, that I win thee ?
  Oh, tell me, lady ! what can ope
The portals of thy heart to me ?
I'd roam the broad earth through and through,
  I'd sail from sea to sea,
But I would find that potent·charm,
  The gift most worthy thee,
That I might make thee all mine own,
That peerless heart, mine, mine alone !

WRECK OF THE "SEGUNTUM."

A Ballad.

The Spanish ship "Seguntum" was wrecked on the Isles of Shoals in the winter of 1813, and all hands on board perished.

FAST o'er the seas, a favoring breeze
   The Spanish ship had borne :
The sailors thought to reach their port
   Ere rose another morn.

As sank the sun, the bark dashed on,
   The green sea cleaving fast :
Ah! little knew the reckless crew
   That night should be their last!

They little thought their destined port
   Should be the foaming surge ;
That, long ere morn again should dawn,
   The winds should wail their dirge!

As twilight fades, and evening shades
   Are deepening into night,
The sky grows black, and driving rack
   Obscures the starry light.

And loudly now the storm-winds blow,
   And through the rigging roar :
They find, too late to shun their fate,
   They're on a leeward shore.

'Mid snow and hail they shorten sail ;
   The bark bows 'neath the blast ;
And, as the billows rise and break,
   She's borne to leeward fast.

The straining ship drives through the seas,
  Close lying to the wind ;
The spray, on all where it doth fall,
  Becomes an icy rind.

It strikes upon the shrinking face
  As sharp as needles' prick ;
And ever, as the ship doth pitch,
  The shower comes fast and thick.

And with it comes the driving snow,
  Borne on the bitter blast :
The helmsman scarce the compass sees,
  It flies so keen and fast.

A sound of fear strikes on the ear :
  It is the awful roar
Of dashing breakers, dead ahead,
  Upon the rocky shore !

"Wear ship ! hard up, hard up your helm !"
  Aloud the captain cries :
Slowly her head pays off, and now
  Before the wind she flies.

Now on the other tack, close braced,
  She holds her foaming course :
Short respite then ! too soon again
  Are heard the breakers hoarse !

Ahead, to windward and to lee,
  The foaming surges roar :
"O Holy Virgin ! save us now,
  And we will sin no more !

We vow to lead a holy life : "
Too late ! alas, too late !
Their vows and plaints to imaged saints
    Cannot avert their fate.

They strike a rock ; O God ! the shock !
    They vanish in that surge !
Through mast and shroud the tempest loud
    Howls forth a dismal dirge.

There lives not one to greet the sun,
    Or tell the tale at home :
A winding-sheet for sailors meet,
    The waves around them foam.

The storm is o'er : the rocky shore
    Lies strewn with many a corse,
Disfigured by the angry surf
    That still is murmuring hoarse.

And thus the Spanish crew were found,*
    Cast on those barren isles :
There, in unconsecrated ground,
    They rest them from their toils.

No mourners stood around their graves,
    No friends above them wept ;
A hasty prayer was uttered there, —
    Unknown, unknelled, they slept.

---

* Thirteen in number. Their graves are still to be seen on one of the Isles of Shoals. These islands lie off the harbor of Portsmouth, N. H., nine miles from the mouth of the Piscataqua.

SAD HOURS.

THE cold winds of autumn are sighing around,
And the leaves sere and yellow lie strown o'er the
    ground ;
By the eddying blasts they are whirled through the
    air,
And the tall trees that bore them are naked and bare.
Ah ! thus has a frost nipped the plans which I cher-
    ished,
And desolate left me : my hopes have all perished !
Disappointment has tracked me, misfortune assailed ;
In vain I resisted, — the storm has prevailed :
The present is misery, the future a void ;
Oh, the foliage of hope is for ever destroyed !

For ever?   Oh, no ! to the heart, tree, and plain,
A spring is approaching ; in verdure again
The tall oak shall be clad, and where chill winter
    hovered,
With a carpet of green the brown heath shall be cov-
    ered.
Bethink thee, sad youth ! were thy hopes placed
    aright?
Didst thou rest on thy God?   Didst thou pray, day
    and night,
For the strength which should bear thee in victory
    through?
In sickness and sorrow he still will be true.

Though friends should forsake, though misfortune as-
  sail thee,
Trust humbly in God, — he never will fail thee :
In the hour of thy trial, look upward to heaven,
Ask strength of thy Father, and strength shall be given.

DEATH ON THE PALE HORSE.

A Painting by Dunlap.

Not thus, not thus, should Death be shown,
  With fearful form and countenance,
With writhing serpent following on,
  With hope-annihilating glance,
With all that's withering to the heart,
  And all that's hideous to the eye,
With hands from which pale lightnings dart,
  With all that tends to terrify.

Not thus should Death, our kindest friend,
  To mortal view be bodied forth, —
Death, in whose bosom is an end
  For all the sin and woe of earth :
Oh ! 'tis a heathen custom, this,
  From which all Christians should be weaned :
The friend who ushers us to bliss
  Should not be painted as a fiend.

Around God's throne in heaven above,
  Death was the mildest of the throng,
His heart most filled with holy love,
  In warmth and charity most strong :

For angels differ in their frame
　Like men, and not to all are given
A mind and heart in each the same ;
　Thus all are not alike in heaven.

When God ordained man's destiny,
　To Death the blessèd task was given
Of setting careworn spirits free, —
　Of ushering souls from earth to heaven :
As downward on this blest employ
　He darted on his pinions bright,
How thrilled his heart with holy joy !
　How beamed his countenance with light !

And ever since that blessèd hour
　Has Death watched o'er each child of clay,
As bends above her darling flower
　A tender girl, from day to day ;
Till, when the long-sought bud appears,
　Expanding to a lovely blossom,
She plucks it from its stem, and wears
　The cherished flower upon her bosom.

Thus tenderly Death watches over
　Each struggling spirit shrined in clay,
Till, at the mandate of Jehovah,
　He bears the ripened soul away.
The bond, the free, the high, the low,
　Alike are objects of his love ;
And, though he severs hearts below,
　He joins them evermore above.

I have a picture in my eye, —
  A bowed-down captive drags his chain
Along his dungeon mournfully,
  And writhes and groans in bitter pain :
But suddenly the walls are burst,
  There rushes in unwonted light ;
Dazzled and blind, he shrinks, at first,
  From his deliverer, with affright ;

And not until his prison-wall
  Is left, although unwillingly ;
Not till his galling fetters fall,
  And leave the long-bound prisoner free ;
And not until his quailing eye
  Is strengthened, — can his gaze embrace
The look of calm benignity
  That beams from his deliverer's face.

And this is Death !   Oh ! paint him not
  As yonder canvas shows him forth, —
Death, who removes us from a spot
  So full of sin and woe as earth !
Oh ! 'tis a heathen custom, this,
  From which all Christians should be weaned :
The friend who ushers us to bliss
  Should not be painted as a fiend.

ALBERT LAIGHTON.

THE MISSING SHIPS.

 THOU ever restless sea !
"God's half-uttered mystery,"
Where all the ships that sailed so gallantly
    away?
Tell us, will they never more
Furl their wings, and come to shore?
Eyes still watch and fond hearts wait : precious freight
    had they.

Precious freight ! ay, wealth untold,
More than merchandise or gold,
Did the stately vessels bear o'er the heaving main :
    Human souls are dearer far
    Than all earthly treasures are ;
And for them we weep and pray : must it be in vain?

In the silence of the night
Did they, with a wild affright,
Wake to hear the cry of FIRE ! echo to the stars ;
    While the cruel, snake-like flame,
    Creeping, coiling, hissing, came
O'er the deck, and up the mast, and out along the
    spars?

As the doomed ship swayed and tossed
　　Like a mighty holocaust,
Did they with despairing cries leap into the waves?
　　Or with folded hands, and eyes
　　Lifted to the peaceful skies,
Calmly go with prayerful hearts to their namcless
　　　　graves?

　　Did the black wings of the blast
　　Poise and hover o'er the mast,
Till at last in wrath they swept o'er the crowded
　　　　deck?
　　Leaving not a soul to tell
　　How the long and awful swell
Of the ocean's troubled breast bore a dismal wreck;

　　How amid the thunder's crash,
　　And the lightning's lurid flash
(Autograph the Storm-king writes on his scroll of
　　　　clouds),
　　High above the deafening strife
　　Piteous cries were heard for life,
Fear-struck human beings seen clinging to the shrouds!

　　Or with shattered hulk and sail,
　　Riding out the stormy gale,
Did the brave ship slowly sink deeper day and night?
　　Drifting, drifting wearily
　　O'er the wide and trackless sea,
Loved ones starving, dying there, with no sail in sight.

　　Or when winds and waves were hushed,
　　While each cheek with joy was flushed,
As they glided gently on, hope in every breast,

13

With a sudden leap and shock,
Did they strike some hidden rock,
And go down, for ever down, to their dreamless rest?

Did the strange and spectral fleet
Of the icebergs round them meet,
Pressing closer till they sank crashing to the deep?
Do these crystal mountains loom,
Monuments of that vast tomb,
In the ocean's quiet depths, where so many sleep?

O thou ever-surging sea !
Vainly do we question thee :
Thy blue waves no answer bring as they kiss the
strand ;
But we know each coral grave,
Far beneath the rolling wave,
Shall at last give up its dead, touched by God's right
hand.

THE SUMMER SHOWER.

A WHITE haze glimmered on the hills,
The vales were parched and dry,
And glaringly the burning sun
Coursed in the summer sky.

The cattle in the distant woods
Sought shelter from its beams,
Or, motionless and patient stood,
Knee-deep, amid the streams.

The house-dog lay with panting breath
　　Close where the elm-trees grew ;
The blue-bird and the oriole
　　To shady coverts flew.

Day after day the thirsty earth
　　Looked up to heaven for rain ;
The gardens held their flower-cups,
　　The fields their lips of grain.

With doubting hearts, men, murmuring, said,
　　" Our toils have been in vain :
We sowed in spring, but shall not reap
　　When autumn comes again."

But while they spoke, within the west,
　　At sunset's glowing hour,
God's voice proclaimed in thunder-tones
　　The coming of the shower !

The deepening shadows slowly crept
　　O'er mountain and o'er plain,
Until in cool and copious floods
　　Came down the blessèd rain.

All Nature smiled ; and when at last
　　The cloudy wings were furled,
The evening star shone regally
　　Above a thankful world.

O love of Heaven ! O fear of man !
　　O faith so cold and dim !
When shall we own the ways of God,
　　And learn to trust in him ?

TO MY SOUL.

GUEST from a holier world,
Oh, tell me where the peaceful valleys lie :
Dove in the ark of life, when thou shalt fly,
    Where will thy wings be furled?

Where is thy native nest?
Where the green pastures that the blessèd roam?
Impatient dweller in thy clay-built home,
    Where is thy heavenly rest?

On some immortal shore,
Some realm away from earth and time, I know, —
A land of bloom, where living waters flow,
    And grief comes nevermore.

Faith turns my eyes above ;
Day fills with floods of light the boundless skies ;
Night watches calmly with her starry eyes
    All tremulous with love.

And, as entranced I gaze,
Sweet music floats to me from distant lyres :
I see a temple, round whose golden spires
    Unearthly glory plays !

Beyond those azure deeps
I fix thy home, — a mansion kept for thee
Within the Father's house, whose noiseless key
    Kind Death, the warder, keeps !

IN THE WOODS.

I WALKED alone in depths of Autumn woods :
  The ruthless winds had left the maple bare ;
The fern was withered, and the sweetbrier's breath
  No longer gave its fragrance to the air.

The barberry strung its coral beads no more ;
  The thistle-down on gauzy wings had flown ;
And myriad leaves, on which the Summer wrote
  Her blushing farewells, at my feet were strown.

A loneliness pervaded every spot, —
  A gloom of which my musing soul, partook :
All Nature mourns, I said ; November wild
  Hath torn the fairest pages from her book.

But suddenly a wild-bird overhead
  Poured forth a strain so strangely clear and sweet,
It seemed to bring me back the skies of May,
  And wake the sleeping violets at my feet.

Then long I pondered o'er the poet's words, —
  "The loss of beauty is not always loss,"
Till, like the voice of love, they soothed my pain,
  And gave me strength to bear again my cross.

O murmuring heart ! thy pleasures may decay,
  Thy faith grow cold, thy golden dreams take wing ;
Still, in the realm of faded youth and joy,
  Heaven kindly leaves some bird of hope to sing.

FOUND DEAD.

A poor vagrant was found by the police wandering in the streets of Philadelphia. He said he wanted to freeze to death; that he had no home, but was afraid to kill himself. The parties left him; and, in the morning, the poor wretch was found a frozen corpse.

Found dead! dead and alone!
  There was nobody near, nobody near,
When the Outcast died on his pillow of stone, —
  No mother, no brother, no sister dear,
Not a friendly voice to soothe or cheer,
Not a watching eye or a pitying tear.
Oh! the city slept when he died alone,
In the roofless street, on a pillow of stone.

Many a weary day went by,
  While, wretched and worn, he begged for bread,
Tired of life, and longing to lie
  Peacefully down with the silent dead:
Hunger and cold, and scorn and pain,
Had wasted his form and seared his brain,
Till at last, on a bed of frozen ground,
With a pillow of stone, was the Outcast found.

Found dead! dead and alone,
  On a pillow of stone, in the roofless street;
Nobody heard his last faint moan,
  Or knew when his sad heart ceased to beat;
No mourner lingered with tears or sighs:
But the stars looked down with pitying eyes,
And the chill winds passed with a wailing sound
O'er the lonely spot where his form was found.

Found dead! yet *not* alone;
    There was somebody near, — somebody near
To claim the wanderer as his own,
    And find a home for the homeless here;
One, when every human door
Is closed to his children, scorned and poor,
Who opens the heavenly portal wide:
Ah, God was near when the Outcast died!

NEW ENGLAND.

WHAT though they boast of fairer lands,
    Give me New England's hallowed soil,
The fearless hearts, the swarthy hands
    Stamped with the heraldry of toil.

I love her valleys broad and fair;
    The pathless wood; the gleaming lake;
The bold and rocky bastions, where
    The billows of the ocean break;

The grandeur of each mountain peak
    That rears to heaven its granite form;
The craggy cliffs where eagles shriek
    Amid the thunder and the storm.

And dear to me each noble deed
    Wrought by the iron wills of yore, —
The Pilgrim hands that sowed the seed
    Of Freedom on her sterile shore.

J O E.

ALL day long with a vacant stare,
Alone in the chilling Autumn air,
With naked feet he wanders slow
Over the city, — the idiot Joe !

I often marvel why he was born, —
A child of humanity thus forlorn,
Unloved, unnoticed by all below :
A cheerless thing is the life of Joe !

Beauty can throw no spell o'er him ;
His inner vision is weak and dim ;
And Nature, in all her varied show,
Weareth no charm for the eyes of Joe.

Earth may wake at the kiss of Spring ;
Flowers may blossom, and birds may sing ;
With joy the crystal streams may flow :
They never make glad the heart of Joe.

His vague and wandering thoughts infold
No dreams of glory, no schemes for gold :
He knows not the blight of hopes ; yet, oh,
A blighted thing is the life of Joe !

Who would not suffer the ills of life,
Its numberless wrongs, its sin and strife,
And willingly bear its weight of woe,
Rather than be the idiot Joe ?

I think of him in the silent night,
When every star seems a beacon light
To guide us, wanderers here below,
To the better land, — the home of Joe.

For He who hears when the ravens call,
And watches even the sparrow's fall, —
He, in his measureless love, I know,
Will kindly care for the soul of Joe.

EBB AND FLOW.

I WANDERED alone beside the stream ;
 The tide was out, and the sands were bare ;
The tremulous tone of the sea-bird's scream,
 Like a winged arrow, pierced the air.

I roamed till the sun in the west was low,
 And the robes of twilight trailed in the sea ;
The waves pulsed in with a rhythmical flow,
 And the nightingale sang a song to me.

All day I roam by the stream of Song ;
 The tide is out, and my life is bare ;
While shadows of evil round me throng,
 And drearily croak the birds of Care.

But at night the waves roll back again,
 And flow in music over my heart,
Till the dusky phantoms of grief and pain
 From the charmed shores of my brain depart.

MY NATIVE RIVER.

LIKE an azure vein from the heart of the main,
    Pulsing with joy for ever,
By verdurous isles, with dimpled smiles,
    Floweth my native river,

Singing a song as it flows along,
    Hushed by the Ice-king never;
For he strives in vain to clasp a chain
    O'er thy fetterless heart, brave river!

Singing to me as full and free
    As it sang to the dusky daughters,
When the light canoe like a sea-bird flew
    Over its peaceful waters;

Or when by the shore of Sagamore
    They joined in their mystic dances,
Where the lover's vow is whispered now
    By the light of maiden glances.

Oh, when the dart shall strike my heart,
    Speeding from Death's full quiver,
May I close my eyes where smiling skies
    Bend o'er my native river!

THE MIDNIGHT VOICE.

FATHER, at this calm hour,
Alone, in prayer I bend an humble knee:
My soul in silence wings its flight to thee,
    And owns thy boundless power.

Day's weary toil is o'er;
No worldly strife my heartfelt worship mars:
Beneath the mystery of the silent stars,
    I tremble and adore.

Not when the frenzied storm
Writhes 'mid the darkness, till in wild despair,
Bursting its thunder-chains, the lightning's glare
    Reveals its awful form, —

I wait not for that hour;
In flower and dew, in sunshine calm and free,
I hear a *still small voice* that speaks of thee
    With holier, deeper power.

Above the thunder-notes,
Serene and clear, the music of the spheres
For ever rolls, though not to mortal ears
    The heavenly cadence floats.

IN MEMORIAM.

When Spring with gladness filled the earth,
To us it brought no sound of mirth;
We cared not if the robin sang;
We watched no blossom as it sprang;
Our eyes with coming grief were wet;
Anemone and violet
Put forth their little lives of bloom;
But *she* was fading for the tomb, —
    Hopefully and trustfully
    Passing to Eternity.

Now winds are wild, and sere leaves fall;
A dying glory mantles all;
I sit and watch the tears of rain
Steal slowly down the window-pane.
The wailing of the Autumn blast
Stirs many a dead leaf of the Past
Within my soul; I seem to hear
The wan lips of the dying year,
    Mournfully, oh, mournfully,
    Chant a low, sad melody!

Old voices mingle in the strain;
Lost dreams of Youth come back again;
Loved forms once more beside me stand;
I feel the pressure of *her* hand
Within mine own; in angel guise
She comes to me from Paradise;

She turns on me her holy eyes,
That overflow with mysteries,
   Lovingly, so lovingly,
   Full of immortality.

O weeping rain! O dying year!
Ye bring her sainted presence near;
O moaning wind! O falling leaf!
Ye shall not fill my soul with grief
For her whose feet so early trod
The starry steeps that lead to God!
Whose heart shall never bear again
Life's weight of weariness and pain.
   Tenderly and joyfully
   Thrill the chords of memory!

THE NECROPOLIS.

Though the sexton, grim and old,
   Turns the mould,
   Damp and cold,
In the churchyard, for the bed
Of the still and holy dead;

Though we see the green turf prest
   On each breast
   Full of rest,
Full of quiet, sweet and deep, —
Yet not there our loved ones sleep.

Oh, the graves where they are laid
　　Sexton's spade
　　Never made !
Nor do sculptured tablets tell
That within the *heart* they dwell ;

Where the winter winds, we know,
　　Cannot blow,
　　And the snow
Never hides the flowers that grow,
Fadeless, from the dust below.

THE AURORA BOREALIS.

With strange, fantastic shapes they haunt my brain ;
A sky of amber, streaked with silver rain ;
A blaze of glory, Heaven's resplendent fires ;
A temple gleaming with a thousand spires ;
A sea of light that laves a shore of stars ;
The gates of Paradise, swift-rolling cars ;
A golden pulse, quick-beating through the night ;
Contending armies mailed in armor bright ;
A gauzy curtain drawn by unseen hands ;
Night's gorgeous drapery looped with starry bands ;
Vast, burning cities, that lie far away ;
Blushes on Nature's face, — pale ghosts of Day ;
A boundless prairie swept by phantom fire ;
The vibrant strings of some gigantic lyre ;
Emblazoned chariots ever skyward driven ;
God writing in the open book of Heaven ;
The flaming banner of the North unfurled ;
The mystery that dares a boasting world !

TO A BIGOT.

You strove in vain, with cunning words
  And subtle arguments, to gain
A convert to your darling creed;
  Then mocked me with your cold disdain.

Ah, well! — sip from your shallow fount:
  The heart hath depths you may not know;
And your philosophy would fail,
  Did you but judge of Nature so.

You do not hate the mountain stream
  Because it floweth wild and free
In hidden channels of its own,
  And finds at last its home, — the sea.

You do not crush the wayside flower
  Because it wears a different hue
From that which decks your garden-walks,
  And only breathes its sweets for you.

You do not wound the forest-bird
  Because your caged canary sings
A sweeter song, — you vainly think, —
  Give me the freedom of *my* wings.

Then if I soar beyond your flights,
  Or if I keep my lowly nest,
What matter, since I am content
  To serve my God as seemeth best?

THE DEAD.

I CANNOT tell you if the dead,
Who loved us fondly when on earth,
Walk by our side, sit at our hearth,
    By ties of old affection led ;

Or, looking earnestly within,
Know all our joys, hear all our sighs,
And watch us with their holy eyes
    Whene'er we tread the paths of sin ;

Or if, with mystic lore and sign,
They speak to us, or press our hand,
And strive to make us understand
    The nearness of their forms divine.

But this I know, — in many dreams
They come to us from realms afar,
And leave the golden gates ajar
    Through which immortal glory streams.

THE VEILED GRIEF.

OH ! think not that my eyes are dry,
    Because you mark no falling tears :
There flows a river deep and dark,
    Whose waters ebb not with the years.

And think not that my lips are mute,
  Because you hear no spoken word
Full-freighted with the tones of grief:
  I hear a voice you never heard.

And think not that my heart is cold,
  Because no passion fires my breast:
There is a chamber in my soul
  That only owns an angel-guest.

My tears fall inward on my heart,
  And, dew-like, keep its memories green:
Sad strains, unheard by other ears,
  Break forth for me from lips unseen.

THE CHIMES.

Ages since, men heard the ringing
Of the song-bells gently swinging
  In the starry domes of thought:
Long they listened to the chimes
That the poet's golden rhymes
  Out of sweetest fancies wrought.

Still the tuneful bells are pealing,
Waking every holy feeling;
  Still they vibrate in the past;
And the poet of to-day
Hears the music far away,
  Clearer than a clarion's blast!

14

SONG OF THE SKATERS.

THOUGH winter winds are whistling loud,
  And skies look cold and gray,
Though earth lies mute beneath her shroud,
  The skaters! what care they?
      A happy throng,
      With mirth and song,
O'er fields of ice we swiftly glide,
As sea-birds sail above the tide.

Oh! well we know the winter hours
  Fly faster as we sing;
That sooner come the birds and flowers,
  And loveliness of Spring:
      So, night or day,
      Away! away!
O'er crystal plains, with mirth and song,
We speed, we speed like the wind along!

The heated room, the crowded hall,
  Where pride and fashion meet,
While waves of music rise and fall
  In time to dancing feet, —
      We seek not these;
      Give us the breeze,
And the gleaming floor o'er which we go
Like arrows shot from the hunter's bow.

Then loud the stormy winds may blow,
　And skies look cold and gray ;
Then earth may wear her robe of snow, —
　We'll laugh the hours away !
　　　With mirth and song,
　　　A merry throng,
O'er fields of ice we'll swiftly glide,
As sea-birds sail above the tide.

UNDER THE LEAVES.

OFT have I walked these woodland paths
　In sadness, not foreknowing
That, underneath the withered leaves,
　The flowers of Spring were growing.

To-day the winds have swept away
　Those wrecks of Autumn's splendor ;
And here, the sweet Arbutus-flowers
　Are springing fresh and tender.

O prophet flowers ! with lips of bloom,
　Surpassing, in their beauty,
The pearly tints of ocean shells, —
　Ye teach me faith and duty.

Walk life's dark ways, ye seem to say,
　In love and hope ; foreknowing
That, where man sees but withered leaves,
　God sees the fair flowers growing.

AN INVOCATION.

RESTLESS phantoms haunt my brain!
Come and ease my nameless pain,
 Sleep, — sweet sleep!
I would own thy gentle power;
It is midnight's holy hour;
Wave thy charmed wand over me,
Let thy mantle cover me,
 Sleep, — sweet sleep!

Clasp me in thy dusky arms,
Soothe me with thy mystic balms,
 Sleep, — sweet sleep!
Let me drink thy Lethean wine,
Press thy dewy lips to mine,
Fold my hands and close my eyes,
Bring me dreams of Paradise,
 Sleep, — sweet sleep!

Linger with me till the dawn,
Leave me not till day is born,
 Sleep, — sweet sleep!
Then shall gates of rosy light
Open for thy silent flight.
Ah! some time thou'lt come, I know,
To my heart, and *never* go,
 Sleep, — sweet sleep!

THE WRECK.

THE Ocean sang to my heart last night,
  When I folded my hands in rest,
A song as sweet as a mother sings
  To the child upon her breast.

But to-day it wails like a funeral dirge,
  As they tell, in the quiet town,
How the English ship, in sight of land,
  With a hundred souls went down!

BENJAMIN D. LAIGHTON.

LINES WRITTEN IN MAY.

WAKE, my Muse! no longer sleep!
　　Once more thy sweetest numbers bring;
The Earth a second Eden shows:
　　Awake, and sing the charms of Spring!

The orchards redolent of bloom,
　　The singing birds, the balmy air,
The bright green fields, the warbling brooks, —
　　To me, all seem divinely fair!

No clouds in yon o'erarching sky
　　To hide the sun's enlivening rays;
No wintry winds to chill my frame,
　　And interrupt my song of praise.

Once more upon my wan worn cheek,
　　I feel the soft ambrosial breeze,
And list the aerial harmony
　　That floats amid the blossomed trees.

Reclined upon some grassy steep
　　That overlooks the billowy sea,
I love to watch the dark-blue waves,
　　And hear their deep-toned melody.

When on the Earth, night's shadows fall,
 Above I gaze with wondering eyes ;
On Fancy's wing delighted soar,
 To pierce the mysteries of the skies,

Still on, above the rolling spheres,
 To where resides the omniscient God, —
The starry realm below is but
 The jewelled floor of his abode !

Oh ! then in awe and rapture whelmed,
 I seek, within that radiant sphere,
Those friends so fondly loved on earth,
 Whose graves received affection's tear.

.   .   :   .   .   .

My harp ! with thy sweet harmonies
 There comes a low and dirge-like strain,
That falls upon my listening ear
 Like the murmur of the distant main.

It may no more be mine, my harp !
 To wake thy soothing melody :
Perchance, when Spring shall come again,
 Silence and dust may on me lie.

Be mine the blissful hope that points,
 Beyond the drear and shadowy tomb,
To that fair clime where the freed soul
 Shall flourish in immortal bloom !

STANZAS.

"If a man die, shall he live again?" — JOB xiv. 14.

WHEN the last struggle's o'er,
  And life this frame hath fled ;
When I shall live no more,
  But lie in my last bed ;

Shall I for ever sleep,
  A senseless mass of clay ;
No more on earth to greet
  The light of opening day ? —

The fingers of decay
  Deep-buried in my breast,
To waste my flesh away
  While I unconscious rest.

The sun shall rise and set ;
  Its shores the ocean lave ;
The grass with dews be wet,
  That grows above my grave.

The years will come and go,
  The past be acted o'er ;
And yet my sleep below
  Will be disturbed no more.

Bright star of Faith, arise !
  And guide me to the way
That leads beyond the skies,
  To the Unclouded Day !

THE FIRST-BORN.

I sit beneath the old elm-tree,
And, Memory! give myself to thee:
Thou sacred Past! thy scenes renew,
Though falling tears may dim the view.

. . . .

Again, as in the days of yore,
Our first-born plays beside the door, —
His little life a constant joy,
A bliss, as yet, without alloy.

Time glides away; with strong arms now
He guides the team or holds the plough;
His smile I see, his tones I hear, —
That smile, those tones, are ever near.

Again I look. O picture fair!
The manly form, the dark-brown hair,
The clear blue eye, the cloudless brow, —
Why wonder tears are falling now?

And still I gaze. Perchance no more
His welcome form will pass our door:
His country calls; he hears the cry,
And gallantly goes forth — to die.

. . . . . .

O God! mysterious are thy ways:
We strive to pierce the dismal maze,
But all in vain; a gloomy cloud
Envelops us as with a shroud.

I dream I've reached the heavenly shore,
— In God's good time a dream no more, —
And, all-entranced, I list the songs,
Sung to his praise by angel tongues.

I see among the shining band
The welcome smile, the beckoning hand ;
And THERE, amid celestial charms,
We clasp our lost one in our arms.

MARY E. B. MILLER.

ON LIFE'S THRESHOLD.

 HE way looks very long and dark and drear,
    That leads through this strange life to life
      immortal :
The great world's din is filling me with fear,
    As I stand, trembling, at its awful portal.

Oh ! I have walked till now in quiet places,
With Nature, in her woods and fields and dells :
The flowers look at me with familiar faces ;
I know the story that the wild-bird tells.

I've watched the Autumn sun's transfiguring splendor
Flood heaven and earth and sea at day's decline ;
I've watched the harvest-moons rise calm and tender,
And fair June mornings wake with smiles divine.

With low, sweet melody of running water,
With wild leaf-music, song of bird and bee,
Has Nature welcomed me, where'er I sought her ;
And never discord mars her harmony.

Oh! none of Earth's sad sights and sounds have ever
Disturbed the quiet of these blessèd years;
And must I bid these joys farewell for ever,
To walk henceforward in a vale of tears?

The world looks very cold and dark and dreary,
As I stand trembling at its open gate:
I hear within the sighing of the weary, —
If I *must* enter, let me longer wait!

I hear, from out its dark and frowning portal,
No sounds but those of sin and woe and death;
No yearning prayers for life and light immortal,
But only cries for bread that perisheth.

And through the open gate of that sad city
Are strange, dark faces gazing out on me:
Oh, how my heart swells, with a shuddering pity,
For these, whose life is one long misery!

For women, with such still and hopeless faces;
For men, whose passions live, whose souls are dead;
For childhood, without childhood's sunny graces;
And age, without the halo round its head.

Are these the sights for which I leave the mountains,
Thy sunlit meadows, and the blossoms fair?
Must I exchange the song of birds and fountains,
For this dread wailing of the world's despair?

O selfish soul! the peace which God hath given,
Which keeps thee safe amid temptation's fires;
The living bread that cometh down from heaven,
And satisfies thine infinite desires, —

With these go bravely forth to meet thy duty :
Within those gloomy gates that duty lies.
Fear not the dimness, — it will change to beauty
When Christ of Nazareth shall anoint thine eyes.

Beneath the weight of this unending sorrow,
Behold *him* bending, — him who died for thee !
Hear how these moans of human anguish borrow
The pathos of his pleading agony !

No time remains for dreams, nor for complaining ;
Childhood is past, — put childish things away :
Christ calls thee by his Spirit's sweet constraining :
Arise and work for him, while it is day.

O world ! thy darkness can affright no longer !
Within its depths the living God doth dwell :
Evil is mighty ; but his Love is stronger, —
Stronger than pain and sin and death and hell !

———

COMFORT.

To God our souls must flee,
When faith and sight grow dim :
The life, to us all mystery,
Is perfect light to him.

Beyond his love's embrace,
We *never* can depart ;
E'en when our sins have hid his face,
He holds us to his heart.

His mercy's depth and height,
No woe, no guilt, can sound :
In him a day for every night,
And life for death, are found.

He, only he, can know
Our heart's despairing pain ;
And he alone can comfort so
That we may hope again.

O death and sin and woe !
Your fury we defy !
For God the souls he loveth so
Will keep eternally.

THE BOOK OF LIFE.

Over the long, long ages,
My weary eyes I strain ;
Old Wisdom's brightest pages
I search, and search in vain :
O earth ! not all thy sages
Can soothe one sinner's pain !

Book of unending ages !
My soul returns to thee :
While vainly toil the sages
To solve life's mystery,
Through these transfigured pages
God speaks eternally.

LITTLE JOSEY'S GRAVE.

O GENTLEST, purest things of all on earth, —
Sweet Flowers! with eyes of tender, tearful blue;
When next the happy fields shall hail your birth,
God hath a holy work for you to do.

This small new grave — oh see! how very small! —
Must have a covering of summer green,
And down among the grasses, fresh and tall,
Your upward-looking, starry eyes be seen.

For aching hearts shall visit this low mound,
Because their little child lies here asleep;
And hot tears rain upon this sacred ground, —
Then must ye comfort those who come to weep.

Ye have no accents musical and tender;
The preacher's pleading art ye never knew:
Yet life's one deep, sweet lesson ye can render,—
" Trust God, — 'tis all that broken hearts *can* do! "

Yes: that is all! The dearest voice is hushed,
And on our hearts a life-long silence falls;
The lips whose smiles made all our light are dust,
And vainly now the sun the day recalls.

Yet angels in this twilight of our pain,
Which shuts us in from all the world beside,
Unto our souls a readier welcome gain,
And we have visions of the Christ that died.

Father, since hearts must ache, and tears must flow,
Oh! let this grief on thy compassion lean ;
And grant us all, when burst the storms of woe,
Thine everlasting love, a shield between!

———

NIGHTFALL.

THE storm has ceased, the winds are still,
　　The weary day is dying;
And deep and white, on plain and hill,
　　The drifted snow is lying.

As slowly through the silent room
　　The twilight shades are stealing,
Old memories glimmer in the gloom,
　　Long-vanished scenes revealing.

Sit here beside me, gentle child,
　　Where I, your face beholding,
May tell you of your mother mild,
　　Close in the grave's infolding.

'Twas fourteen weary years ago, —
　　Ah me! how life is flying! —
When earth, as now, was white with snow,
　　Your mother sweet lay dying.

Without, the tempest's fitful wail
　　The starless night affrighted ;
Within, we saw her features pale,
　　With wondrous splendor lighted.

She heeded not the dreary night,
Heard not the tempest's wailing :
Before her death-illumined sight,
Heaven's glories were unveiling.

She gazed in deep ecstatic calm ;
Then, with a smile upspringing,
Her soul sang one exulting psalm,
And passed away in singing.

Come, darling, let us kneel ; and so,
To God our sorrow bringing,
Dwell near him, praying thus below,
As she in heaven, singing.

EVENING ASPIRATIONS.

FATHER in heaven ! thy watchful love I claim, —
Thy full forgiveness for this day's deep sin,
Not in my own, — in Jesus' blessed name,
I ask, and, asking thus, shall surely win.

O Father ! will the shadows always stay ?
Must every day, like this, with guilt be stained ?
Oh ! bid me go rejoicing on my way,
To find each night a nobler height attained.

When shall this heart, so cold and thankless now,
Be full of joyous love, my God, to thee ?
When shall I wear, resplendent on my brow,
The seal that shows thou hast adopted me ?

Be it by hours of bitter agony,
By storms that darken all my joys on earth ;
But wake me from this deathly lethargy,
And let me find the glorious second-birth.

Oh ! fill me with the spirit of the cross ;
Let me go forth to conquer evermore, —
To walk, despising shame and pain and loss,
Wherever my Redeemer trod before.

Arise, my soul ! with quenchless hope and zeal,
All selfish thoughts renouncing from this hour :
Each day that passes shall to thee reveal
Some new evangel of God's love and power.

Oh, onward, upward press ! forgetting all
The sin and sorrow in the weary past !
Strive for a living faith like that of Paul ;
And thou, like him, shalt overcome at last.

One more competitor for life's bright crown,
One more aspirant after holiness,
See, Lord, before thee humbly bowing down,
Waiting for thee to strengthen and to bless.

Send me not faith alone to run the race ;
For there are dangers only thou canst see,
And there are foes I should not love to face,
If thy dear hand were not upholding me.

Oh, then abide in me, my blessed Lord !
And I in thee ! so shall I see the throne,
And gain at last — exceeding great reward ! —
A home where I shall " know as I am known."

SNOW.

THE sunset tints have faded from the leaves ;
The smile of death is on the withered flowers ;
And winter's wind, in mournful music, grieves
The flight of summer's golden-wingèd hours.

The feathered songsters fled with summer's glow,
To seek the shores of never-fading green ;
The woods are wrapped in solemn silence now,
And all is drear where life and joy have been.

The brilliant blue of heaven is changed to gray ;
The sunny glow has left the mountain's brow ;
No gush of music ushers in the day ;
No crimson glory crowns its closing now.

But see ! how, falling from the sombre sky,
In silent gracefulness, those pearly things,
So pure, so fragile too, come floating by,
Like tiny feathers from an angel's wings.

And myriads now are floating calmly down
To clothe the fields so desolate and bare :
Each withered blossom wears a crystal crown ;
Each leafless bough, a robe of ermine rare.

The wood that looked so gloomy now appears,
As if by magic, tastefully arrayed ;
From every twig are pendent frozen tears ;
And wreaths of white are hung in every glade.

Oh! softly, softly falls this gentle snow
Upon the quiet graves of some we love, —
Pure as the robes of light they're wearing now,
In perfect happiness, we trust, above.

There falls no snow on Heaven's glorious hills,
But ever there a golden summer reigns :
Immortal flowers their fragrance there distil,
And life's pure river feeds those happy plains.

A few more summers, with their gentle rains ;
A few more winters, with their silent snows ;
A few more tempests on these earthly plains ;
A few more struggles with our sins and woes :

And then shall break the day of endless rest ;
The raptured soul forget its stormy past ;
The shades of sorrow flee the tranquil breast,
Exchanged for joys that shall for ever last !

THOMAS P. MOSES.

TO A MINIATURE OF THE DEPARTED.

EWEL more dear than pearls or gold,
 Bright impress of the loved and lost!
Thee to my bosom will I fold,
 While on Life's changeful sea I'm tossed.

Dear image of a soul refined!
 There's inspiration in thine eyes;
And on those lips seem whispers kind,
 Like soothing music from the skies.

I gaze upon thy features fair,
 Till fancy paints a breathing glow:
Thy smile then dissipates my care,
 And frees my breast from every woe.

Thy voice seems raised in seraph song,
 And sweetly echoes in mine ear:
O heart! deem not my fancy wrong;
 Still would I dream that voice I hear.

THE RETURNED RING.

TAKE back the ring I wore for thee :
  The shining gem is worthless now ;
It hath no magic charm for me, —
  'Twill mind thee of thy truthless vow.

Oh ! take it back, — 'twas gift of thine
  When thou wert true, and life was fair :
No longer will I call it mine, —
  False vows are mirrored in its glare.

Yet I'll not murmur at my fate,
  Nor crave a passing thought of thee ;
No ! calmly to the end I'll wait,
  To learn a false one's destiny.

Then take the ring I wore for thee ;
  It lends no inspiration now :
Nought in the cherished boon I see,
  But emblems of a broken vow.

SYMPATHY.

Art's glittering domes and towers must fall,
  Gay cities crumble with the dead ;
All things must yield to Time's stern call, —
  Thus the Omnipotent hath said.

But mark the sympathetic breast,
  That melts when Misery's sons are nigh :
In golden palace, with the blest,
  His name shall brightly shine on high.

JOHN N. MOSES.

BORN 1811; DIED 1837.

THE MIDNIGHT VOICE.

"Then a spirit passed before my face; the hair of my flesh stood up: it stood still, but I could not discern the form thereof: an image was before mine eyes; there was silence, and I heard a voice, saying, Shall mortal man be more just than God? shall a man be more pure than his Maker? Behold, he put no trust in his servants, and his angels he charged with folly: how much less in them that dwell in houses of clay, whose foundation is in the dust?"—JOB iv. 15-19.

H! there is in the midnight air a Voice,
When hushed in silence is the dreaming
world:
The magic breathings of that voice are heard
In whispering tones, but awfully distinct,
As of some spirit-monitor from heaven,
Charged with a message to the sinner's heart.
It comes not often to false Pleasure's bower;
Nor does it visit oft the gilded halls
Where glittering Wealth stalks down, and stately Pride
Swells in her puny, weak magnificence.
Ah, no! it may not linger there, that Voice,
To hold its friendly warnings out too long
To such as spurn the thought of penitence;
For He, whose promise never fails, hath said
His spirit shall not always strive with man.

There is a glen where silent Solitude,
In ashy paleness, sits enthroned alone ;
And oft to that secluded spot I stray,
When earth is wrapt in midnight's holiest veil ;
And her pale, lovely satellite above,
In all her mellow brightness, marches on,
As if the captain of yon glittering host,
To storm, with smiles, the erring Atheist's heart ;
When all is breathless, and when those harsh sounds
As of a world in clashing arms have died,
Or into that one murmuring echo sunk
Of distant ocean, beating on the shore
With its broad, foamy crest and ceaseless roar ;
And when the flowers, the beauteous, fragrant flowers,
Are sending up their incense to the skies, —
Then, then that holy messenger will come,
As he will come to all who shun him not ;
And, holding out the page of crime and sin,
He slowly points to errors unforgiven.

Callous and cold and proud,
And rank in sinfulness, my heart had grown,
Forgetting all the bounties Heaven had given,
In mercy too, — the blightings all withheld ;
And I had murmured at that Sovereign Power
Who wields the sceptre o'er our destinies,
Murmured that one in beauty, youth, and hope, —
Too true, alas ! my heart's own idol dear, —
Was snatched away by the grim hand of Death ;
And, as I leaned beneath that drooping tree
Whose boughs seemed weeping as in sympathy
With hearts shorn of their dearest cherished hopes,
I trembling heard that solemn step approach ;
And in reproachful, yet in soothing tones,
Thus spake the spirit voice : —

" Vain man ! dare ye presume to be —
  All sinful thus — more wise than God?
More mighty, holy, just, than He
  Who holds the eternal judgment-rod?
That haughty brow all crimsoned o'er
  With deepfelt guilt and shame must be,
And that proud heart must learn to pour
  Its gushings of humility !

A single link in that vast chain
  Of wisdom, reaching where the eye
Of mortal strives to gaze in vain,
  Would ye subvert God's harmony?
It cannot be ! ye may not scan
  What angels long in vain to see, —
Why, in his dealings, God to man
  Should wrap his wand in mystery.

Oh ! be content that he has spread
  The hills with bounties, fields with food ;
That all earth's fruits for thee are shed, —
  Earth's every blessing for thy good :
And though thy heart has now been crushed
  While basking in Hope's sunny ray,
Peace ! — let thy murmurings be hushed :
  Shall He who gave, not take away?

He who is infinite in love ;
  Who fills the earth with bliss for you,
And spreads that glorious arch above
  To cheer thy path in mercy too, —
A hope of richer bliss hath given
  Beyond the uncertain bounds of time ;
And hearts, by sorrow worn and riven,
  Shall find a balsam in that clime ! "

. . . .

Thus spake the spirit, ere it soared afar,
On its bright pinions, to the realms of day.
But, while I bowed beneath that weeping tree,
It lingered yet to take a falling tear,
That, like a film from off my stricken soul,
Had rolled in silence. Then was I alone!
Nought, save the night-bird's warbling melody
Among the gently waving leaves, was heard;
And, with a humbler heart, I joined his praise, —
No more resolving to repine at Him
Before whose brow the starry hosts above,
In all their splendid brilliancy, are dim;
But humbly to repent of errors past,
And eager strive to gain an entrance there
Where all is harmony and joy and love.

JAMES R. MAY.

AT YORKTOWN.

HE army slept around the stream ;
The camp-fires cast a ruddy gleam

O'er tents that shone like marble domes.
With dreams of war and dreams of homes,

The army slept without a fear.
Danger must reach the sentinel's ear.

Before the foe to them may come,
The alarm must sound from ready drum.

And so, in showers of rain and sleet,
The sentry marched his weary beat,

Acting with zeal a patriot's part,
With shivering frame, but sturdy heart.

But not all did their duty well:
To one poor soldier it befell,

That wearied-out with labor done,
While still he grasped his slippery gun,

His strength, despite resolve, gave way,
And slumbering at his post he lay.

Justice had doomed the man to die ;
But Mercy passed the verdict by :

She loosed the chains the prisoner wore,
And set him free to strike once more.

He whom a friendly power may save,
A grateful heart makes doubly brave.

Soon the contending armies meet.
With gallant rush and sturdy feet

Our banner's borne toward the foe,
A beacon in war's ebb and flow.

Around the flag in deadly fight
Rebel and patriot host unite,

Resolved to do all that man may
In battle-field to gain the day.

The soldier met the death he sought,
As in the foremost rank he fought ;

And there's no shadow now of shame
Upon the brightness of his fame.

Valor and gratitude unite !
A nation thanks thee for the sight.

Wise mind ! who knew, that, to the heart
Of soldier true, no keener dart

May come than a dishonored death ;
Who knew, that, with the joyful breath

Of pardon, Mercy lights a fire,
Never while memory lasts to expire.

The holy truth is proved again, —
Mercy ne'er bends to save in vain !

CATHERINE M. McCLINTOCK.

———◆———

WHEREFORE?

 SAW Life binding myriads
    In utter slavery;
I saw her smite them with disease,
    Crush them with poverty,
And break their hearts, for human love that yearned
With scornful faces ever from them turned.
Life seemed to work these deeds of misery,
As if compelled unto it, sorrowfully.
    But, when I asked her " wherefore?"
      She only bowed her head:
      With rain of tear-drops shed,
    She gave me back my " wherefore?"

I went unto Life's victims, — Hope,
    Whose wings lagged wearily,
Whose flowers were trampled beneath Life's feet:
    Why was her agony?
The flowers fell faster as I questionèd;
The wings dropped down as with a weight of lead;
The smiles grew fainter, though she strove to smile,
And struggled bravely, for a little while,

Against that cruel *wherefore?*
Hope could not find it out;
Death came to her with doubt,
His arrow barbed with " wherefore? "

To Love, — she held upon her heart
A body without breath,
That in the silence lay embalmed, —
A casket that held death.
And when she found it only this contained;
To see but this, Love, watching, still remained,
Till " earth had taken earth ; " then veiled her face.
I asked no wherefore? for it filled the place, —
Love's bitter, despairing " wherefore? "
At each new pang, she'd start
With shrinking, bleeding heart,
And utter, moaning, " wherefore? "

I saw upon a mountain-top,
The nearest unto God,
And such a one of needs must be, —
A mountain Christ had trod, —
A form, that could not but a shadow be ;
A shining rather seemed it unto me :
There stood a shape betwixt the earth and heaven ;
The human and divine both to her given.
And, when I asked Faith " wherefore? "
From Holy Scroll she read, —
" God is love." Thou, like the dead,
Should'st know all things are therefore.

FAITH.

FAITH that is born of sunshine;
  Faith that's a sunbeam only,
Dead on the storm-cloud's bosom,
  Leaving life dim and lonely.

Faith that is born of darkness;
  Child, too, of eternal light;
Ray from the star unsetting,
  That glorifieth night.

Faith that is born of quiet, —
  A fair and delicate thing,
That faints at the first o'ersweeping
  Of cloud or shadowy wing.

Faith that is born of struggle, —
  Sinewy, elastic, strong
In the soul, not soul's surroundings,
  It shall aye to the soul belong.

Faith that is born of ignorance,
  Unquestioning, blind from its birth:
The lightning that openeth its eyelids
  Striketh it dead to the earth.

Faith that is born of knowledge,
  Its elder brother Doubt,
Whom it wrestleth with, and o'ercometh,
  And shall live evermore without.

Till we have passed beyond him
　Who stops at the gate of heaven,
With thanks our guide dismissing,
　Whose sight for faith is given.

DEATH IN SPRING.

Nature's life-throb strengtheneth, quickeneth ;
　Count we a pulse-beat faint and slow ;
Passing beneath her arches of triumph,
　Vanquished, graveward her child must go.

Vanquished ! but not so for ever :
　Keep thy triumph, O Nature life !
Heaven and earth shall pass together,
　Soul shall see their parting strife.

Tree and plant and flower upspringing,
　Fades life's nobler bloom away?
Death the pictured form effaceth,
　Faintly drawn upon the clay.

Bird and breeze and brook in chorus,
　Striving with one dying tone, —
Soul shall sing when ye are silent ;
　Drown that breathing faint — swell on !

Catching a tone that falls from heaven,
　Sings this life like a mocking-bird :
Let the notes die ! soaring God-ward,
　The immortal skylark's heard.

Father! to thee we commend the spirit
  Over the waters drifting to thee;
Down in the black gulf, O white Angel diver!
  Rescue the soul — Immortality!

" There shall be no more sea," cries the Angel:
  Crieth the soul, the sea could not drown:
Safe on the shore where the God-beloved season,
  Spring-time eternal, weareth the crown.

EDWARD P. NOWELL.

---•---

THE DESERTED HOMESTEAD.

DECAYED and brown the old house lonely
        stands
    Beneath the elm-trees' flecked and shifting
        shade,
Denoting Time's imperative commands, —
    That earthly things but bloom to early fade.

The great square chimney with its gaping top,
    The windows leering like lithe spectres grim, —
While summer evening's stealthy shadows drop, —
    Their peak-like fragments render them less dim.

The mossy curb-roof, of its shelter shorn,
    Whose fissures wide the spider strives to close ;
The hingeless door, reclining, seems to mourn
    Its long-lost friend, the fragrant climbing rose.

No path now leads adown the gentle slope
    To where the broken well-sweep marks the place,
Where once rose sweet and cool the bubbling rope
    Of globules, in the limpid water's face.

The circling stones that saw the bucket pass,
  So oft o'erflowing, to the sphere of light,
Have, one by one, dropped in ; and now, alas !
  The ruined well will weep in endless night.

Within, the creaking floors a tale relate,
  Of vanished scenes now with the Past entombed,
When all these rooms re-echoed with the prate
  Of those whose hearts to claim no care presumed.

Unfeeling Time ! what changes hast thou wrought
  Within this dwelling, all forsaken now ;
In which the worthy parents early sought
  With traits of truth their offspring to endow.

Where are the members of this household good,
  Who erstwhile gave these rooms a pleasing guise ;
Who by their footsteps, where the tables stood,
  Wore thin the floor, and made the nails uprise?

Down by the winding wall a willow waves,
  The ivy clings around a modest pale :
In this enclosure lifts a line of graves, —'
  Yon home yields all to that within the vail.

The little ones were smitten by the stroke
  Of cureless maladies, and borne away
O'er Death's cold, sullen stream, which wholly broke
  The mother's heart upon that tearful day.

Like Rachel mourning for her loved and lost,
  Refusing comfort from her Ramah friends ;
So was this mother on the ocean tost
  Of bitter sorrow, which no solace lends !

But Death, the sable sovereign, loosed the cord
  Which bound the broken-hearted to her grief;
And all her tears were dried, when with the Lord
  She knelt, — adoring Him who brought relief.

Alone the stricken father walked on earth,
  Alone he lived beneath his humble roof;
Yet not alone, — since of the second-birth
  His heart in resignation gave the proof.

The dear Redeemer dwelt with him below,
  And gave him faith and trust, with calm content;
Life's river flowed where fruitful fig-trees grow, —
  His peace was sure, because 'twas heaven-sent.

Thus age crept on the head of this good man;
  And, with the precious Bible on his knee,
He sat upon his door-stone, where began
  The life beyond Time's rough and stormy sea.

Thus was he found, — his head bowed o'er that Book
  Which was his rod and staff in life and death;
His face wore heavenly smiles, as though he took
  And kissed the Saviour's hand with latest breath!

WINTER.

THE sly Frost-king has blown his bitter breath
  O'er Summer's bright-eyed children in an hour,
And shown in Autumn's hues the stroke of death,
  The gorgeous painting of his wondrous power.

Scene beyond scene of forest and of field
 View Winter's frigid reach from Iceland's hills ;
And through the land his potent stamp has sealed
 The mouths of rivers and the voice of rills.

Enrobed in white lie Nature's withered forms, —
 Their place of rest marked by the leaf-shorn trees,
On earth's cold plains to sleep 'neath howling storms,
 Till Spring's loud trump shall wake the birds and
 bees.

While wintry blasts dirge through the gloomy street,
 Where starving beings dread the coming dawn ;
To these, oh, may the Watcher guide the feet
 Of Charity, ere life's last spark is gone !

TO JOHN B. GOUGH.

GREAT Champion of the Right ! Thy clarion voice
 The erring world checks in its thorny path,
 Securing oft absolvement from God's wrath !
Thy rare persuasive power makes those rejoice
 To whom life had before been baleful blight.
Thou hast outvied the Alchemist of old, —
Hast turned the brass of Wrong to Truth's pure gold !
 Thy armor girded on in fearless fight
'Gainst Error and Oppression's base array,
 Combating Sin with all its hydra heads, —
 The blood of Acratus thy sharp sword sheds !
Brave Conqueror ! Truth's standard high display,
 Till, for thy shining soul, the angel's hand
 Shall lift the veil before the Better Land !

PÆAN FOR VICTORY.

SHOUT, shout, the tidings o'er
The land, from shore to shore, —
    All shall be free !
The Knights of Bondage bleed,
Rebellion's ranks recede,
Our arms triumphant lead
    To victory !

All hail the glorious sight !
Columbia's martial might
    Traitors astounds !
Fair Freedom's valiant host
Has silenced Slavery's boast,
Along Secessia's coast,
    And through her bounds !

God grant we soon may see
Enduring unity,
    And sheathe the sword ;
Our Country's foemen felled,
Secession's spirit quelled,
The smoke of strife dispelled,
    And Peace restored !

Then Union's banner bright
Shall herald Freedom's light
    On shore and sea,
And Heaven's benignant rays
Illume the Nation's days, —
Our hearts ascribing praise,
    Great God, to thee !

IN MEMORIAM.

HE is gone, the Christian philanthropist,
Dear Nature's student, beloved of all compeers;
His eyes are closed, his ears no longer list
To catch the subtile music of the spheres!

The starry skies their mysteries revealed
To his untiring, scrutinizing gaze;
And shifting clouds afforded him a field,
Whose wealth did e'en his sapient mind amaze.

His years with studious introspection fraught, —
The fleeting moments were to him like gold;
Yet if, to evolve a giant truth, close thought
Of years were spent, these years gave joy untold.

With what intrepid, marked enthusiasm
He wrestled with his problems dark and dense,
And bridged by patient toil as wide a chasm
As challenged minds of keen Baconian sense!

Removed from life's vast and diffuse concerns,
In which his ease to care did oft concede,
The destitute with tearful sorrow learns
A friend is gone who was a friend indeed.

His sympathetic heart acutely felt
The wants of the down-trodden and oppressed:
Full many say, to whom in need he dealt,
The name of MERIAM be for ever blessed!

A noble life is lost to us on earth,
A soul as pure as angel robes of white :
This life in brighter realms receives its birth,
This soul exults in heaven's transcendent light !

———

THE SEA.

I STOOD, and listened to the Ocean's roar,
 As on the scowling crags he leaped and raved,
And spent his fury on the rugged shore,
 Where many sink, and where how few are saved !

O treacherous Deep ! to-day thou art a friend
 To trusting man upon thy tranquil main,
But mayst to-morrow prove his fatal foe :
 He sinks — his foe thou canst not be again !

The beat of ocean-waves sepulchral sounds,
 As on the darkened air they strangely moan :
To me it seems as if their countless dead
 Were now just gasping their expiring groan !

. The fierce Storm-king hides not his form to-night ;
 In his cloud-car he comes forth to destroy ;
His yell terrific makes the sea run mad,
 And in his grasp whole fleets are but a toy !

The demon cliffs are lurking in the gloom,
 And trembling ships haste to white spectral shoals :
O God of Pity ! stay their fearful course,
 And snatch from restive graves despairing souls !

THE OLD OAKEN CRADLE.

SWEET scenes of my boyhood! I love to recall them,
Electric they shimmer on mem'ry's warm sky, —
The radiant river, the hills grand and solemn,
And all the dear haunts in the forest near by.
I watch these fresh views on the Past's panorama
Unfold as among the enchantments of earth, —
The ancient red house, in which Life's devious drama
Commenced in the cradle which stood by the hearth :
    The old oaken cradle, the rocker-worn cradle,
    The high-posted cradle which stood by the hearth.

Near two generations from earth have departed
Since home in high state this quaint cradle was
    brought,
Attesting the advent of one who, light-hearted,
Gave joy pure and holy, of sad sorrow nought.
Dear relic of dream-days! what rest have you granted
To mother and infant when hushed was his mirth !
How grateful was sleep when the babe for it panted ! —
A boon is the cradle which stands by the hearth !
    The old oaken cradle, the rocker-worn cradle,
    The high-posted cradle which stands by the hearth.

Not all mem'ry's promptings of by-gones that gather
Are free from a sadness made sacred by space,
Since angels led two from our home, — and for ever
Seraphic behold they Immanuel's face ;

And we who remain live more or less distant,
But never forget we the place of our birth :
The light of our mem'ry, in realms reminiscent,
Reveals the staid cradle which stood by the hearth :
  The old oaken cradle, the rocker-worn cradle,
  The high-posted cradle which stood by the hearth.

CHILD AND CHERUB.

Baby Nora, peering out
Through the casement, gave a shout
      So full of glee,
      Its melody
Blending with the thrush's trill,
Like the breeze with rippling rill, —
'Twas a scene so sweet to see,
That I gazed admiringly.

Passing by her home next day,
All is mute ; no child at play,
      No open blind,
      No face I find !
Baby Nora, why so still?
Dost thou sleep or art thou ill?
Hush ! give ear ! her spirit is
Hymning heavenly harmonies !

ROCKY GLEN.

DEAR Rocky Glen! to thee belong
Minerva's praise, Apollo's song!
Thy name the sparkling brooks rehearse,
To thee sing woods in varied verse:
Green hills o'erlook thy quiet view,
Through vistas grand gleam waters blue,
And tender vine climbs friendly tree
In Rocky Glen, down by the sea.

From bough and nest in leafy shade,
Where birds their homes secure have made,
They, sweet-voiced warblers, strive to tell
With what delight their bosoms swell;
Gay fairy sylphs glide through thy bowers,
And dance away the sunny hours;
And wild sweets woo the honey-bee
In Rocky Glen, down by the sea.

Thy azure windows, golden doors,
Gild thy green walks, and gem thy shores,
Abode of peace and purity!
Fair sunbeams linger long with thee;
Clear streamlets bathe thy spangled feet;
Thy face is with rich charms replete;
To realms of bliss is found a key
In Rocky Glen, down by the sea!

MRS. C. E. R. PARKER.

LOST AND WON.

LOST the freshness of life's morning,
　　Lost the tints of rosy light,
　Which, like daylight's perfect dawning,
　　Covered all with glory bright;
　Lost the golden locks which shaded
　　Brow so smooth, and eyes so blue;
　And the happy smile has faded
　　Round those lips of rosy hue.
　　　　　　I have lost, — but I have won.

　Lost the kind oblivious sleeping
　　Which enshrouds the little child,
　Like the holy angels' keeping, —
　　Saintly watches, calm and mild.
　　Lost the dreams of sunny hours,
　Where no terror dare intrude;
　Lost the dreams of love and flowers,
　　Of the beautiful and good.
　　　　　　I have lost, — but I have won.

　Lost, — oh most of all the losses! —
　　Lost the childlike, earnest faith,
　Loving on 'mid joys and losses,
　　Thankful still for all it hath.

I have lost youth's simple blossoms;
  Each hath departed, one by one;
But, oh, blessing without measure!
          I have lost, — but I have won.

I have won, through earnest striving,
  Guerdons above all the loss;
Hopes once faded, now reviving,
  Twining round the sacred cross.
Sorrow pale hath been my teacher;
  Hopes bereft, my gentle friends;
Graves of the loved, my silent preachers,
  Where dust with dust so sadly blends.
          I have lost, — but I have won.

I have won, through tribulation,
  Title to a heavenly home,
Working out my own salvation,
  Through the blood of Christ alone.
Oh! my future brightest seemeth;
  Eye of faith, exchanged for sight,
With celestial splendor beameth
  On through darkness into light.
          I have lost, — but I have won.

I have won bright hopes immortal
  Of a heaven of peace and rest;
E'en now I linger at the portal
  As a kindly bidden guest.
Lost and won! — O earth, O heaven!
  Hark! — I list the angels' strain,
Voices in the silence even!
  Small the loss, and great the gain!
          I have lost, — but I have won.

"LORD, IS IT I?"

" Lord, is it I?" I ask in tears and sadness,
  I, thy disciple at thy sacrèd board,
Who from thy cup hath drank, thy bread hath broken;
  Oh! is it I who shall betray my Lord?

" Lord, is it I?" I ask in deep emotion!
  " Exceeding sorrowful," my heart would say
Though I should die with thee, I'll not deny thee:
  Forbid it, Lord, that I thy trust betray.

" Lord, is it I?" Thou knowest that I love thee;
  " I love thy habitation and thy seat;"
I love to hear thy gospel's holy teaching:
  With Mary, I could worship at thy feet.

" Lord, is it I?" I tremble at the question:
  Oh! is my faith so weak in Christ, my God,
That I for worldly gain *could* sell my Master, —
  That I for worldly joys deny my Lord?

" Lord, is it I?" Thou knowest my temptations,
  My spirit willing, though my flesh is weak;
My earnest striving, and my often failing,
  Sinning, repenting, still thy grace I seek.

" Lord, is it I?" Oh, cheer my drooping spirit!
  Unto thy cross I cling in humble prayer,
Distrusting all but thee and thy great merit:
  O blessed Saviour, take me in thy care!

THINE FOR EVER.

THINE for ever ! Thine for ever !
　What to me is chance or change?
Can the love I once have plighted
　Ever to my heart be strange?

Thine for ever !　So I whispered,
　When thy lips first spoke of love ;
Thine for ever ! though now severed,
　I on earth, and thou above.

Thine for ever ! was thy promise ;
　Not " *till death us part* " was mine :
Through this life, and still for ever,
　Thou art mine, and I am thine.

Thine for ever ! what though anguish —
　Oh most deep ! — did rend my heart,
When on earth our bliss was severed,
　And I saw thy life depart ;

Saw thine eyes (most tender gazers)
　Fade in death while fixed on mine ;
Felt *my* life was fast departing,
　While I trembling watched for thine ;

Saw thy form borne sadly from me,
　Laid beneath the grassy sod ;
Knew my eyes no more would greet thee,
　Till we meet before our God !

17

What though many suns have lingered
   O'er thy lonely grass-clad bed?
What though nights and days have found me
   Weeping o'er my blessèd dead?

Thine for ever! still for ever!
   Oh! no death can part us twain;
Thine on earth, and thine in heaven,
   Blessèd thought, — we meet again!

Meet! — we never yet have parted:
   Thy dear form is lost to sight;
.But *the hearts which God united*,
   Death can never disunite.

Thine for ever! — others whisper
   Words of love into my ear:
Know they not the deathless feeling,
   Which will ever linger here?

Know they not that love as ours,
   On through life and death the same,
Knows no change, — that earthly sorrows
   Cannot quench the sacred flame?

Thine for ever! — soon I meet thee,
   Still thine own as thou art mine;
Meet thee, never more to sever,
   Still thine own, for ever thine!

THE OLD KITCHEN-FIRE.

Oh ! happy were my early days,
  And pleasant was my home,
And sunny was the green hillside
  Where I was wont to roam.
No scenes, which memory recalls,
  My thoughts with joy inspire,
Compared to my own little seat
  Beside the kitchen-fire.

The quiet winter evening,
  When, with my simple book
Or knitting-work, I claimed my seat :
  In that snug, cosy nook
I listened to the older folk ;
  For I could never tire
Of all the twice-told tales I heard
  Beside that kitchen-fire.

The spacious chimney deep and wide,
  The broad old kitchen-hearth
Of bright-red bricks, that in the blaze
  Would blink as if in mirth ;
The kettle, sending forth its steam,
  And cheery little song ;
The low, calm ticking of the clock,
  Speeding the hours along.

The cricket, from his hiding-place,
  His little voice would lend ;
The merry heart ! I welcomed him
  As if he were a friend.

The smiling basket, full of chips,
  Did screen the little thing :
I did not care to hunt him out,
  I'd rather hear him sing.

And pussy sat, with half-shut eyes,
  And black and glossy fur,
Dozing the sleepy hours away
  With low, contented purr.
How the great logs would blaze and roar,
  And crackle as in glee !
While the bright sparks went flying up, —
  A goodly company !

What magic power that bright fire had !
  No artist ever drew,
With skilful hand, such glowing scenes,
  All beautiful and new :
Bright colors from dear fairy-land,
  The happy limner blends ;
And, 'mid the embers, shadowed forth
  Faces of little friends.

Old happy times ! My heart goes back,
  And wonders at the change,
While painful memories press around,
  And whisper, " Is it strange ?
Oh ! where has gone the simple heart,
  The humble, calm desire,
Which made that little seat so dear
  Beside the kitchen-fire " ?

BLUE FLOWERS.

You ask which flowers I love the best,
When Spring calls forth her pretty train,
And, each in cheerful garments dressed,
She sends them forth o'er hill and plain.
    Give me blue flowers,
    To grace my bowers!
The "*perfect color*,"—heaven's own blue,
    Meek violet
    In emerald set,
And glistening with the fragrant dew;
    Or by the brook,
    With downcast look,
The nodding harebell's fairy form
    I love to see,
    Where, lowly, she
Doth bend her head to meet the storm.

Blue flowers!—oh, give me fair blue flowers!
So pleadingly their azure eyes
Uplook in mine at morning's hour,
Taking their color from the skies:
    Of heaven they learn,
    To heaven they turn
Their opening bells at break of day;
    And heaven doth shed
    On each fair head
A blessing on them where they lay,—
    A blessing meet
    For flowers so sweet,

A portion of her glory bright.
Our prayer should be,
Oh, thus may we
Be clothed upon with robes of light!

GOOD NIGHT, LITTLE DAUGHTER, GOOD NIGHT!

Good night, little daughter, good night!
Sleep sweetly, oh, quietly sleep!
Send down thy kind angels, our Father in heaven,
 A watch o'er the slumberer to keep:
  Good night, little daughter, good night!

Good night, little daughter! good night!
Dream sweetly, oh, quietly dream!
Send down blessèd dreams, our Father in heaven,
 Beneath her closed eyelids to gleam:
  Good night, little daughter, good night!

Good night, little daughter, good night!
Wake brightly, oh, cheerfully wake!
With the fresh morning dawn, our Father in heaven,
 Oh break her light slumbers, oh break!
  Good night, little daughter, good night!

Good night, little daughter, good night!
She is thine, blessèd Jesus, — is thine:
Oh, cease not thy care, gracious Father in heaven!
 This treasure to thee we resign:
  Good night, little daughter, good night!

MY CROSS.

It is not heavy, agonizing woe
Bearing me down with hopeless, crushing weight;
No ray of comfort, in the gathering gloom;
A heart bereaved, — a household desolate.

It is not sickness, with her withering hand,
Keeping me low upon a couch of pain;
Longing each morning for the weary night, —
At night for weary day to come again.

It is not poverty, with chilling blast;
The sunken eye, the hunger-wasted form;
The dear ones perishing for lack of bread,
With no safe shelter from the winter's storm.

It is not slander, with her evil tongue;
'Tis no " presumptuous sin " against my God;
Not reputation lost, or friends betrayed, —
That such is not my cross, I thank thee, Lord!

Mine is a daily cross of petty cares,
Of little duties pressing on my heart;
Of little troubles hard to reconcile;
Of inward struggles, overcome in part.

My feet are weary in their daily rounds,
My heart is weary of its daily care;
My sinful nature often doth rebel, —
I pray for grace my *daily cross* to bear.

It is not heavy, Lord, yet oft I pine ;
It is not heavy, but 'tis ever here ;
By day and night, each hour my cross I bear :
I dare not put it down, — thou laid'st it there.

I dare not put it down : I only ask,
That, taking up my daily cross, I may
Follow my Master, humbly, step by step,
Through clouds and darkness unto perfect day.

UNDER THE SNOW.

BEAUTIFUL things lie hidden
    Under the snow :
Tulips and daffodils sleeping,
Myrtles with broad leaves are creeping,
And blue-eyed forget-me-nots peeping,
    Under the snow.

Beautiful things lie hidden
    Under the snow :
The crocus and dear little daisies,
Arbutus in wonderful mazes
Its sweet-scented tendrils upraises,
    Under the snow.

Beautiful things lie hidden
    Under the snow :
But they will awake in the morning ;
When spring with warm sunshine is dawning,
They will peep out from under their awning
    Under the snow.

Our dear little Alice lies hidden
    Under the snow :
The angels their kind watch are keeping,
O'er our beautiful treasure safe sleeping, —
No pain and no sorrow or weeping
    Under the snow.

Yes! beautiful Alice lies hidden
    Under the snow !
But she will awake in the morning,
When the bright resurrection-day dawning,
No more to lie down 'midst our mourning,
    Under the snow !

OUR LAMB.

TAKE away the little baby,
    Folded in his garments white ;
Place him in the rosewood casket,
    Close the lid upon him tight ;
Throw the pall upon the coffin,
    Bear our little one away ;
Leave me in my quiet chamber, —
    We have lost our lamb to-day.

Bear the casket and its jewel
    Out beneath the open sky :
Dust to dust, our little treasure
    With its mother-earth must lie.
Heap the sod upon the coffin,
    Hide our darling quite away ;
Leave me in my quiet chamber, —
    We have lost our lamb to-day.

Let him sleep on, while the daisies
    Bloom upon the grassy sod:
Leave him there, our fairest flower,
    Leave our darling with his God!
Very lonely, sad, and heart-sick,
    On my bed I weep and pray;
Leave me in my quiet chamber, —
    We have lost our lamb to-day.

Only three short weeks I had him
    Folded in my arms of love;
Then the Heavenly Shepherd called him
    To that other fold above.
Oh! I know my child is safest,
    Borne on angel wings away;
Yet my tears are falling, falling,
    For we've lost our lamb to-day.

Bear him, angels, far above us,
    To the regions of the blest:
No more pain, no sin, no sorrow, —
    Safe within the fold of rest.
Throbbing heart-aches, tears of anguish,
    Let me banish you away!
Oh, rejoice! though sick and lonely, —
    Heaven has gained our lamb to-day.

God, in his good time, will send us
    Blessèd comfort from above:
He who wept o'er Lazarus sleeping
    Looks on us with pitying love.
Little lamb, in Jesus' keeping,
    Christ himself hath called away;
Heavenly Shepherd, gently, gently,
    Guide our little lamb to-day.

NIGHT.

'Tis holy night! The stars are out
Upon their watches, far on high ;
The moon's slight shell upon the edge
Of the horizon's verge doth lie,
Looking a fair " good night " to me
Who watch her course thus silently !

'Tis holy night! The moon hath gone,
With timid steps, to seek her lord :
The sun her master is ; and she,
Ever, with loving, sweet accord,
Through night and day, doth follow him,
Lest her pale light should grow more dim.

'Tis holy night! God grant that I
A lesson from its page may borrow :
Just like the moon, through night and day,
Through present joy and coming sorrow,
May I, with meek and lowly heart,
Follow *my* Lord with trusting love ;
Keeping an eye, undimmed and clear,
Upon his glory far above ;
Knowing, like her, more and more dim
My light and life, if far from him !

MRS. ADELAIDE E. M. PARKER.

THE BENIGHTED TRAVELLER.

EARILY the day has passed,
Drearily night comes at last,
While, upon the driving blast,
      Driveth on the snow :
Faster now the day declines ;
And the piercing winter-winds
Whistle through the moaning pines
      In the vale below.

Down the mountains whirls the snow ;
And the torrent there below
Rushes on with thundering flow
      To its deeper bed,
Gathering, as it speeds, new force ;
Bearing in its headlong course,
From its distant, hidden source,
      Leaves all brown and dead.

Now the darkness doth efface
From the wild scene every trace,
Till, in seeming endless space,
      Falleth on the ear,

'Mid the torrent's awful roar,
Thunders from the wave-lashed shore ;
And the winds wail evermore,
      Shrieking as in fear.

Now the tempest gains in might ;
Deeper, blacker grows the night ;
Blustering on, from height to height,
      Faster falls the snow :
Feebly struggling 'gainst despair
And the fast benumbing air,
Gropes along a traveller there
      From the pass below.

Fast around him drifts the snow,
Keener still the air doth grow,
Still more fierce the wind doth blow :
      Only Heaven can save.
Life is ebbing fast away,
Death is waiting there his prey,
And at dawn the snow will lay
      Around him for a grave.

Now, far-off amidst the hills,
As rapidly his life-blood chills,
He hears a sudden sound which thrills
      Through his heart and brain ;
Pausing with his ear bent low,
Till his cold cheek meets the snow,
Mingling with the torrent's flow,
      Hark ! the sound again !

Surely 'twas a watch-dog's bark ! —
Suddenly he sees a spark
Faintly glimmer through the dark,
      Up the rocky way.
Hope rekindles at the sight ;
But his strength has failed him quite,
And, along the slippery height,
      Faint and stiff he lay,

Till a something snuffing round,
Pawing on the frozen ground,
Uttering a strange wild sound,
      Rouses him with fear.
But the shaggy creature there,
Trained to brave the mountain air,
Trained to rescue from despair,
      Tells that aid is near.

Soon, with cordials and with light,
From the convent on the height,
Come three brethren through the night,
      Guided by the sound
Uttered by the dog below ;
And they hurry through the snow,
Scarcely heeding where they go,
      So the spot be found.

Then they bear the fainting frame
Up the rugged way they came,
Praying in Christ's holy name
      Life might be retained ;

And that earnest, heart-felt prayer,
Breathed upon the frozen air,
In the depth of midnight there,
   Speedy answer gained.

A P R A Y E R.

FATHER, I have wandered far ;
Oh ! be now my guiding star ;
Draw my footsteps back to thee ;
Set my struggling spirit free !
Save me from the doubts that roll
O'er the chaos of my soul ;
Let one ray of truth illume
And dispel the thickening gloom !
God of truth and peace and love,
   Hear my prayer !
Draw my restless thoughts above ;
   Keep them there !

Father, save me, at this hour,
From the tempter's fearful power ;
Purify the hidden springs
Of my wild imaginings !
I have thought till thought is pain, —
Searched for peace till search is vain ;
Out of *thee* I cannot find
Rest for the immortal mind.
Now I come to thee for aid :
   Peace restore !
Let my soul on thee be stayed
   For evermore !

THE VAGARIES OF A DREAM.

I KNOW not how it was, — I seemed
   In a frail bark, far out at sea,
Where the hot sunbeams fiercely streamed,
   And the whole ocean seemed to be
Stagnant and slimy.   I could see
   No sign of life to which to cling :
In that almost infinity
   I was the only living thing.

Alone, and fixed in mute despair, —
   No hope, no thought, my life to save ;
I floated on, I knew not where, —
   To this no single thought I gave ;
But rapidly I skimmed the wave :
   There was no breath to aid me, none ;
All was quiet as the grave,
   And yet I still kept floating on.

I had no power to judge or mark
   The space I passed, the course I sped ;
For, ever high above that bark,
   The sun was fixed all fiery red.
It fell on my unsheltered head ;
   I felt it burning through my brain
Like a swift stream of molten lead :
   Madly and loud I shrieked with pain.

This was the first sound I had made :
  I had no feeling until now ;
But all earth's waters, all its shade,
  Would not have cooled my burning brow :
And, horrid sight! around the prow,
  As if suspended in the air,
Serpents with human heads did bow,
  Waiting to dart upon me there.

But suddenly a monstrous bird
  Rose from the bosom of the deep :
The flapping of his wings I heard,
  And saw him round and round me sweep,
Till, with a sure and rapid leap,
  He fixed his talons in my hair ;
And, as the serpents nearer creep,
  He bore me darting through the air.

Away he swept, I knew not where ;
  But high he soared, and ever higher :
At length I caught a sudden glare,
  As if a world were all on fire ;
And here and there a glittering spire,
  Shooting unto the zenith's height,
Made other paler ones retire
  Like phantoms vanishing from sight.

And all around one silent scene
  Of sparkling and unsullied snow ;
Ice-mountains stood, as they had been
  Watchers since ages long ago,

O'erlooking all the world below ;
   And, from each pointed glittering height,
Reflecting all the solemn glow
   That luminates the polar night.

No object could a shadow fling,
   All was so bright above, around ;
But 'twas a painful, fearful thing
   To see no life, to hear no sound,
To *feel* a silence so profound,
   And know that thus the scene would be
Waiting, in this same stillness bound,
   The dawning of Eternity.

. Above this frozen, silent scene,
   This brilliant, ever-changing glow,
With not a single cloud beneath
   Me, and the salient fires below,
He loosed his hold, he let me go ;
   The stillness of the scene it broke ;
I heard a rushing sound below,
   I shuddered, started, and — awoke.

THE DIVINE COMFORTER.

Wanderer.

I WALK amidst the darkness that surrounds me,
  Like a pale spectre through the shades of night:
The shadows deepen, and the storm is gathering;
  One only star emits a glim..iering light.

Daylight has vanished; and the night, increasing,
  Has round my pathway every terror thrown, —
Obscured each trusted landmark; and in darkness
  I wander on, uncertain and *alone.*

The way grows rougher, and my limbs are weary;
  My eyes are heavy, and my heart opprest:
Must I, my Father, perish here in darkness?
  Here, midst these terrors, must I sink to rest?

Aid me, my Father! Let thy powerful hand
  Scatter the darkness, and my strength renew!
Give me the courage still to struggle onward,
  Until the dawn shall break upon my view!

The Divine Comforter.

Child, when thou thinkest I am far from thee;
  When faith and hope have ceased to be thy guide;
When thou no shelter and no aid canst see, —
  Then is it I am ever by thy side.

And when thou thinkest almost all is lost,
    That nothing more on earth remains to thee,
Then art thou in the way to merit most;
    Though, in thy blindness, this thou canst not see.

Then trust to me, and let thy fears away;
    Walk in the darkness as in daylight sure :
Did I but will it, it would *now* be day :
    'Tis not my will, — then patiently endure.

SONG.

        I watch in vain !
        When the morning breaks,
The hope of my heart with the day awakes ;
        But it dies away
        At the close of day.
        Oh ! I watch in vain,
    Alone in silence, in tears and pain,
For a gleam of his sail on the waves again !

        I watch in vain !
        On this rocky height
I weep through the long and the silent night,
        When the storms are out,
        And the winds about ;
        But I watch in vain,
    With an aching heart and a burning brain,
For a gleam of his sails on the waves again !

TO A FRIEND.

Like night-blooming flowers, which, in darkness and
   dews,
Expand into beauty, and perfume the air
With odors, that startle the senses, and throw
A charm over earth of which day might despair;
So we, who have bloomed in the night of neglect, —
A night long and dark, — and whose dew has been
   tears,
May shine with a lustre which ever shall gild
The gloom with which fate has surrounded our years.

And as some will remember, when daylight returns,
The fragrance that sweetened their vigils of gloom,
And treasure for ever the flowerets that thus,
In darkness and silence, so humbly could bloom;
So patiently wait; and hereafter, when *we*
Are gathered from earth, like these night-blooming
   flowers,
Our memory to some may a talisman prove
To lighten the gloom of their desolate hours.

AURIN M. PAYSON.

—◆—

SEDES MUSARUM.

F thou wouldşt love to strike the lyre,
And wake the choral song of heaven,
Believe not inspiration's fire
Burns brightest at the dusk of even.

But haste to where the laurels bend
Their graceful boughs at morning dawn,
And Nature's voices sweetly blend
In joyous music o'er the lawn.

In whispering branches o'er thy head,
And laughing brooks beneath thy feet,
Around the graves of hallowed dead,
The sacred Muses hold their seat.

On hill-tops and in grottos green ;
Amid the strife of tempests dire ;
Or where we watch the nightly queen,
Whose silver light sweet thoughts inspire ;

Amid lone silence, deep, profound ;
Up where no creature's foot hath trod,
Or voice was ever heard to sound
On mountain-peak, but that of God !

Within the halls of Memory, too,
Where legends of the past are hung ;
And o'er whose tablets, waiting you,
Are gems of beauty loosely flung ;

In pattering rain-drops on the towers ;
The heaving ocean's low bass-tone ;
Beneath the grass, 'mid tiny flowers ;
The sighing zephyr's gentle moan ;

Along Piscataqua's sunny shore,
Where sweeps the deep resistless tide, —
Their echoes answer, evermore
Down toward eternity we glide !

Out on those dark sequestered strands,
When forms were transformed into ghosts
In years long past, bright laurelled bands
Of Muses strolled along the coasts.

Could some clear panoramic view
Of dusky olden time be given,
And scenes of centuries lost renew,
Beneath this deep blue vault of heaven,

Perhaps those spirit-forms might *now*,
All floating toward the dark-blue sea,
Be seen, with garlands on their brow,
Waking the harp's sweet minstrelsy.

THE SUFFERING POOR.

I saw just before me, on the street, a poor fellow thinly clad, shivering with the cold, and his feet almost destitute of covering, just as the storm was coming on. — January, 1856.

LIST! as the chill winds blow,
And force the drifting snow,
     How sad they moan!
Hear in their mournful wail,
Sweeping along his trail,
     The poor man's groan!

Let's hasten down the street,
And mark well where his feet
     Trace out his home.
To-morrow may too late
Reveal his wretched fate, —
     Death and the tomb!

My friend, whose manly form
Bore down the opposing storm,
     Quick led the way.
There, near the beating tide,
That home we soon descried
     In deep dismay.

We enter first the hall,
(If such we may it call),
     And pause for breath.
Hark! hear that suppliant's tone,
Uprising toward His throne
     Who succors e'en in death!

And hear him pray, " God, save
From hastening to the grave
   My child and wife !
Send some kind hand with aid,
Let this distress be stayed,
   Nor take my life !

Oh spare the suffering poor,
Who, prostrate at thy door
   Of mercy, call !
Oh help in this our need,
And let thy blessing speed,
   And on us fall ! "

God heard that upborne prayer :
It seemed the very *air*
   Had felt the thrill !
We found upon the floor,
Kneeling, the starving poor ! —
   That room how chill !

No light, no wood, no bread,
By which they could be fed
   Or warmed or cheered :
We bade them hope and wait,
Then hasted from the gate,
   For worse we *feared.*

So, fast from friend to friend,
Our hurried steps did bend,
   And found relief :
Good food, a generous store,
With wood and oil, we bore,
   And stayed their grief.

Go, then, whoe'er ye be
That live in luxury,
 Go, bless the poor :
Turn not in proud disdain
From suffering and pain,
 When at your door !

There is a mind that knows
Each mite you give to those
 In want or woe :
A cup of water given
May wake the smile of Heaven :
 Your *bread* bestow !

Then He, by whose command
The wide extended land
 Its fruitage yields,
Will pay in hundred-fold
Your sacrifice of gold,
 Through all your fields.

Nay, more, — beyond the sky,
Each prayer, each burdened sigh,
 Will plead anew ;
And, at Heaven's mercy-gate,
Angelic guards will wait
 To welcome you !

THE CHARACTER OF NAPOLEON.

From the Prose of Phillips.

At last, the victor Death has found the room
Where lay the Hero, waiting for the tomb :
    His " sweet repose " is sung.
Now pause before that prodigy of might,
Which, like some ancient tower's giddy height,
    In ruins o'er us hung !

Exalted on a throne, in gloomy grandeur sat
This sceptred hermit, wielding o'er the State
    His awful magic wand :
A mind decisive, unrestrained, and bold ;
A will despotic, all his acts controlled ;
    Of martial glory fond.

A conscience, too, like steel to interest bent,
Distinct to shade, her finer pencils lent
    The extraordinary man.
A stranger at his birth, flung into life
Amidst a people maddened into strife,
    Dependent he began.

With sword and talents, these his only friend,
'Gainst rank and wealth and genius to defend
    His hopes of future fame ;
His potent arm, all competition fled,
As from the glance of fate, and honor shed
    Around the victor's name.

By interest moved, success inspired his breast;
His god ambition, there he made request
    In that proud idol's fane :
All creeds professed, and favor thus would court;
For thrones and crowns the crescent he'd support,
    Hope's lofty height to gain.

To win divorce, beneath the cross he'd fall;
St. Louis' orphan, ready at his call,
    The State relief would bring :
And yet, with parricidal hand, he rent
The throne and tribune, with the full intent
    To make himself the king.

The Roman faith professed, the Pope he bound;
The country soon in poverty was found,
    Confiding in his care :
In Brutus' name, he, bold without remorse,
The crown of Cæsar grasped ; and, what is worse,
    No shame his heart would share !

To all his whims, proud fortune played the clown ;
Since beggars he set up, and kings threw down,
    And systems came and went :
Now victory crowned his march, sometimes defeat ;
And yet his *ill*-success oft made him great,
    And gave his power extent.

Though fortune great, his genius rose sublime ;
Decisive words he spake ; and, prompt in time,
    The deed, the work, was done !
Those smaller minds, not competent to scan
Such combinations, *his* own well-wrought plan
    Bewildered ere begun !

But, in his might, his hand the action pressed,
And quick success oft proved his wisdom best ;
 His *will* obeyed, 'twas done !
So, like his mind, his constitution lost
No strength against the rain and polar frost,
 Nor 'neath a torrid sun !

'Mid Alpine rocks or on Arabia's plain,
His nature ne'er would yield ; with proud disdain,
 He'd tread opposers down ;
And trembling States, beholding his designs,
Would move their rulers, by some timely signs,
 To offer up their crown !

When *he* performed, past prodigies were dumb ;
Romance was history : what, then, could become
 A check upon his path,
When, o'er her ancient capitals displayed,
The dark imperial flag, the world dismayed,
 Once saw in sullen wrath !

All visions of past ages soon became,
In his proud thought, but commonplace, the same
 His flashing mind composed !
And kings his people were ; and nations, scouts :
Of courts and crowns and kingdoms on his routes,
 With ease he oft disposed !

Amid all changes, undisturbed he stood,
With mobs, levees, or in the field of blood,
 Or in the drawing-room ;
Though bonnet of a Jacobin he chose,
Or iron crown, o'er every hope arose
 That same despotic gloom !

The jailer of the press, yet friendly *then*,
As patron of the arts and learnèd men ;
    But cruel as the grave
To Palm, De Staël, who crossed the despot's way ;
While David's art, and others 'neath his sway,
    High patronage he gave.

Without a model yet, a shadow none,
Complex, consistent self, he stood alone,
    Subaltern, sovereign king !
Such medley, too, of contradictions he,
To God or Reason's shrine, he'd make a plea,
    And there his offerings bring !

O earthly fame ! how fading, yet how fair !
Delusive phantom, bubble of the air,
    Thou cheat'st the soul of bliss !
Man, flushed with pride, devotes time's fleeting hours
In search of fancied good, and wastes his powers
    On such a world as this !

THE PULSE OF FREEDOM.

1861.

WHEN the first torch had lighted the fires on his path,
And the war-god had mustered his hosts in his wrath,
O'er the hills, through the vales, Freedom's quick
    blood was stirred,
As the deep-toned responses from Sumpter were heard !

Then the pulse of true liberty beat quicker far
Than the steam-pulse that forces the swift-moving car ;
And the shout of defiance, on that fearful morn,
Rang with " Strike for the Union," from curled lips of
scorn !

Soon the cry rent the air from the workshop and field,
And from rich homes of ease, " To the foe never yield !
Sooner die 'neath our flag, on the land, on the sea ;
Be our watchword for ever, ' Our country is free ! ' "

Forth there flashed o'er the wires an appeal from the
State
To the brave, to deliver their homes from a fate
Far more dreadful than death, on the proud field of
fame,
In a contest for freedom, in God's sacred name !

As the dark clouds come slowly, foretokening a night
Full of tempests, whose thunders e'en stout hearts
affright ;
So the brave hosts of freemen, more direful than storm,
At the call of their country, in deep columns form !

They had armor, equipments, with spirits elate,
That would grace a king's guard, as they move from
his gate ;
But of drill they had none, for sweet peace through
the land
Had long lulled to repose every disciplined band.

Why were *they* then so fearful in power and in might,
That the nation's check crimsoned with pride at the
sight?

'Twas because they were freemen, resolved to defend,
Each his altar and hearth-stone, or die in the end!

Oh beware! then, ye tyrants, nor trifle with men
Who inherit their freedom, on hill, plain, or glen;
For at last they must conquer, — the world must be
    free,
And humanity's triumphs oppressors shall see!

Then the star-spangled banner shall wave o'er the
    State,
Far aloft, and defiant to oppression and hate,
Till the down-trodden millions shall suffer no wrong,
And proclaim their redemption, though baffled so
    long!

EDWARD A. RAND.

POND-LILIES.

ALL through the day the lilies float,
  Swayed gently by the drowsy streams,
As tired thoughts in sleep obey
  The changing impulse of our dreams.

Through waters dead, who thought such life
  Was creeping up the tangled stems,
To burst in bloom of snow and gold,
  And sprinkle wide those floral gems?

In those dark depths, who thought such light
  In folded bud was thus concealed,
To open into stars, with rays
  As pure as those by night revealed?

Take heart, faint soul! and stay the grief
  In whose sad presence man e'er weeps:
Up through life's dark and shaded depths
  Some bloom of beauty ever creeps.

Some rays of light, in darkness hid,
  Wait God's appointed, better time,
To break in stars whose peaceful beams
  Shall round our darkened pathway shine.

19

RAIN ON THE ROOF.

Is that a step upon the stairs,
    That makes its echo in the night?
Not that: the rain is creeping down the roof;
    I hear its footfall hushed and light.

I do not wonder that I seemed
    To hear soft footsteps on the stairs:
I've fancied so before, and e'en
    Amid the silence of my prayers.

I cannot see, but fancy still
    My sainted child looks in my face,
And think the shadow of a wing
    Makes heavenly twilight in the place.

How oft within her eyes' blue depths
    I looked, as down some shaded aisle
That into Heaven ran afar:
    God only let me look awhile!

The bitter rain has dripped but twice
    Since last I heard her little feet
Drop music all adown the stairs:
    And *now* — they press the golden street.

Such music as the raindrops make,
    Those passing feet made every day:
One eve they stopped, and then I knew
    That they had climbed the heavenly way.

WAITING.

THIS wind that cools my burning brow,
   What soothing peace it brings !
As if this summer-air were stirred
   By countless angel-wings.

It is not strange, this golden light
   That plays about my head :
Are not the angels of the Lord
   Encamped around my bed?

All through these days that tarry long,
   These nights of pain, I wait :
I only wait a little while
   The opening of the gate.

At night, my pillow, hard and rough,
   A peaceful Bethel seems :
I sleep, yet only sleep to watch
   The angels in my dreams.

They flash along this heavenly way,
   As if, to Heaven's door,
A vine had climbed up through the sky,
   And white-winged blossoms bore.

So now I know my home is near,
   That I am near the gate :
I only fold my hands in prayer,
   Then knock, and knocking — *wait !*

PEACE.

PEACE on the calm, blue western sea,
    And in the calm, soft Autumn sky;
And peace within the heart of pain
    That lays its heavy sorrow by.

And yet how slow we are to learn,
    That in the daily, changing life,
The fullest peace must follow pain,
    As calm the storm, and rest our strife!

Our knowledge comes from opposites,
    And gain of tearful loss is born,
And rest is known through weariness:
    The haven's shelter follows storm.

Each day's contentment is not peace:
    Our song will never turn to psalm,
Till feet that press the bars of pain
    Shall feel the Master's soothing balm.

For him who suffering ne'er has known,
    There is a joy not yet begun;
Who, finding Christ within the storm,
    Shall come out in the morning sun.

Oh, peace from Christ, sweet end of pain!
    We welcome all that brings alarm,
If, after troubled waves, we reach
    The soul's eternal, heavenly calm!

THE MIST.

THE mist is coming in from the sea,
  As white as the shelving sand ;
Some huge sea-bird hath spread its wings
  To hide the rock-ribbed land.

The mist is coming in from the sea,
  As cold as the waves below :
So white, so cold ; and can it be
  The white December snow?

O mist ! why lie so white and so cold,
  So still in the Autumn night?
Wouldst deck with bridal veil the moon
  That casts such ghastly light?

Not that, not that, — a *shroud* for the *ship*
  That sinks in the bay below !
Ah, me ! I would that this had been
  The white December snow !

GONE.

I MISS the hand that pointed out
  A heaven of rest from care ;
And yet, if here, my soul would lose
  The hand that leads it there.

I miss the smile whose constant light
  Made bright each clouded place ;
And yet, if here, my dreams by night
  Would want one sainted face.

I miss the form whose shadow fell
  Like sunshine on the floor ;
And yet, if here, one angel less
  Would hover round my door.

JONATHAN M. SEWALL.

BORN IN 1748; DIED IN 1808.

——◆——

THE TRANSFIGURATION.

THEN took he with him Peter, James, and
  John
  (His three disciples), to a mount alone ;
And suddenly, ere they distinctly knew,
He stood transfigured to their wondering view.
His face was radiant as the mid-day sun,
And, whiter than the light, his lucid raiment shone.
Lo ! Moses, and Elias too, revealed
Celestial colloquy with Jesus held.
The wondering three, lost in the effulgence bright,
Stood gazing with ineffable delight,
Till Peter, ever zealous 'bove the rest,
His Lord and Master ardent thus addressed :

" 'Tis good for thy disciples to be here !
Let us three tabernacles instant rear ;
And each a solemn sanctuary be
For Moses and Elias and for THEE ! "

While thus he spake (scarce knowing what he said).
A bright o'ershadowing cloud the mount o'erspread ;
And, from amidst the brightness that appeared,
These solemn accents audibly were heard :

" This is my Son BELOVED! in whom alone
I am well pleased : hear him, and reverent own ! "

A secret terror through each bosom spread ;
And all fell prostrate, wrapt in holy dread !
Till Jesus, with compassion moved, drew near,
And touching, raised them, and dispelled each fear,
Forbidding them the vision to disclose
Till from the dead the Son of man arose.

But we've a *surer word of Prophecy*,
Which we do well to mark with heedful eye,
As a celestial, all-disclosing light,
Refulgent beaming through the shades of night ;
Till, in each heart. this DAY-STAR of the skies
With inextinguishable splendor rise.
For PROPHECY came not of old by *man*
(Whate'er blaspheming infidels maintain) ;
But godly men, for sanctity approved,
Spake as the Holy Ghost impulsive moved.
The irrevocable word no power repeals ;
Unerring Wisdom stamps. Omniscience seals,
And uncontrolled Omnipotence fulfils.

EXTRACT FROM "EPILOGUE TO CATO."

RISE then, my countrymen ! for fight prepare,
Gird on your swords, and fearless rush to war !
For your grieved country nobly dare to die,
And empty all your veins for LIBERTY.
No pent-up *Utica* contracts your powers,
But the whole boundless continent is yours.

Canst thou, by searching, the Omniscient find,
Or to perfection scan the Eternal Mind?
Vain aim!—its height the heaven of heavens trans-
    cends,
Deeper than hell the unfathomed line descends!
'Tis longer than the earth's unmeasured plain,
And broader than the illimitable main.

If He, in wrath, shut up a guilty land,
Or fierce consume them with his red right hand;
Humbled in dust beneath Almighty power,
Trembling they groan, bow prostrate, and adore:
Then, touched with pity, he their prayer receives,
Repents him of the evil, and forgives.

Thus oft doth God: what power can stay his hand?
Who his fixed counsels question or withstand?
He knows, vain man! no thought escapes his eyes;
And canst thou stand, if wrath eternal rise?
Yet dares proud dust presumptuously revolt,
To folly born, like the wild ass's colt.

Oh, then learn wisdom, much-enduring land!
Implore thy God to stay his wasting hand!
He'll not be deaf, if humbly thou prepare
Thine heart, and stretch thy hands in fervent prayer.
If in them wrath or wickedness be found,
If fraud, extortion, violence, abound,
Far, far remove them; let no guilty stain
The tabernacle of thy God profane.
To him with filial confidence repair:
He'll lift thee up, nor suffer thee to fear.

Thy miseries shall be all forgot, or seem
Like gliding waters or an empty dream.
Then shall thy light be as the morning ray,
Thine age more glorious than meridian day ;
Confirmed by hope, thy terrors all shall cease ;
And, 'midst contending worlds, thou shalt have peace.
Thy sons, reposing in Almighty aid,
Shall dwell securely, none to make afraid.
Before thee, Britain shall abashed retire,
And mightiest nations deprecate thine ire ;
Thy favor court, from thy just vengeance flee ;
And, for their great example, copy thee.
Resembling in thy morals, laws, police,
The glorious kingdom of the PRINCE OF PEACE.
Then faith shall triumph, envy rave in vain ;
Oppression tremble, slavery drop her chain :
To law, proud rapine, fraud to justice, yield ;
Fierce discord raging bathe no more the field ;
But perfect love, joy, harmony, and peace
Crown thy millennium with transcendent bliss.

PARAPHRASE ON THE LAST CHAPTER OF ECCLESIASTES.

WHILE life's warm current revels in each vein,
And youth, health, joy, uninterrupted reign,
Attend the dictates of celestial truth,
Remember thy Creator in thy youth,
Before the evil days come hastening on,
When thou shalt say, " My every joy is flown ; "

Ere day's bright orb, and milder queen of night,
With every twinkling star, withhold their light;
When azure skies no more succeed the rain,
But clouds, involving clouds, return again ;
When palsies seize the trembling limbs, and make
The strong men bow ! the palace-keepers quake !
The lessening grinders from their office fail,
While darkness round the windows spreads her veil.
In every street the sullen portals close,
And the cock's clarion interrupts repose ;
Imaginary snares the way beset,
The tumbling ruin, the deep yawning pit ;
While ceaseless terrors every sense alarm ;
Even Music's tuneful daughters cease to charm.
Strewn o'er with blossoms, blooms the almond-tree ;
The grasshopper a burthen seems to be ;
Life's glimmering taper shoots a feeble fire,
Just ready in the socket to expire ;
All sense of joy extinguished, all desire,
Till man to his long-destined home is borne,
And the slow minstrels through the city mourn.
Ere the fine silver cord be snapt in twain,
Or broke the golden bowl that holds the brain ;
The wheel around its cistern cease to turn,
Or at Life's fountain fails the vital urn.
Then shall the dust return to earth again,
The soul to God ascend, with him to reign.

ON A QUACK WHO DIED OF ASTHMA.

HERE lies death's caterer, breathless with the phthisic,
Who lived by what killed all his patients, — PHYSIC.

THE SEASONS.

SPRING.

Soft gales to Winter's chilling blasts succeed;
Perfumed with odors, blooms the enamelled mead;
Re-echoing music fills the vocal grove,
Inspiring every sense with joy and love;
Nature to its great Author homage pays,
Glowing with rapture, gratitude, and praise.

SUMMER.

See, glowing ether sheds one boundless blaze!
Unclouded Phœbus darts intense his rays:
Mercy! not one kind breeze? Ye clouds, arise;
Melt in soft showers, and mitigate the skies.
Enough, I hear the distant thunder's voice:
Rejoice! it pours amain; ye grateful fields, rejoice!

AUTUMN.

Adieu, ye vernal fields: now Autumn reigns,
Unloads her gifts, rewards the peasant's pains.
Then, while your crowded barns scarce hold the grain,
Unasked, like Boaz, let the stranger glean:
More plenteous crops shall crown each fertile vale,
Nor your rich, ponderous harvests ever fail.

WINTER.

Winter, dread Winter, reigns! each joy o'ercasts,
Involved in tempests, armed with piercing blasts!
Nature's locked up! whole rivers as they run,
To flint converted, mock the feeble sun;
Enrobed in fleecy garb, the fields are bright,
Revealing to the eye one boundless, shining white.

ANNIVERSARY SONG.

When our great Sires this land explored,
  A shelter from tyrannic wrong ;
Led on by heaven's Almighty Lord,
  They sung and acted well the song, —
Rise united ! dare be freed !
Our sons shall vindicate the deed.

In vain the region they would gain
  Was distant, dreary, undisclosed ;
In vain the Atlantic roared between,
  And hosts of savages opposed.
They rushed undaunted : Heaven decreed
Their sons should vindicate the deed.

'Twas Freedom led the wanderers forth,
  And manly fortitude to bear :
They toiled, succeeded, — such high worth
  Is always Heaven's peculiar care.
Their great example still inspires,
Nor dare we act beneath our Sires.

'Tis ours undaunted to defend
  The dear-bought, rich inheritance ;
And, spite of every hostile hand,
  We'll fight, bleed, die ! in its defence ;
Pursue our Fathers' path to fame,
And emulate their glorious flame.

As Jove's high plant inglorious stands,
  Till storms and thunders root it fast;
So stood our new, unpractised bands,
  Till Britain waved her stormy blast.
Her soon they vanquished, fierce led on
By Freedom and great WASHINGTON!

Hail, godlike Hero! born to save!
  Ne'er shall thy deathless laurels fade,
But on thy brow eternal wave,
  And consecrate blest Vernon's shade;
Thy spreading glories still increase,
Till earth and time and nature cease.

TO S. S., ESQ.

On his joining the American Army in 1777.

WHEN once the die is cast, vain all regret!
Sense, virtue, duty, teach us to submit.
Go then, my friend! in quest of glory go,
Defend your country, and repel the foe.
With native fortitude and valor blest,
Let your example animate the rest;
Arouse the torpid, and the dull inspire,
Till each bold brother burns with all your fire.
'Tis not for conquest, but defence, you fight:
Think, 'tis your Country's cause, and think it right.
Whate'er began the desolating woe,
A cause apparent, or some secret foe,
The ill so universally is spread,
'Tis now too late to alter or recede;
And arms and blood alone can terminate the deed.

If generous Cathmos, Priam's godlike son,
And glorious Brutus, gained such high renown,
Who waged, perhaps, unvindicable war,
Because their Country's safety was their care ;
Much more will you, who, faithful to your trust,
Defend a cause which half the globe thinks just.
But, O my brother! happier fates attend
My Country's, mine, and virtue's noblest friend !
Heaven crown thee with their glory on the plain !
But, ah, return thee to our arms again !

TO A LADY SINGING.

How oft, Eliza, have I thought,
   Since first I heard those notes of love,
I'd rather listen to thy voice
   Than hear a radiant saint above !

And by those lips that sang so sweet,
   And by that warbling voice divine,
I vow, to hear a seraph's lyre,
   I'd not forego one note of thine.

Then how divinely blest the youth
   Ordained by Heaven to share thy love !
Raptured, he'll listen, gaze, adore ;
   Nor envy seraphims above.

Thus will the fond, enamoured youth
   Sink, overwhelmed in love's abyss ;
And, snatching treasures from those lips,
   Dissolve in ecstasies of bliss.

PSALM XCIII.

Thy boundless sway, Almighty Lord!
    Earth. heaven, all nature, own :
Strength, majesty, omnipotence,
    Are thine, great King, alone.

The strong foundations of the globe
    Were fixed at thy command :
Unshaken still from ages past,
    They shall to ages stand.

But thy firm throne before all time
    Immutable hath stood,
The eternal mansion where resides
    The self-existent God.

The floods, O Lord ! with fury rise
    And roar and foam on high ;
Still urged by storms, they rage, they burst.
    And tempest all the sky.

But thou with ease canst still their noise,
    And make their fury cease ;
One breath of thine their rage subdues,
    And softens all to peace.

Since such thy power, Eternal God !
    What wretch shall dare rebel?
Unspotted holiness alone
    Can with thee ever dwell.

EPIGRAM.

THE famous Peter Porcupine,
   Who loved a joke full well,
In merry humor advertised
   "*Porcupine's quills* to sell."

One, who the advertisement read,
   Sent quick, and bought a score :
On viewing them, his choler rose ;
   He raved, he stamped, he swore !

Away to Cobbet's shop he hies,
   And cursed him for a rogue, —
" These are not what you advertised,
   You lying, cheating dog !"

I lie not, cheat not, Peter cried
   With grave and solemn tone :
When *mine*, these quills *were* Porcupine's ;
   They're GOOSE-QUILLS *now*, I own !

EPITAPH ON A PETTIFOGGER.

To elude the bailiff, Quibble vainly tries :
Death served the Writ, and here tongue-tied he LIES.
When summoned to the bar with trumpet shrill,
What will the lying varlet do ? — LIE still.

B. P. SHILLABER.

THE THREE LOCKS.

I LAY them gently on my open palm, —´
Three locks of hair, — the golden, dark, and white:
My spirit wakes from apathetic calm,
As the known tokens greet my eager sight.

And Memory beckons from the distant past
A train of spectral fancies to my ken, —
Age, Youth, and Childhood, — oh, how sweet and fast
Come love and joy to my cold heart again!

FATHER! I see thee now, as when thy prime
Gave vigorous promise of thy lengthened years, —
That a broad lapse would intervene in time,
Dividing present joy from future tears.

And the assurance given *was* fulfilled;
A garner full of years was life to thee;
And, when that kindly heart in death was stilled,
We kissed the rod, and bowed to Heaven's decree.

Calmly to death, to sleep serene, thou passed;
    World-worn and weary, thou wert ready now!
Strange that my tears should flow so free and fast
    As when this lock I took from off thy brow!

Brother! the raven's sable plume ne'er shone
    With glossier lustre in the eye of day,
Than this last trophy, which affection won
    From the loved form that cold before me lay.

O Death! how bitter was the pang when riven
    Became the tender bond which bound him here!
O Death! a sadder blow thou ne'er hast given
    Than that which brought him to his early bier.

In the young spring-time of his days, he passed
    From youth's allurements and from scenes of earth;
As the bright morning may be overcast,
    Ere many hours shall smile upon its birth. ·

My Child! my dimming eyes behold thee still,
    As when thy little hand in mine was pressed;
As when my pulse with rapture wild would thrill
    To feel thy young heart throb against my breast;

As when that golden curl would sweetly blend
    With the bright glory of thy radiant eye,
And such a beauty to thy face did lend
    As stilled the thought that thou couldst ever die;

As when thy prattling tongue would greet mine ear
    With the glad accent of a dawning love;
As when thy promise made my pathway here
    A blessèd forecast of the bliss above.

I weave a braid, — the gold, the dark, the white ;
 They mingle well, these types of human life !
The calm of Age, Youth's hope, the Child's delight, —
 The simple cord with eloquence is rife.

Brief is the time dividing old and young, —
 A step between the cradle and the grave :
Death's shadow o'er the manly oak is flung,
 Ere yet its youthful glories cease to wave.

THE SPRING ON THE SHORE.*

Upgushing through the pebbly strand,
 Here flows a fairy crystal stream ;
Its waters, sparkling o'er the sand,
 Like threads of liquid silver seem.

The music of its note is sweet,
 As singingly it speeds along,
The river's stormy lord to meet,
 And soothe his harshness with a song.

The cattle from the grassy lea
 Come gratefully its wealth to drink ;
And birds of land and birds of sea
 Meet peacefully beside its brink.

----

* Upon the shore of the Piscataqua, in Newington, N.H., is
a spring of pure water, over which the salt river flows at every
high tide.

The sunbeam on the rippling tide
  Smiles gayly down from heavenly height,
To see its glories magnified
  In myriad beams of golden light.

And men, with foreheads red and warm,
  Bow down before the crystal shrine ;
And girlhood bends her graceful form,
  And shadowy lips with real join.

But see the rapid river rise !
  Fast, fast it gains upon the shore, —
A moment ; and the spot we prize
  The angry billow closes o'er.

But gushing still, though hid from view,
  The little rill yet pours its tide,
As constantly, as pure and true,
  As when by sunlight glorified !

And when the rolling river wanes,
  And cravenly deserts the shore,
The rivulet new strength obtains,
  And sings and sparkles as before.

And this the lesson it may teach, —
  That thus Truth's crystal streamlets rise,
And trickle on o'er Time's dark beach,
  To bless the heart and glad the eyes ;

And that, though Error's tide o'erflow
  The gentle stream, and hide its power,
Its silvery wave again will glow,
  And Truth's fair spirit rule the hour.

BENEVOLENCE.

A BENEVOLENT man was Absalom Bess:
At each and every tale of distress,
 He blazed right up like a rocket;
He felt for all who 'neath poverty's smart
Were doomed to bear life's roughest part:
He felt for them in his inmost heart,
 But never felt — in his pocket.

He didn't know rightly what was meant
By the Bible's promised four hundred per cent
 For charity's donation;
But he acted as if he thought railroad stocks,
And bonds secure beneath *earthly* locks,
Were better, with pockets brim full of rocks,
 Than *heavenly* speculation.

Yet all said he was an excellent man;
For the poor he'd preach, for the poor he'd plan, —
 To better them he was willing:
But the oldest one who had heard him pray
And preach for the poor in a pitiful way
Couldn't remember, exactly, to say
 He had ever given a shilling.

Oh! an excellent man was Absalom Bess;
And the world threw up its hands to bless,
 Whenever his name was mentioned:
But he died one day, he did; and oh!
He went right down to the shades below,
Where all are bound, I fear, to go,
 Who are *only* good-intentioned.

THE LITTLE RIVULET.*

I KNOW a gentle rill
That springs beside a hill,
    In the shade
Of the birch's emerald screen,
And the alder's cheerful green,
And the sweet-fern in between,
Where the sun's bright glow, I ween,
    Ne'er hath strayed.

Down through the meadow wide,
Down by the deep wood-side,
Cheerfully its crystal tide
    Moves along;
And the cattle on its brink,
As they bow their heads to drink,
Seem to linger there, and think
    On its song.

That song, — how sweet its notes,
As on the air it floats!
    And the birds
On the willow spray that's near
Oft turn a raptured ear,
And stoop the bliss to hear
    Of its words.

---

* Chase's Pasture, Portsmouth.

The trees their branches wave,
As their roots the waters lave;
   And the grass
Receives a brighter hue,
And the flowers of gold and blue
Their brilliancy renew
   As they pass.

And on its placid breast
The lilies fondly rest,
As if supremely blest
   With content;
And the sedges by its side
Look down upon its tide,
With love and trust and pride
   Sweetly blent.

And the living eddies swirl,
And their graceful ripples curl
Like the tresses of a girl;
   And the sky
Sends troops of gorgeous clouds
To gaze on it in crowds,
   From on high.

Like the joyous tide of youth,
Like its virtue, like its truth,
Like its guilelessness and ruth,
   Sweetly gay,
Blessing all it glides among,
Cooling fevered brow and tongue,
Ever marked with smile and song,
   On its way.

And the gentle flow of song
Like its waters moves along,
Busy paths of men among ;
    And its word, —
Though the tempest din of life
Drown it, mayhap, in its strife,
Still its voice, with heaven rife,
    Shall be heard.

SPIRIT LONGING.

For ever wakefully the ear is turning
    To catch some token from the shadowy sphere ;
For ever is the full heart strongly yearning
    Some word of promise from its depths to hear.

When the dark shadows flit along the ceiling,
    As the dull firelight trembles in the grate,
Fancy, fond yet with old remembered feeling,
    Striveth the loved and lost to re-create.

It feels their presence in the hush of even,
    When day's excitement settles to repose ;
It sees them in the twilight hues of heaven,
    And in the beauties that the stars disclose.

It heeds the breezes that around are playing,
    And in their music fain that voice would hear,
Whose melody, it deems, may yet be straying
    To glad the faithful hearts yet sorrowing here.

When midnight, resting like a pall above us,
    Within its dusky arms infoldeth all,
We list for those whom hope says still may love us,
    And sigh as their unanswering names we call.

We dream, and ever-faithful Memory bringeth
    Old happiness we may not know awake ;
The rose of pleasure in our pathway springeth,
    And rills of joy where we our thirst may slake.

But, oh ! returning consciousness dispelleth
    The sweet illusion in whose thrall was bliss ;
And strife renewed in life's encounter quelleth
    Regrets, as we our dreams of joy dismiss !

And are there kindred spirits dwelling by us,
    And mingling yet their loving thoughts with ours,
For ever drawing in communion nigh us,
    In virtue's way to cheer our lagging powers?

Oh ! are there voices that may, at our asking,
    Come to assure us of that better state,
Where, evermore in endless pleasures basking,
    Those gone before, our fond re-union wait?

The seeking soul asks for prophetic vision
    To penetrate the dark, mysterious cloud
That intervenes between the land elysian
    And this dull earth, where sins and sorrows crowd.

The grave is not a bourn whose sombre portal
    Closeth eternal o'er the bright and fair ;
But through its gate to blessedness immortal
    The spirit passeth, endless life to share.

Still old affection hereward back is turning,
 And whispering words to us of joy and peace ;
And spiritual eyes are round us burning
 With holier love as heavenly powers increase.

A PICTURE.

1857.

THERE's a little low hut by the river's * side,
Within the sound of its rippling tide :
Its walls are gray with the mosses of years,
And its roof all crumbly and old appears ;
But fairer to me than a castle's pride
Is the little low hut by the river's side.

The little low hut was my natal nest,
Where my childhood passed, — life's spring-time blest,
Where the hopes of ardent youth were formed,
And the sun of promise my young heart warmed,
Ere I threw myself on life's swift tide,
And left the dear hut by the river's side.

That little old hut, in lowly guise,
Was lofty and grand to my youthful eyes ;
And fairer trees were ne'er known before
Than the apple-trees by the humble door,
That my father loved for their thrifty pride,
Which shadowed the hut by the river's side.

---

* The North Mill Pond, Portsmouth.

That little low hut had a glad hearthstone,
That echoed of old with a pleasant tone;
And brothers and sisters, a merry crew,
Filled the hours with pleasure as on they flew:
But one by one have the loved ones died
That dwelt in the hut by the river's side.

The father revered, and the children gay,
The grave and the world have called away;
But quietly all alone there sits
By the pleasant window, in summer, and knits,
An aged woman, long years allied
With the little low hut by the river's side.

That little old hut to the lonely wife
Is the cherished stage of her active life:
Each scene is recalled in memory's beam,
As she sits by the window in pensive dream;
And joys and woes roll back like a tide,
In that little old hut by the river's side.

My mother! — alone by the river's side
She waits for the flood of the heavenly tide,
And the voice that shall thrill her heart with its call,
To meet once more with the dear ones all,
And form, in a region beatified,
The band that once met by the river's side.

That dear old hut by the river's side
With the warmest pulse of my heart is allied;
And a glory is over its dark walls thrown
That statelier fabrics have never known;
And I still shall love, with a fonder pride,
That little old hut by the river's side.

AN ANALOGY:

A Fancied Resemblance between a Little Stream of Water
and a Little Life.

A GENTLE rill gushed from the breast of Spring,
   And flowed in beauty through the summer-land;
Stealing along, just like some bashful thing,
   Half-hidden by the boughs that o'er it spanned.

But the wild blossoms in its mirrored sheen
   Beheld themselves in all their rustic pride;
And the tall trees assumed a brighter green,
   Because they stood the little rill beside.

So humble was it, that the dallying grass
   Asked not the question whence the wanderer came;
And the proud lilies, as they felt it pass,
   Looked down upon the stream of modest name.

Yet tenderly the sweet rill loved the flowers,
   And the great trees that grew upon its brink:
It saved for them the bounty of the showers,
   And filled their empty cups with needed drink.

It asked for no return: unselfishly
   It moved, content that it was doing good;
Delighted, from its ministry, to see
   The gladness of a green beatitude.

Anon, a change came o'er the little stream, —
The loving sun had claimed it for his own;
And, like some fleeting picture in a dream,
In all its quiet beauty it had flown.

The flowers grew sickly that had erewhile dwelt
Upon its banks in queenliness of state;
The sturdy trees its unlooked absence felt;
The lilies withered, — beautiful of late;

The grasses sighed in sallow discontent;
And all confessed the rill a friend most true;
Contrite that its sweet life should thus be spent
Before its loving offices they knew.

'Tis thus we've seen some gentle, loving one
Noiselessly moving through the paths of life;
Here cheering sadness with her voice's tone,
There giving tears as mollients to strife;

Singing with bird-like sweetness on her way,
From the outgushing of her teeming heart,
As the airs blow, or the bright waters play,
Unknowing the blest influence they impart.

We value not the blessing by our side,
Until, down-stricken by some fatal blight,
We feel it with our joy identified,
And mourn the star now hidden from our sight.

The noisy consequence of life may claim
The tribute of attention at our hand;
But 'tis the little acts of humble name
That make our hearts with blessedness expand.

FRENCHMAN'S LANE.*

'Twas a brave old spot, and deep was the shade
By the fast-locked boughs of the elm-trees made,
Where the sun scarce looked with his fiery eye,
As he coursed through the burning summer sky,
Where breezes e'er fanned the heat-flushed cheek, —
Old Frenchman's Lane, up by Islington Creek.

Most lovely the spot, yet dark was the tale
That made the red lips of boyhood pale,
Of the Frenchman's doom, and the bitter strife,
Of the blood-stained sward, and the gleaming knife,
Of the gory rock set the wrong to speak,
In Frenchman's Lane, up by Islington Creek.

But the grass sprung green where the Frenchman fell,
And the elder-blossoms were sweet as well,
And the pears grew ripe on the branches high,
And the bright birds sang in the elm-trees nigh,
And the squirrels played at their hide-and-seek,
In Frenchman's Lane, up by Islington Creek.

The blessèd shade on the greensward lay,
And quiet and peace reigned there all day;
The fledglings were safe in the tall elm-tops,
More safe than the pear-trees' luscious crops:
For the pears were sweet, and virtue weak,
In Frenchman's Lane, up by Islington Creek.

---

* Frenchman's Lane was the scene of a fearful murder,
where a sailor belonging to the French fleet that lay at Portsmouth, N.H., nearly a century ago, was found with his throat
cut. Hence its name, and the mystery connected with it.

But at times when the night hung heavily there,
And a spirit of mystery filled the air,
When the whispering leaves faint murmur made,
Like children at night when sore afraid,
Came fancied sounds like a distant shriek,
In Frenchman's Lane, up by Islington Creek.

And gleaming white at times was seen
A figure, the gloomy trees between ;
And fancy gave it the Frenchman's shape,
All ghastly and drear, with wounds agape !
But fancy played us many a freak
In Frenchman's Lane, up by Islington Creek :

For lovers' vows those dark shades heard,
Their sighs the slumbering night-air stirred ;
And the gleaming muslin's hue, I ween,
Was the ghostly glimpse, the limbs between !
There was arm in arm, and cheek by cheek,
In Frenchman's Lane, up by Islington Creek.

Ah, blissful days ! how fleet ye flew,
Ere from life exhaled its morning dew !
When children's voices sweet echoes woke,
That often the brooding stillness broke,
As the meadow strawberry's bed they'd seek,
Through Frenchman's Lane, up by Islington Creek.

Those days have long been distant days,
Recalled in memory's flickering rays ;
And the boys are men, with hearts grown cold
In the world whose sun is a sun of gold,
And their voice no more in music will speak
In Frenchman's Lane, up by Islington Creek.

And Frenchman's Lane has passed away :
No more on its sward do the shadows play ;
The pear-trees old from the scene have passed,
And the blood-marked stone aside is cast ;
And the engine's whistle is heard to shriek
In Frenchman's Lane, up by Islington Creek.

But, true to ourselves, we shall ever retain
A love for the green old Frenchman's Lane,
And its romance, its terror, its birds and bloom,
Its pears and the elderblow's perfume ;
And a tear at times may moisten the cheek
For Frenchman's Lane, up by Islington Creek.

BALLAD ABOUT BUNKER.

'Twas dreadful hot on Bunker's height, —
    The patriots in their trenches lay, —
While, bellowing with a bitter spite,
    The British cannon blazed away !

When Parson Martin wiped his brow,
    And, turning round to Prescott, spoke, —
" I guess I'll go, if you'll allow,
    A while among the Charlestown folk.

I feel there's danger to the town ;
    I see the clouds there gathering thick ;
And, ere the storm comes rattling down,
    I think I'll tell them cut their stick."

21

And then he took a glass, — good man ! —
    And through the village made his way ;
A glass, I mean, with which to scan
    The hostile vessels in the Bay.

He saw the British barges fill
    With armèd soldiers, fierce and strong,
And told the folk it boded ill,
    And that they'd better push along.

But no ! not they : a doggèd trait
    Impelled them to incur the pinch ;
And so they thought they'd better wait,
    And vowed they wouldn't budge an inch.

Again good Parson Martin went
    Down to the village all alone :
From digging hard his strength was spent,
    From watching he was weary grown.

" Now rest ye," Goodman Cary said ;
    " Your tottering limbs pray here bestow ; "
And pointed to a bounteous bed,
    A solace meet for weary woe.

And on the bed the parson fell ;
    But scarcely had his eyelids closed,
When, crashing through the roof, a shell
    Disturbed the dream in which he dozed.

" I think," quoth he, upstarting straight,
    " 'Twill be here somewhat warm to-day ;
And that, if you should hap to wait,
    You'll find the Ancient Nick to pay ! "

And then from out the fated bound
  The people sadly made their tracks ;
But Parson Martin — he was found
  Where fell the most determined whacks.

His heart to Heaven went up in prayer,
  That it would aid each mother's son ;
And Heaven made vocal answer there
  In every deadly patriot gun !

————

A COURTING REMINISCENCE.

My brow is seamed o'er with the iron of years,
  And the snow-threads are gleaming the dark locks
    among ;
My eyes have grown dim in the shadow of tears,
  And the flowers of my soul have died as they sprung ;
But Memory bears to me, on its broad wings,
  Bright images true of my earliest life ;
And there, 'mid the fairest of all that she brings,
  Is the little low room where I courted my wife.

That low humble room seemed a palace of light,
  As Love held his torch and illumined the scene,
With glory of state and profusion bedight,
  Where I was a monarch, my darling a queen :
Ourselves were our subjects, pledged loyal to each ;
  And which should love best was our heartiest strife :
What tales could it tell, if possessing a speech, —
  That little low room where I courted my wife !

Warm vows has it heard, — the warmest e'er spoke, —
　Where lips have met lips in holy embrace ;
Where feelings, that never to utterance woke,
　It saw oft revealed in a duplicate face !
The sweet hours hastened, — how quickly they flew ! —
　With fervor, devotion, and ecstasy rife :
Our hearts throbbed the hours, but how I ne'er knew,
　In the little low room where I courted my wife.

The romance of youth lent its rapturous zest,
　And fairy-land knew no delight like our own :
Our words were but few, yet they were the best, —
　A dialect sweet for ourselves all alone ;
So anxious to hear what the other might say,
　We scarcely could utter a word, for our life :
Thus the hours unheeded passed fleetly away
　In the little low room where I courted my wife.

Long years have since passed o'er my darling and me,
　And the roses have faded away from her cheek ;
But the merciless seasons, as onward they flee,
　Leave love still undimmed in her bosom so meek :
That love is the light to my faltering feet,
　My comfort in moments with sorrowing rife,
My blessing in joy, as with joy 'twas replete
　In the little low room where I courted my wife.

THE DISMISSAL:

Showing the Feeling of a Patriotic young Lady, on the Occasion of her Lover's Recreancy.

THE time has come that we must part:
 I own no more the tender tie
That lately bound us heart to heart,
 And say to all my hopes — good-by.

I loved a MAN. My love is dead ;
 For, when his country claimed his sword,
He from the trial meanly fled,
 And died in living shame abhorred.

He died to *me :* I'll own no more
 The sway that once my heart inthralled :
The time that's passed I may deplore,
 But do not wish the past recalled.

Take back your gifts. The golden chain
 You hung about my neck of old
Would now a burden be of pain, —
 Your cowardice pollutes the gold.

I from my fingers tear the ring
 I long have worn in loving pride :
'Twould be from hence a hated thing,
 Since all that gave it value died.

I read your words with burning brow,
  So full of tender love for me;
But I absolve from every vow,
  And set you from your bondage free.

I would have borne with you the toil,
  The burden, of obscure estate:
I'd not complain to be the foil
  Of adverse and invidious fate.

With honor left to shed its light,
  We, self-sustaining, hand in hand,
Might well have dared misfortune's spite, —
  The poorest, proudest in the land.

But now I shudder as I think,
  Like one awakened from a dream,
Of slumbering on the awful brink
  Of that black-moving hideous stream,

Whose course leads on its darkling way
  Through ignominiousness and shame,
Lit only by one lurid ray,
  To show my coward-coupled name.

Escaped, thank God! — I rend the chain,
  And stand up disinthralled and free:
The riven steel, the human pain,
  I give, my country's cause, to thee.

'Tis duty's throb that stills complaint, —
  No human love must intervene;
And better far than recreant taint
  Were early grave and memory green.

GRAPE-SKINS.

I SAW a man of portly estate
Walking the street with regal gait;
Just the man that the eye well suits,
Proper and nice, from hat to boots.
So perfect his coat, so neat his vest,
An exquisite taste was manifest;
And every one who chose to scan
Could only say, what a tasteful man!

Alas, for the glory of human pride,
As frail and fickle as the tide!
For the polish of blacking and brush and oil
One little spatter of mud may spoil.
E'en as he walked the pave along,
With head exalted and footstep strong,
He trod on a grape-skin in his way;
And a man disgraced in the dirt he lay!

This moral I drew from what I saw:
There are men in the world without a flaw,
Who are in such robes of sanctity found,
And such rare virtues engirt them round,
That we humble ourselves as we pass them by
With reverent and admiring eye,
Saying, while viewing such merits rare;
Bless us, what very good men they are!

But, alas, for the glory of human pride,
As frail and fickle as the tide !
In the world of men they exalt their horn,
As though of a better clay they were born ;
But there in their path, the grape-skins wait, —
Temptations hidden perhaps till late, —
One step of the foot, one curvetting lurch, —
And down they come from their eminent perch !

In dress or morals, 'tis much the same ;
And happy is he, who wins his fame,
If he die at its zenith, nor has to wait
Till he slip, and fall through invidious fate.
He may dodge the rock, and shy the cloud
That threat his step and bearing proud,
But let him not crow till danger's past, —
He may by a grape-skin be overcast.

POOR BOY!

" Poor boy !" the mother fondly sighed,
    When she had bid the lad farewell ;
But in her eye was a lofty pride
    That spoke more than her tongue would tell.

And, though her nature said " Poor boy,"
    He in her breast held grander place,
And thrilled it with a nobler joy,
    Than were he heir of wealth and grace.

His was the heart to do and dare
    In manly battle with the wrong:
She might not in his conflict share;
    But she could yield him, and be strong.

"Poor boy!" Oh, epithet misplaced!
    Not poor by laws that reckon worth:
The noblest record fame has traced
    Has had no more exalted birth.

The soul that thus in Duty's path
    Bounds forward at its first appeal
More grandeur in the humblest hath
    Than titled state that cannot feel.

Mother, though heavy with your fears,
    Throw all your burdening doubts away;
Discard the ministry of tears, —
    Your boy is crowned a king to-day!

Not poor! could you but see the goal
    For those the race have nobly run,
'Twould glad your yearning mother-soul,
    To mark the glory he has won.

Not eighty years of golden sands,
    Nor life, though spotless of a shame,
So high an eminence commands
    As the young hero's laurelled name.

Thank God, O mother, who hath given
    This treasure of immortal price,
That you might render back to Heaven
    Your wealth of love as sacrifice!

MASTER WEEKS'S OLD FERULE.

GRIM relic of a distant time,
More interesting than sublime!
Thou'rt fitting subject for my rhyme,
    And touch'st me queerly, —
Unlike the touch that youthful crime
    Provoked severely.

It was a dark and fearful day
When thou held'st sovereign rule and sway,
And all Humanity might say
    Could not avert
The doom that brought thee into play,
    And wrought us hurt!

Ah, Solomon! that dogma wild
Of sparing rod and spoiling child
Has long thy reputation soiled,
    And few defend it:
Our teachers draw it far more mild,
    And strive to mend it.

Oh! bitter were the blows and whacks
That fell on our delinquent backs,
When, varying from moral tracks,
    In youthful error,
Thou madest our stubborn nerves relax
    With direst terror.

I know 'twas urged that our own good
Dwelt in the tingle of the wood
That scored us as we trembling stood,
    And couldn't flee it;
But I confess I never could
    Exactly see it.

The smothered wrath at every stroke
Was keenly felt, though never spoke;
And twenty devils rampant broke
    For one subdued,
And all discordances awoke, —
    A fiendish brood.

And impish trick and vengeful spite
Essayed with all their skill and might
To make the balance poise aright;
    And hate, sharp-witted,
Ne'er left occasion, day or night,
    To pass omitted.

I see it now! — the whittled doors,
The window-panes smashed in by scores,
The desecrated classic floors,
    The benches levelled,
The streaming ink from murky pores,
    The books bedevilled.

Small reverence for Learning's fane,
For master's toil of nerve and brain:
They saw Instruction marred with pain,
    And Alma Mater
Was thought of only by the train
    To deprecate her.

'Tis strange to have thee in my grasp,
My fingers round thy handle clasp,
No sense of pain my feelings rasp,
    As last I knew thee !
Then thou didst sting me like an asp,
    Foul shame unto thee !

But gentler moods suggest the thought,
That still thine office, anguish-fraught,
For our best good unselfish wrought,
    Had we but known it ;
And we, with grateful spirit, ought
    To freely own it.

Perhaps, — but I am glad at heart
That thou no more bear'st sovereign part
In helping on Instruction's art
    By terror's rule ;
That other modes will prompt the smart
    Than thee in school.

Thanks ! old reminder of the past,
For this brief vision backward cast :
We measure progress to contrast
    Times far and near,
Rejoiced, on summing up at last,
    We're not arrear !

TRANSMUTATION:

Showing the Operation of a quick Fancy in working out spiritual Results from a real Subject.

I SEE him every week,
With his thin and wrinkled cheek,
And a wealth of wintry hair falling round his aged
neck ;
And his coat of homespun blue,
That's brushed the texture through,
Bears many awheres about it a white and seedy
speck.

He's in the strangers' seat ;
For no bending hinges greet
The old man hoary, when he comes with slow and
lagging pace ;
And the velvet-cushioned pews
All sympathy refuse
With the waiter at the table for the crumbs of God's
free grace.

There he sits, with eager ear,
To catch the heavenly cheer,
As the minister unfolds the glories of the Word ;
And a smile his face illumes,
As the apple gives its blooms,
When, in its secret depths, the call of Spring is
heard.

At times a tear I'll trace
Steal down his care-worn face,
As though some memory of eld were passing through
his brain ;
Then the smile will come once more,
As, when the storm is o'er,
The sun appears more bright through the lenses of
the rain.

His name I cannot guess ;
But interest no less
Attracts my eager gaze to the old white-headed man ;
For in his face I see
A mighty mystery
That awes me, as with earnest eye its depths I strive
to scan.

Not with the pride of wealth,
Not with the thrill of health,
The human soul is strong in its world of joy and trust ;
And, though drop away
The props of mortal clay,
There's a glory born within not dimmed by earthly
dust.

I see upon his brow
A regal glory now ;
And the poverty and pain are transmuted in its ray :
No longer poor and old
Is the form that I behold,
But a soul rejuvenate, and risen on a life of endless
day.

BLESS YOU!

THERE is a prayer of simple art,
  That from the tongue the readiest slips;
That springs spontaneous from the heart,
  And breaks in blessing on the lips:
    Bless you!

When joy's bright beam about us rests
  As some dear hand our cup o'erfills,
In this our gladness manifests,
  And with love's fondest cadence thrills:
    Bless you!

The sympathy with other's woe,
  That melts the heart to loving tears,
No sweeter form of speech may know
  Than this the sorrowing spirit hears:
    Bless you!

When weary limb and aching brain
  Attest the weight of busy care,
How lifts the dulling cloud of pain
  To catch the accent of that prayer:
    Bless you!

In love's pure sacrament of bliss,
  When lip meets lip in fond embrace,
Rises with blest approval this,
  To give the chrism a holier grace:
    Bless you!

As failing pulse and dimming eye
　Proclaim some loved one's exit near,
How like a whisper from on high
　Comes the faint murmur to our ear!
　　Bless you!

But yet no language it may need:
　A glance, as well as words, may pray;
All speech kind action may exceed,
　A smile a deeper sense convey:
　　Bless you!

Oh, may our hearts be tuned aright,
　Unselfishly this prayer to feel!
And fill our measure of delight
　By supplicating others' weal:
　　Bless you!

LOUISA SIMES.

TO A CHILD.

To a Child of Impulse, who in a Moment of beautiful Enthu-
siasm uttered, "Jesus of Nazareth passeth by."

E passeth by, — when thy full heart is lifted
    Urgently upward on thought's radiant
      wing,
His breath is that elastic bound within thee,
  Momently breaking from each earthward thing!

When o'er thee steals a cataract of feeling,
  Leaping the mountain of the world's restraint,
His the felt shadow 'neath which form is kneeling, —
  Of all aspiring soul, the Guardian Saint!

He passeth by, — when mesh by mesh of pleasure
  Weareth its subtle veil o'er inner light,
With love more gentle though it rend the treasure,
  Than Time's slow rust of never-breaking night.

When, like the tide, the "lesser light" is swaying,
  The fulness of thy spirit laveth earth,
Let not the shimmer, o'er the surface playing,
  Hide the dark rocks retreating waves bring forth.

22

He treads *life's* waves *most visibly* to *mortal,*
　　When o'er them sweep the tempest and the gloom ;
Yet ever waiteth at the glad heart's portal,
　　Hallowing e'en joys which have but pilgrim's home !

He passeth by, on every varied pathway,
　　With the sweet lessons of far-reaching love :
Jesus of Nazareth ! sink thy teachings inly.
　　So from earth-guile the soul shall wide remove !

Bear up in hours of joy, or days of sorrow,
　　Heart, greatened by thy panoply of truth :
Link with each act of now the might of morrow :
　　Breathe o'er each right intent, perpetual youth.

So, on the page of life, eternal glowing,
　　New purpose with new holiness shall write —
God's spirit still the *dear Immortal* showing
　　Where Jesus passeth not, — home, home to light !

TO A THOUGHTFUL BRIDE.

'Tis well, — that look of pensiveness
　　Upon thy brow, young bride !
The stream of Life is not all peace :
　　It hath its varying tide.

And never was a time for thee
　　To watch with closer care
That gentleness and purity
　　Which glorify the fair.

It is no light thing thou hast done
   To take the name of wife,
To make or mar the joy of one
   Dearer to thee than life!

A lover's eye may beam delight
   On beauty of the dust:
A husband asks the abiding bloom
   Of a mind in graces dressed.

His heart, thy chosen earthly rest,
   Thou mayst not ever wield;
For thousand things may be impressed
   On man, where *none* are sealed!

He will not live upon the past
   As thou in memory;
He needs the love that blesses now,
   To light his future way.

The hasty word or look unkind
   Thy frown could once repel;
Thy lip must learn to smile away,
   Though pain thy bosom swell!

What's dignified as maiden's pride
   Is madness in a wife;
The act which bends a lover's knee
   May poison wedded life!

Whatever were the charms which won,
   Oh! bid them brightly glow:
E'en though they all unheeded be,
   Thou must be winner now!

If gathering frowns or cold reproof
   Should e'er be offered thee,
Oh, bear it with an humble heart!
   This is love's victory.

With hand as gentle as the light,
   Dispel the shades of care;
And, should it be thy pain to chide,
   Be tenfold gentler there!

Sorrows must come, and many a care
   And disappointment: when
Did maiden ever wed her heart,
   Nor find its dreams in vain?

Man wins by arts he seldom feels,
   And woman trusts them all;
He points her high imaginings,
   And then permits their fall.

Yet be thou patient, meek, and kind;
   And He who formed the tie
Shall bless the effort to thy soul,
   Though man its power defy!

— A tear! amid the bridal gems
   Tears are not wont to flow:
At such an hour, Hope's fairy gleams
   Bid earth too brightly glow.

Yet weep! As falls the dew, at even,
   Back whence it gently rose,
Giving new glory to the flower;
   My fervent prayer so throws

Those drops upon thy heart again,
To make the pearls of life ;
For thou dost feel it is not light
To take the name of wife !

TO AN EARLY ROSE.

BEAUTIFUL mingling of water and dust,
Oh ! where were thy glories hid,
When the branch which now bears thee in fondness
up
By the wintry blast was laid?   .

Wert thou there in the fold of that withered thing,
Or down in the frozen earth ?
Or did part of thee lie in a wreath of snow,
Which could boast of a cloudlet's birth?

Wherever thou wert, O beautiful Rose !
A lesson of truth thou dost bring,
For much that seems dross to the human eye,
May up into glory spring :

But thou hast been nought save a simple bud,
Through cloudy and sunny days ;
Now thy tunic of green on thy stem is cast,
And thou art all fragrance and grace.

So I, if unscared by the world's bright sun,
And calm by its tempests driven,
May throw off my vestment of changing dust,
And bloom like thee, rose, — in heaven.

.

To J. K. C.

"We have lost two sons in battle: were another called, I would bid him go, that our country may have power for an honorable peace." — *Words of a Mother.*

WHEN the strong staff is broken,
   And the beautiful rod of trust
Is laid, like a withered token,
   Back, back, to the pitiless dust;

When hands, after long sustaining,
   Outreach for returning aid,
And only the void remaining
   In their trembling grasp is laid;

When hearts that have warmed in the sunshine
   Of hope, on a loved one's brow,
Grow suddenly chill in the folding
   Of the mantle enwrapping it now, —

What word that may reach benediction,
   ʼWhat whisper uprising to prayer,
What balm for the cup of affliction,
   Can the breath of our sympathy bear?

O father! so brave in thy sorrow,
   O mother! so calm in your grief,
From the house of such mourning we borrow
   The might of your lofty belief.

We shrink with our poor consolation,
  We rise by a faith so sublime :
Far more than the soul's resignation,
  Its glory and triumph are thine !

Can the spirit of sacrifice falter,
  Can Freedom grow pallid again,
When Pain, from her sanctified altar,
  Uplifteth that hallowed "Amen"?

" Amen ! if by new consecration,
  Our hearts with new anguish be torn :
We give the word ' Home ' to our Nation,
  Till of Purity, Peace shall be born."

THE NEW YEAR.

Welcome, New Year ! what hast thou
For the light of heart and brow?
Many an hour with rainbow wings
Gayly tinting earthly things?

Hast thou for the views of youth
Graver shadows cast by truth?
Nay, I fear me they too weave
Webs which could no blast survive !

What of age ! Hath all the past
Taught how temporal glories waste?
Does the dim eye turn from thee,
Asking for eternity?

Answer me, thou New-born Year!
Hast thou most of hope or fear,
Joy or woe, sweet peace or strife,
In thy store for human life?

" Listen! I can only bring
Unto mortals what hath been;
No new mission is mine own,
With no stranger gifts I come.

As on tireless feet I range,
I must scatter, I must change:
Is there gloom in my reply? —
It is life's reality!

I the cherished flower shall crush,
Which hath waked affection's gush!
Make a stream of bitterness,
That which seemed but born to bless!

To the bride whose dreams have won
Fairy visions of her own,
I may bring the grief of life,
Wrung from a neglected wife!

Parents, round whose cheerful board
Laughter's merriest tone was heard,
Now may list the spirit's moan
Of a household broken, — gone!

Where Life's current gladly flows,
Death shall seal a stern repose;
Young and old, the wise and gay,
Swift with me shall pass away!

I new sepulchres shall make
In the heart that pines to break,
As the silent host I swell
With the loved and beautiful!

Many, ay all, all must know
Thousand changes ere I go ;
Not one bosom can retain
Feelings, hopes, and joys the same!

Were the world all happy now,
Sad would be my journey through ;
But where past made desolate,
I shall many a joy create!

Doubts of truth shall pass away,
Souls be knit in constancy, —
Erring ones to virtue turn,
Healing what they've pierced again.

Beauty shall from ashes rise ;
Smiles shall light the weeper's eyes ;
Many a cheek shall gain its bloom ;
Many a heart shall lose its gloom.

Love that could neglect defy, —
Buried love that *would not* die, —
Shall come forth to life renewed,
Bright from tears and solitude!

Hope, that dared not stir its wing,
To its voyage of light shall spring ;
Richest music shall be breathed
From the soul which pain has writhed!

Who that lives would choose to stay
Where, and as they are to-day?
None! for every heart has set
Treasures on the *distant* yet!

Bid me welcome then, though change
Mark my broad and speedy range;
For ye would not ONE be blest,
If the present were your rest!

Higher than the things of time
Bid the undying soul to climb!
Give it strength; the joys of earth;
The deepest note woe utters forth, —

All may purify and bless;
All may fit for happiness
In that land of spirits, where
Never sighs a changing Year!"

STANZAS.

"Thou renewest the face of the earth."

SWEET is the face of earth,
Which God renews again
With the sunbeam's lengthened smile,
And the gently soothing rain!

The laughing waters haste
From Winter's bonds away,
To wake their song of joy
In the valleys where they stray.

The foamy rill will die
To nurse the hidden flower,
Which waits in the bosom of earth,
Like a gem, for her festal hour.

Sweet is the gracious light
Which bids the young blade spring,
And generous is the air
Which buoys the songster's wing.

The heirs of promise doubt
The fruit while the bud is green ;
But the trusting bird will come
When scarce a leaf is seen.

They come, and make their nests,
With songs of gladness now ;
Nor shall they miss reward,
For green will be the bough,

And softly sweet the path,
Through which the rays shall fall,
Led by the graceful leaves,
From their Father's palace-wall.

Oh, earth and sea and air
In the blessèd sun are glad !
The flowers and trees rejoice,
One only thing is sad, —

The heart of its light bereaved
Since last the spring-time came,
Whose fondest hopes have fled,
To return no more again.

Oh! sad indeed it is
To see from the dust appear
All things to life and bloom,
But those which the heart lays there;

'Mid the voices of the loved,
To know that one is hushed;
To sigh 'mid beaming eyes
For those now sealed in dust!

The wild with hope and joy,
And those who prayed release,
Pass on to deep tranquillity,
Where life's strange throbbings cease.

The sunny curls of youth
Are laid as moveless there
As are scattered locks of gray,
Platted by thorny Care.

Oh, earth and sea and air
In the blessèd sun are glad!
The flowers and trees rejoice;
The heart should not be sad.

Shall there not come a Spring
Bright with eternal flowers,
Where the treasures of the soul
Shall be for ever ours?

ONE IN SYMPATHY.

I HAVE been with thee, thou belovèd one,
With trackless footsteps and with voiceless tone,
When slumber's mantle lay about thy heart:
Hast thou not felt its foldings gently start?
   I sighed for thee.

I have been near thee, when, with gladdened light,
The world has beamed, and all within was bright:
I knew its transient radiance, yet I know
The depth to which its milder rays may go, —
   I hoped for thee.

I drew me near thee when thy heaving breast
Betrayed the billows of its wild unrest:
Thy sorrow, whatsoe'er its cause, its course,
I shared in sympathy, and wept its force, —
   I mourned with thee.

I would infold thee, if affliction chill,
Or if temptation, deck the path of ill
With mocking blossoms, which at touching die;
Kindly I'd bend thy step, and point thine eye, —
   I'd watch with thee.

Smile of God's spirit! when, with trusting glance,
Thou cleavest the cloud for thine inheritance,
And, upward tending to the fount above,
Dost consecrate thy life, thy heart, thy love,
   I'd pray with thee.

I would be near thee when life's jewel breaks
From its earth-setting, and the dust forsakes
What it has shrouded, but could never mar, —
The glory of a beaming, quenchless star!
   I'd soar with thee.

I'd dwell with thee beloved in our near home,
One Father and one childhood for our own!
One spirit-note to swell the blissful strain
Of blended life, — " Never to part again
   From Heaven and thee!"

LIFE.

"The everlasting powers are twined into *one* Chord, and that is — LIFE."

LIFE is before us, — of trial and trust, —
A voyage of the spirit, on pinion of dust;
Through clouds, and o'er mountains, unknown till we
 climb,
And the windings of peril beguiling all time!

Life is around us, — temptation and snare;
The fetter of joy and the poison of care;
The music of good and the mocking of ill;
The weakness of wishes, the sternness of will:
The calmness of hope and the tempest of fear;
The surges of passion, the wreck of despair;
The staff of high purpose oft laid in the sand,
For baubles which fancy but offers the hand;
The flowers of beauty, the ashes of death, —
Have met, and are mingled; and this is life's wreath!

Life is within us, — a kingdom of power
Whose strength is increased by the need of the hour :
Life is within us, through trial to trust, —
An heirship of glory, through pathway of dust.
Illusion may wilder ; but truth will reveal,
If, piercing the outward, we seek the ideal
Through the silver-toned whisper outbreathing from
    heaven,
Which an infinite One to the finite hath given.
O mystical book ! where our purposes write
The records of fate with the pencil of light ;
Where hope paints her rainbow, and sorrow her cloud,
Faith her wings of ascension, and terror her shroud ;
Where sadness may gather the folds of despair,
And joy's springs be dried by the furnace of care ;
Where the penitent tear is as bitterly shed
O'er the darkened intent as the day-revealed deed ;
Where love o'er the chaos may brood, and control
The elements' jar to a musical whole ;
And the passions refined in each note may express
The *fulness* of *life* in the anthem of peace !

Is such life within us ? a God-written deep
Which tempest may trouble, yet angels would keep !
How clear should its depths be, — how true to the
    light,
That its waters be never a cradle of night,
But onward to truth, — in the pathway of love,
It may bear back its waves to the ocean above !
Then, ashes of earth into flowers shall spring
To garland eternal the home-cleaving wing ;
All the shadows of life shall in brightness unroll,
And cares stand revealed as the jewels of soul ;
All pure aspirations shall bless as they rise.
For the true voyage of life is with God in the skies !

IT IS BETTER TO BE REMEMBERED IN THE PRAYER OF THE POOR THAN IN THE PRAISES OF THE KING.

Seek ye the Poor:
From cheerful homes go forth,
Ye favored, to the suffering ones of earth ;
While Winter in his sternest mood is found,
Oh, let the summer of the heart abound !

Give to the Poor:
Hath not their toil procured
A thousand blessings for your hearth and board,
Which never come to theirs?   Oh, then, impart
Of your abundance to the sad of heart !

Give to the Poor:
The wealth of harvest came
To gladden all : one fount supplied the rain,
One urn the sunlight, let your mercies spread
The gifts of bounty, God hath richly shed !

Blend with the Poor:
We are one family,
Bound by one Father to one destiny :
Shall darkness, penury, suffering, on our way,
Mar the high claim of our humanity?

Plead for the Poor :
The struggles they o'ercome,
Strangers to wildering want have never known :
Oh, save from sin by charities of Heaven
The oppressed, whose graveward path to gloom is
    given !

Learn from the Poor :
If it be sweet to hear
Praise from the lip, where life hath given cheer,
Hath it not tenfold sweetness, tenfold power,
Where hardship, sorrow, storm, their shadows lower?

Learn from the Poor :
When the full heart is stung
By anxious cares, and every feeling wrung
With sound and sight of woe, *if then there live
Virtue, undimmed, where may she not survive ?*

Learn from the Poor :
The moral light they shed
Shall gather as a halo round thy head ;
For meekness, gratitude, and purity
Glow from the furnace of adversity !

Learn from the Poor :
Glean of their lowliness,
As ye approach them with the wish to bless ;
For gifts that perish with the using, bind
Their humble graces on the heart and mind.

23

THERE IS A MIGHT IN THE PRESENT, OF WHICH WE DREAM NOT TILL IT BE PAST.

To–morrow, ay, *to-morrow* is the time for which we
  live ;
We sow not in the *present*, for the harvest life might
  give ;
And yesterday, ay, *yesterday*, with its varied joy and
  pain,
Distracts us by its shadows, and we dwell in it again :
In listless musing on the past, in thought of what may
  be,
We let life's richest moments fly, uncrowned by victory
O'er passion's fires, o'er fevered hopes, o'er fears that
  storm the soul,
And fancies whose exuberance needs immediate con-
  trol !

Oh ! memory's thousand stores are dear ; and haply
  from the past
Come lessons of experience, with the whispers of the
  lost :
From out that one deep fountain where such bitter
  waters flow
May still be quaffed the sweetest draughts the spirit's
  thirst can know ;
That one word " gone " doth purify the heart's idola-
  tries,
And " never more " impels it on to seek unbreaking
  ties.

And that wide world before us, to which we well may
    bear
The anguish of our bosoms, and lay it trusting there,
Or, from our joyous gladness, anticipate to bless
Those who in quick-toned sympathy would share our
    happiness, —
For these, — for more, — 'tis well indeed the eye should
    onward turn ;
For it lights life's holiest fires, it feeds affection's urn :
The present feels its touch of power, and, like a harp
    new strung,
Gives out deep music from the chords which else had
    silent hung.

A threefold life is ours, — the Past, the Future, and
    the *Now*,
Whereon is written, line by line, our solemn journey
    through :
It is the future realized, it is to-morrows past, —
The bosom of an ebbing stream, whose waves must
    die at last.
It is the field of action where all our duties throng,
Where Virtue gathers priceless pearls to give her
    golden crown :
These are the " few things " given, our living faith to
    prove,
Which shall win from Him who marks it, that highest
    good, — his love !

TO A FRIEND IN SADNESS.

I KNOW that life has never been
  That fairy scene to thee,
Where skies are aye too bright to weep,
  And flowers too fair to die.

For, on thy heart's horizon, oft
  The threatening cloud has hung;
And leaden-footed Care has crushed
  Hope's bright buds as they sprung.

But from the baptism of grief,
  If faith hath risen strong;
And dying flowers have breathed to thee
  That after-life their own;

If friends, the kind, the warm, the true,
  Have been and still are thine, —
Oh! with these jewels spared the heart,
  What can we not resign?

Long may these bless thee! long mayst thou
  Their equal blessing be!
To soothe, to comfort, and to cheer,
  Is no mean destiny.

And for each trial meekly borne,
  Each well-imparted joy,
There beams new lustre on the soul,
  Which time can ne'er destroy.

Thus be ye brightening for that world
Where change can never mar,
Where sorrow could not dare be guest,
Nor bliss be wanderer!

"THE FIRST GRAY HAIR."

To A. S. B.

WHAT meaneth it, — that " silver thread "
Those rich dark locks among,
Had Time no veteran brows to wreathe,
That he must deck thine own?

The roses of youth have not left thy cheek,
Nor the sunlight of life thine eye ;
And still, as in childhood, on thy lip
Doth Joy sit trustingly.

The touch of a spoiler it cannot be ;
For thy heart hath not chilled to care,
And its world of affection is bright and warm :
Then wherefore that " first gray hair"?

It may be that Time hath weary grown
Of waiting till youth goes by,
And would give his honors to worth alone, —
Then — could he have slighted thee?

My hope shall make it an augury ;
My spirit shall breathe its prayer,
That thy years into silver lines may fall,
Like the coming of that gray hair.

Life hath around thee a garland cast
  With buds for an after-bloom ;
Blight be afar from their delicate leaves,
  In that beautiful garden, — home !

The richest blessings to mortals given
  Be ever with thee and thine !
And when age shall have right to thy cheek and brow,
  And thy head wear the crown of Time ;

Then, still as now, may thy treasured ties
  Their strength and their glory bear ;
And thy soul be reflecting a smile as sweet
  As welcomed that " first gray hair " !

TO A FRIEND AT PARTING.

Could human wisdom mark our path,
  Or human wishes bless,
Our skies would have no lowering clouds ;
  Our earth, no wilderness.

No purifying storm would come
  Across the ocean's breast :
To save *one little bark* from harm
  We'd give its billows rest !

'Tis wisely fixed : another's way,
  How dear that other be,
We may not plant with thornless flowers,
  Or I might err for thee,

Making thy life so beautiful,
That thou its chains might love,
Unlinked to·that inheritance
Awaiting thee above!

ELIZA O. SHORES.

BORN SEPT. 14, 1796; DIED FEB. 3, 1863.

---◆---

ON VISITING THE SCENES OF EARLY LIFE.

O scenes, to friends in childhood dear,
In after-life we fondly stray :
But, oh, how sad these scenes appear,
When those loved friends have passed away !

With pensive pleasure we renew
Acquaintance with the dreamy past;
And, as the picture starts to view,
We wish it would for ever last.

We wander o'er the well-known sward
Where we in childhood loved to play ;
Where mother's kiss, that best reward,
Could lure us from our sports away ;

With chastened hearts bend o'er the spot
Where friends beloved now sleep in death.
(No : there the spirit slumbereth not :
'Tis but their dust that rests beneath.)

We seek a flower, — a sprig of green,
Which we, when far away, may view ;
A something to be touched and seen,
That may our early days renew.

This blade of grass, these fading leaves,
Are all the barren sod would yield ;
But to my heart more dear they are
Than gorgeous lilies of the field.

REFLECTIONS ON THE CLOSE OF THE YEAR.

TIME with untiring wing has brought
Another solemn space for thought :
Pause, O my soul ! reflect, and hear
The record of the dying year.
Say, does it speak of duties done,
Temptations met, of victories won?
Of secret sins subdued and slain,
For ever vanquished to remain?
Of love to man, that thinks no ill,
But loves him, though ungrateful still?
Unwearied seeks his present good,
And feeds his soul with lasting food?
Of trust in Heaven, which, firm and sure,
Sees God in all, and rests secure?

Or does the faithful register
Show thee still weak, and prone to err?
Knowing the right, yet following still
The dictates of thy wayward will?

Remiss in duty, far from God,
Unmindful of his gracious word?
Though fair to men, dost thou appear
To God, "a whited sepulchre,"
To whom the unerring Judge will say,
Thou painted hypocrite, away?

Say, O my soul! say, dost thou fear
Time's long and dread account to hear?
If so, arise, repent and pray,
Nor let another New-Year's Day
Find thee still far from God and Heaven,
Thy many sins yet unforgiven;
Awake, and in Christ's strength arise,
And strive to win the immortal prize!

Then, if another dying year,
Shall find thee still a pilgrim here,
Time's record thou mayst hear with joy;
For nought will then thy peace annoy.

· THE HOUR-GLASS.

THE hour-glass on the desk is placed,
    Its sands are gliding through;
And silently, but solemnly,
    It speaks to me and you.
It tells us that our term of *years*
    Is made of fleeting hours,
That soon — ah! soon — they pass away
    As do the early flowers:

That as in youth the sands run slow,
 While we impatient wait,
As life advances, they too glide
 With step accelerate ;
Till, as we near "life's western gate,"
 More swiftly still they run,
As down behind the distant hills
 Swift sinks the setting sun.
A lesson fraught with import may
 Thus to our hearts be given ;
And from the hour-glass we may learn
 To use our time for heaven ;
That when the sands have all run through,
 The spirit's time-work done,
Our souls may rise to glory too,
 As mounts the rising sun.

WILLIAM B. TAPPAN.

BORN IN 1795; DIED IN JULY, 1849.

———◆———

THE OLD NORTH BURIAL GROUND IN PORTS-
MOUTH, N.H.

 STAND where I have stood before in boy-
hood's sunny prime, —
The same, yet not the same, but one who
wears the touch of Time, —
And gaze around on what was then familiar to the
eye,
But whose inconstant features tell that years have
journeyed by,

Since, o'er this venerable ground, a truant child I
played,
And chased the bee and plucked the flower where
ancient dust is laid ;
And hearkened, in my wondering mood, when tolled
the passing bell ;
And started at the coffin's cry as clods upon it fell.

These mossy tombs I recollect, the same o'er which I
    pored ;
The same these rhymes and texts with which my
    memory was stored ;
These humble tokens, too, that lean, and tell where
    resting bones
Are hidden, though their date and name have per-
    ished from the stones.

How rich these precincts with the spoils of ages
    buried here !
What hearts have ached, what eyes have given this
    conscious earth the tear !
How many friends, whose welcome cheered their now-
    deserted doors,
Have, since my last sojourning, swelled these melan-
    choly stores !

Yon spot, where in the sunset ray a single white stone
    gleams,
I've visited, I cannot tell how often, in my dreams, —
That spot o'er which I wept, though then too young
    my loss to know,
As I beheld my father's form sepulchred far below.

How freshly every circumstance, though seas swept
    wide between,
And years have vanished since that hour, in vagaries
    I've seen ! —
The lifted lid, that countenance, the funeral array, —
·As vividly as if the scene were but of yesterday.

How pleasant seem the moments now, as up their
  shadows come,
Spent in the domicile that wore the sacred name of
  home! —
How, in the vista years have made, they shine with
  mellowed light,
To which meridian bliss has nought so beautiful and
  bright!

How happy were those fireside hours, how happy
  summer's walk,
When listening to my father's words, or joining in the
  talk!
How passed like dreams those early hours, till down
  upon us burst
The avalanche of grief, and laid our pleasures in the
  dust!

They tell of loss; but who can tell how thorough is
  the stroke
By which the tie of sire and son in death's for ever
  broke?
They tell of Time! — though he may heal the heart
  that's wounded sore,
The household bliss thus blighted, Time! canst thou
  again restore?

Yet if this spot recalls the dead, and brings from Memory's leaf
A sentence wrote in bitterness, of raptures bright and
  brief,

I would not shun it, nor would lose the moral it will
   give
To teach me, by the withered Past, for better hopes to
   live.

And though to warn of future woe, or whisper future
   bliss,
One comes not from the spirit-world, a witness unto
   this ;
Yet, from memorials of his dust, 'tis wholesome thus
   to learn,
And print upon our thought the state to which we
   must return.

Wherever then my pilgrimage in coming days shall be,
My frequent visions, favorite ground! shall backward
   glance to thee :
The holy dead, the by-gone hours, the precepts early
   given,
Shall sweetly soothe and influence my homeward way
   to heaven.

AN OATH ON WOMAN'S LIPS!

Though pouting out with youth and health,
'Twould blast their rich and tempting red :
I cannot join such living wealth
Of sweets with what is sour and dead. ·

An oath on woman's lips!—let *man*
Touch rudely strings that jar above :
She snaps the cord and breaks the plan
Of Heaven by other word than Love.

An oath on woman's lips!—in vain
Her eyes are starry worlds of light;
Her voice as when soft lyres complain;
Her skin of the celestial white :

'Tis lost to me. She only seems
The twofold wonder fables tell,
That charm and fright the sleeper's dreams, —
An angel, and a fiend of hell.

GETHSEMANE.

'Tis midnight, — and on Olive's brow
The star is dimmed that lately shone ;
'Tis midnight, — in the garden now
The suffering Saviour prays alone.

'Tis midnight, — and, from all removed,
Immanuel wrestles, lone, with fears :
E'en the disciple that he loved
Heeds not his Master's grief and tears.

'Tis midnight, — and for others' guilt
The Man of sorrows weeps in blood ;
Yet He that hath in anguish knelt
Is not forsaken by his God.

'Tis midnight, — from the heavenly plains
Are borne the songs that angels know :
Unheard by mortals are the strains
That sweetly soothe the Saviour's woe.

WALKING ON THE SEA.

TIBERIAS battles with the storm ;
  And hark ! its waters cry
To weeping winds, that answer give
  From out the troubled sky.

And, lo ! upon its raving tide,
  How awfully serene
He walks, who, in the furnace, once,
  Unscathed the " Fourth " was seen.

He walks the waves ! — the rebel waves
  In deep submission lie ;
The wild winds hear his tread, and cease
  When Jesus passes by.

And in my spirit lurks a storm :
  Here chafes the angry sea ;
And wild winds here lift up their voice,
  And rage continually.

Rebuke these waves, Redeemer ! they
  Shall slumber at thy call ;
Oh, move amid these winds ! — the winds
  Shall at thy presence fall !

THERE IS AN HOUR OF PEACEFUL REST.

THERE is an hour of peaceful rest
    To mourning wanderers given ;
There is a joy for souls distressed ;
A balm for every wounded breast, —
    'Tis found alone in Heaven.

There is a soft, a downy bed,
    Far from these shades of even ;
A couch for weary mortals spread,
Where they may rest the aching head,
    And find repose — in Heaven.

There is a home for weary souls
    By sin and sorrow driven ;
When tossed on Life's tempestuous shoals,
Where storms arise, and ocean rolls,
    And all is drear, — 'tis Heaven.

There Faith lifts up her cheerful eye,
    To brighter prospects given,
And views the tempest passing by,
The evening shadows quickly fly,
    And all serene in Heaven.

There fragrant flowers immortal bloom,
    And joys supreme are given ;
There rays divine disperse the gloom :
Beyond the confines of the tomb
    Appears the dawn of Heaven.

FOR AMERICA.

God of earth, the only Ruler,
 Why should earth forget thee so?
God of nations, shall the nations
 Thee, their only Ruler, know?

Old dominions, proud dominions,
 How they rose, the boast of men!
But they knew not God, and therefore
 Sank they into dust again.

Where art thou, imperial Tyre, —
 City from the ocean won?
Hundred-gated Thebes and Memphis,
 Nineveh and Babylon?

God, how slow to learn are nations!
 Else should *we* have spelled thy name, —
In their end have read thine anger:
 Grant that ours be not the same!

New Republics, great Republics,
 Homes of free and fearless men,
As the ancient, proud dominions,
 Thou wilt sink to dust again,

If they know thee not. O Ruler,
 Let not *ours* forget Thee so;
God of nations, let our nation
 Thee, its only Ruler, know!

THE WEST.

Valley of the Mississippi.

O ʏᴇ to whom God's word reveals its privileges blest,
Who hold the pearl without a price, — think, think
    upon the West!
And think, as every precious boon of Heaven comes
    up in view,
Of those that dwelt where now ye dwell, that wor-
    shipped once with you.
For we have left our sunbright homes, the scenes of
    early day,
Our pleasant hearths, and all we loved, to wander far
    away
In wilds where voice of Sabbath bell breaks not upon
    the air ;
Where lifted not are hands in praise, nor bent the knee
    in prayer ;
And where come o'er the laboring heart its white-
    winged, happy hours,
While warm tears gush, a tribute given to light that
    once was ours.
O ye who prize the heavenly light lit up within the
    breast,
Think what it is to mourn it quenched ; oh, think
    upon the West!

The past! — we fain would dwell upon the pages of
    the past,
Though sad it is to read of joys too beautiful to last ;

Yet we will yield in thought again unto his fond
 caress,
Who listened to our lisping prayer, and said that God
 would bless ;
Ay, and we feel the mother's kiss, which only she
 could give,
When teaching us to bow the heart to Him who bade
 us live :
We think, too, of the white-haired man who chid our
 careless youth,
And well remember where his lips dropped sacred
 words of truth,
And sadly comes to aching thought, with memory's
 quickened power,
The Bible class, the Sunday school, and Prayer's
 rejoicing hour !
O ye who revel in their light, who hear the gospel
 blest,
Give praise to God, and succor here, — oh, think upon
 the West !

Here, where tall forests wave their tops, the wild beast
 hath his den ;
The eagle hath her eyry built, unknown to steps of
 men ;
And small birds hang their mossy nests on many a
 branching limb,
And yield, at evening's peaceful hour, their pure and
 joyous hymn :
But rise for us no temple-walls, nor points the spire to
 heaven,
And many faint for Bread of Life, — to break it none
 are given !

Oft, too, by men who lust for gain, these solitudes are
    trod,
Who cast off fear, refrain from prayer, foes to them-
    selves and God :
The stillness of these lovely vales is broken by their
    curse ;
By reckless sires the children led, soon wax from bad
    to worse.
O ye that hail the Sabbath morn, ye with the Bible
    blest,
Speed, speed the Rose of Sharon here, to blossom in
    the West !

THE ANGEL'S WING.

There is a German tradition, that, when a sudden silence takes place in a company, an angel at that moment makes a circuit among them ; and the first person
who breaks the silence is supposed to have been touched by the wing of the passing seraph.

AND why should Wisdom smile at this?
   Are not those perfect beings nigh,
To witness and to share our bliss,
   To hear and hush the secret sigh?
Yes : they may heaven's solace bring ;
Then scorn not thou the Angel's Wing !

Thou who, alone, thyself dost deem
   A solitary in thy grief, —
List ! soft as footfall of a dream
   Comes one to bear thee sweet relief ;
And fled is all thy hoarded care :
The passing Seraph's Wing is there !

Thou who, forgiven, dost possess
  The penitent's intense delight,
When the dark cloud of guilt's distress
  Reveals to thee its edge of light, —
Think, as unhallowed tempests fly,
Thy soul is touched, the Wing is nigh!

And thou of contemplative mood,
  Who dost at eve in wild-woods stray,
Where nought of this world may intrude,
  When fancy might in others play;
And hearest the voice that zephyr flings, —
No! 'tis the rush of Angel Wings.

Oh! I have paused a space as 'twere
  Bewildering thoughts to gather up,
To put aside the draught of Care,
  And taste of Mind's exalted cup;
Nor knew what o'er my soul could bring
Such calmness, — 'twas the Seraph's Wing.

When brooding tempters caused me shame,
  And, in its company of sin,
My spirit sat, the Angel came,
  And swept with wings the heart within;
A moment made its circuit there,
And broke my silence into prayer.

I knelt beside my precious boy,
  Who went at childhood's fairy time, —
My hope, my life, my being's joy, —
  From this to Love's unclouded clime;
And, while around wept pitying men, .
Rejoiced, — the Angel touched me then!

And at my own departing hour,
  When earth recedes and follies fly,
To comfort me with heavenly power
  Descend! some Herald of the sky;
And, while of victory I sing,
Bear me away on upward wing!

THE NATIVITY.

Judæa's plains in silence sleep
Beneath the cloudless midnight sky,
And o'er their flocks the shepherds keep
Kind watch, to David's city nigh:
That royal city! — nobler Guest
Is she awhile to entertain
Than proudest monarch, whose behest
It is o'er earthly realms to reign.
By him salvation is to mortals given,
On earth is shed the peerless noon of Heaven.

For, see! along the deep-blue arch
A glory breaks; and now a throng,
From where the sparkling planets march,
Comes trooping down with shout and song;
And o'er those pastures, bathed in light,
The sacred legions stay their wing,
While on the wakeful ear of Night
Steals the rich hymn that seraphs sing.
And sweetly thus the mellow accents ran,
" Glory to God, good-will and peace to man! "

WAKE, ISLES OF THE SOUTH.

Written November, 1819, on occasion of the departure from the United States of
the first Missionary band for the Sandwich Islands.

WAKE, Isles of the South! your redemption is near;
No longer repose on the borders of gloom :
The Strength of His chosen in love will appear,
And light shall arise on the verge of the tomb.

The billows that gird ye, the wild waves that roar,
The zephyrs that play when the ocean-storms cease,
Shall bear the rich freight to your desolate shore,
Shall waft the glad tidings of pardon and peace.

On the Islands that sit in the regions of night,
The lands of despair, to oblivion a prey,
The morning will open with healing and light,
The glad Star of Bethlehem will usher the Day.

The altar and idol in dust overthrown,
The incense forbade that was offered in blood,
The Priest of Melchizedek there shall atone,
And the shrines of Hawaii be sacred to God!

The Heathen will hasten to welcome the time
The day-spring the prophet in vision once saw,
When the beams of Messiah shall gladden each clime,
And the Isles of the Ocean shall wait for his law.

And thou, Obookiah! now sainted above,
Wilt rejoice as the heralds their mission disclose ;
And the prayer will be heard that the land thou didst
      love
May blossom as Sharon, and bud as the Rose!

THE THUNDER-STORM.

THE storm is up! — along the sky
Swiftly the ebon rack is driven ;
And, look! yon curling cloud floats nigh,
Charged with the panoply of heaven ;
It rends, and, gathering to a heap,
Of angry billows takes the form :
How troubled is that upper deep !
God! thou art awful in thy storm.

'Tis past, — and, see! o'er fields again
Sunbeams their laughing light unfold ;
On tower and tree the sparkling rain
Drops like a shower of molten gold ;
On yonder hill-top rests the bow,
The air is redolent of balm :
How bright is all above, below !
God! thou art glorious in thy calm.

So when the tempest shrouds my skies,
And grief holds empire in my soul,
I see the desolation rise,
The waves already o'er me roll :
Thou speak'st, and, like a tender sire,
Thou dost thy child's frail fears reprove.
Lofty art thou when storms retire :
God! thou art dearer in thy love.

JAMES P. WALKER.

—◆—

SEVEN YEARS TO-DAY.

IS seven years, my love, to-day,
 Since, hand in hand, we started,
In faith, to tread life's devious way,
 Till we by death are parted.

And, God be thanked!—though Fortune's smile
 Our pathway has not lighted;
And many hopes, indulged long while,
 Have ruthlessly been blighted,—

We're spared to one another yet,
 And blessed with "troops of friends;"
No daily want has not been met;
 And, thanks to Him who sends

Life's choicest blessings,—love and hope!
 We are stronger now to bear,
And abler with life's ills to cope,
 Than if we'd known no care.

And though those ills we may not cure,
  Nor taste unanxious rest,
With the " kings and priests of literature "
  Our constant welcome guests, —

With childhood's laugh, domestic peace,
  And ready willing hands,
We murmur not, though no increase
  Is ours, of " house or lands."

MARCH 17, 1859.

NEW FRIENDS AND OLD.

An Album Dedication.

As the generous fruit of the vine
Is enriched by added years ;
As fire will gold refine,
Till each vestige of dross disappears :
    So time is the lover's test ;
    And the heats of adversity prove
    That old and tried friends are the best,
    However our fancy may rove.

As of flowers the odor is sweetest,
While still with the morning dew wet ;
And, of the family group, it is meetest
That the youngest should ever be pet :
    So fresh love some chord may awaken
    Which vibrated never before ;
    And to hearts which bereavement hath shaken,
    New friendship lost peace may restore.

Then we'll cordially welcome the new,
While yet firmly retaining the old;
Let fortune prove fickle or true,
We have treasures more precious than gold.
    But the future we may not command,
    And the past to the present gives place;
    Death stiffens the readiest hand,
    And darkness the sunniest face:

Since the substance so surely must fade,
At least let the shadow be spared;
And here let the record be made
Of delights which affection hath shared.
    No vain tribute to beauty or pride,
    Which melt at the touch of old age,
    But TO VIRTUE AND WORTH, which abide,
    WE DEDICATE EVERY PAGE.

NECESSITIES AND LUXURIES.

"Give me but the luxuries of life, I will do without the necessities."

How needs of sense and senseless needs
    Enthrall our human kind!
The nobler wants, alas! who pleads,
    Of heart, or taste, or mind?

The claims of appetite, and all
    That helps the body's ease,
Necessities of life we call;
    All else, its *luxuries.*

What fashion dictates or decrees
　In manners, dress, or home,
Are manifest necessities ;
　And luxury must succumb.

For luxuries of art, too poor !
　Necessities take all :
Persian or Brussels on the floor,
　And nothing on the wall !

An idle luxury to read ;
　To spend for books a sin :
Small care, so fashion *cover* the head,
　How empty 'tis *within !*

That hospitality's too great
　A luxury, we own,
Unless the necessary plate
　And china can be shown.

Must social life become a cheat,
　And friendship a pretence !
Measured by what one has to eat,
　And governed by expense !

Might not a cultivated mind,
　An hospitable heart,
The treasures of a taste refined,
　Enable one to part

With e'en some " necessary " things,
　Deemed such by shallow pride?
These needs of life oft take to wings,
　While luxuries abide.

Be to your friends a feast yourself,
  When any chance to call ;
Have " Lamb " and " Bacon " on the *shelf*,
  And " plates " upon the wall :

Then, though your larder should be lean,
  All your appointments plain,
Play thou the host with mind serene :
  Be sure they'll come again !

The luxuries of life grant me, —
  An understanding mind,
A heart to feel, an eye to see
  Beauties of every kind :

From those whose fadeless glories bright
  The universe adorn, .
The matchless wonders of the night,
  The splendors of the morn,

The emerald turf, the towering tree,
  Bird, insect, flower, and vine,
The placid lake, the boundless sea,
  Symbol of love divine :

To those of literature and art,
  Painted or pictured thought,
The subtler beauties of the heart
  With noble deeds inwrought.

Possessed of these, I'm rich indeed ;
  And well may I despise
The claims of fashion, sense, or greed, —
  All *false* " necessities."

TO LILLIE G——.

DEAR LILLIE, I've read your Album through,
From titlepage to " finis ; "
I find you're " fair " and " wise " and " true,"
" Good-tempered," " loving," " guileless."

I find no end of wishes kind,
No lack of blessings prayed for ;
Which clearly prove your friends not blind
To what an Album's made for.

Have admonitions, ranging, say, —
Diverse opinion showing, —
From " Gather ye rosebuds while ye may,"
To " Now's the time for sowing."

Abundant store of cautions, too,
Of warning, hint, suggestion,
And all that sage advice can do
To produce a moral congestion.

To all this store of kindly phrase,
Heaped in o'erflowing measure,
My friend, what word of mine, or praise,
Can magnify your treasure?

In vain I search with anxious care,
No love can better the best :
Be this my comprehensive prayer
" AMEN TO ALL THE REST ! "

TO MY WIFE.

With a Seal-ring, enclosing two Locks of Hair.

Accept, dear wife, this token
Of the living and the lost,
And cherish in remembrance
Of the two who love you most.

Purer than its crystal,
More precious than the gold,
Is her memory that tenderly
Within our hearts we hold.

MRS. CAROLINE E. WHITON.

—◆—

MAY.

II! the air is laden with a rich perfume
  From a shower of blossoms prophesying
     June;
  And the sweet anemones, hidden where they
     grow,
Kiss the purple violets with their lips of snow:
From the damp earth rises vapor full of Spring;
And a perfect freshness is on every thing.

Beautifully azure is the sky serene;
Only a few fleecy, floating clouds are seen;
And the soft wind stirring, playing in the trees,
Makes the sunshine ripple into golden seas;
And the lights and shadows seem to rise and fall
With the pulse of Nature beating through it all.

And the distant spires, catching up the light,
Flash a crystal glory on my dazzled sight:
I can see the river sparkling in the sun,
And the distant hill-tops, rearing one by one:
Full of wonder stand I, drinking in the whole,
While a flood of silence falls upon my soul.

From the waving pine-trees to the waving grass,
I can see the squirrels as they downward pass;
And the early robin, stretching out its wings,
Shaking off the dewdrops as it soaring sings;
And the gurgling waters, running cool and sweet,
Drop their silver music at my lingering feet.

In the deepest shadow of a leafy dell,
Something seems to murmur like the sighing of a shell:
Perhaps it is the petals, bursting into sight,
Ringing out their odors with a soft delight;
Or, perhaps, the bushes on the mossy ground,
When their leaves entangle, shiver into sound.

Hark! the undertone is swelling up to me,
Swelling through the silence like a distant sea;
Waves in solemn surges break upon the shore,
In eternal motion beating evermore:
Through the distance look I, but I look in vain;
This mysterious murmur I cannot explain.

Be the revelation whatsoe'er it may,
I have lived a life-time in one perfect day.
May preludes the Summer, so the poets sing;
But my heart is beating to the heart of Spring:
Hush! the tears are falling; but they fall, I see,
Into countless prisms, catching light from *thee*.

With a rainbow glory always on my sky,
Springs may bloom and wither, *this one cannot die;*
Never day in Summer can be half as bright,
Never fall of music as ecstatic quite:
In this one sweet picture all the tints are *fast;*
It will live for ever; *Heaven* will touch it *last*.

SUMMER SUNSET.

I watched the golden Summer sun
    Fade slowly down behind the sea, —
God's token that the day was done
    In crimson flushing left to me.

Fainter and fainter grew the skies ;
    My heart was dropping noiseless tears :
For, ah ! I thought of closing eyes,
    Whose lids I have not kissed for years.

Oh ! softly as the setting sun,
    My darlings sank behind the sea, —
God's token that his peace was won,
    The looks of glory left to me.

By that seraphic light which fell
    Ineffably divine and sweet,
I know, beyond the soul's farewell,
    Behind the sea, that we shall meet.

AUTUMN SUNSET.

There is a pathos in the Autumn sun,
    That reddens as it lingers in the west ;
And gorgeous leaves, that, crimsoning one by one,
    Drop slowly into rest.

The tops of silver poplars, and the elms,
  Are lifted into such a rapturous glow,
It seems as if from some enchanted realms
    The light had dropped below.

The dying flush that bathes the hills serene,
  And leaves a purple glory on the sky,
Is like the rapture that is often seen
    Ere immortality.

The leaves so crisp, that rustle to the ground,
  Are like the requiems of the soul's farewell:
The light that gilds them is the hope profound
    That whispers, All is well.

Oh! as I watch the Autumn fires arise,
  And spread in sweeping splendor through the west,
My soul is sure, beyond the purple skies
    That there is perfect rest.

MY FLOWERS.

I HAVE three flowers as fresh and bright
  As ever heart could wear;
A Morning-glory and a Rose,
  A Lily white and fair.
They cluster round me in the morn,
  With petals opening sweet;
And the first sounds that greet mine ear
  Are sounds of little feet.

My Rose has large brown eyes that look
  As limpid as a stream:
They always wear a softened light
  As tender as a dream;
They make me think of moonlights past,
  When youth was in its flush,
Whose waves of glory, as they fell,
  Dropped with a silver hush.

Her smile is beautiful and rare,
  Toned down from childish mirth,
Just as the calm uprising
  Of a star above the earth:
Her little heart is so mature,
  Her love so warm and deep,
I sometimes think my peerless Rose
  I may not always keep.

My Morning-glory has a face
  Just like an April day:
The sunlight catches up the rain,
  And dries it all away;
It ripples into winsome smiles,
  It sparkles into glee,
Yet has an earnest depth behind,
  That loving eyes may see.

My Lily with her baby hands
  Is clinging to my fold;
The sunshine on her silken hair
  Makes shining waves of gold;
Her eyes are fringed forget-me-nots,
  Just shaking off the dew,
As if remembrance of the skies
  Had left its trace of blue.

I have three clustering flowers on earth
    That blossom fresh and fair ;
And two I would not dare describe,
    Unless it were in prayer :
Yet sometimes, when the others lead
    My Lily unto me,
I think that *those* two lilies crowned
    May crown these other three.

INDIAN SUMMER.

AT the open window I sit, and see
The gorgeous clouds that are passing by ;
And the soft south air is bringing to me
Perfumes as sweet as in June buds lie ;
Even the bees are humming to-day ;
And I catch the sound of children at play.

Did I not see the changing leaves
Brilliant in coloring as the sky,
And the reapers binding their golden sheaves,
I should say the Summer had not gone by :
It seems as if Nature had paused to think,
Before it should reach October's brink.

But, with every breath of the scented breeze,
There is rustling down a withered leaf ;
And I hear the sighing among the trees,
That is like the prelude to bitterest grief ;
And, though the sun shines with a splendor like June,
By this I should know 'tis a Fall afternoon.

At the open window I sit, and see
Clouds that are passing, hopes that are past;
And the soft south air is bringing to me
Memories crowding thick and fast;
And some of the dreams I recall to-day
Are swept like the withered leaves rustling away.

At the open window I still remain;
And my soul is vainly trying to see,
Over the losses, on to the gain;
Knowing how much that gain would be.
Teach me, oh teach me, how to wait
For the Summer so endless, — Heaven so great!

THE LOST VERSE.

I was writing a poem the other day,
When one of the verses slipped away.
I have searched every corner of my brain
For the missing verse, but all in vain!
Not a word or a rhyme can I recall:
It fell just as snow-flakes sometimes fall,
That are melted before they reach the ground;
And so, as *snow-flakes*, are never found.

The snow-flakes form into drops of rain:
Perhaps the verse is still in my brain,
But melted, by some mysterious heat,
Into a vapor, yet just as complete;
Perhaps an angel, when passing by,
Breathed it away while breathing a sigh:
But the poem I write will never be
Finished without that verse to me.

Oh, *this* is but one of my losses here :
I have lost many thoughts that were shining clear ;
I have looked at my treasure, and found — the rust ;
I have gathered my dreams, but they fell to dust ;
I have seen the flowers belonging to Spring
Withered before their blossoming.
I have seen all these losses ! Is it in vain?
Shall I reap in a harvest of *tares* — or of *grain?*

Yet *nothing* is lost. 'Tis our dimness of sight :
What looks like the shadow may still be the light ;
What seems in the dark like our heaviest pain,
When brought to the light, may be glorious gain.
What if the angel breathing the sigh
Carried my verse *up* — up to the sky?
Oh ! when Life's poem perfected shall be,
All of the missing lines shall we not see,
And reap in one harvest — *eternity?*

————

OUR COUNTRY.

HAIL ! men of the North so loyal and true,
The strength of the Union is vested in you :
With courage your armor, and right for your shield,
Face traitor and foe, if you die on the field :
Strike, freeman ! the flag that waves over your head
Is red as your heart's blood, and white as your dead ;
But let it wave not o'er a nation of slaves :
Better, O men of the North, in your graves !

O flag of our Union, raised proudly on high !
We welcome your rainbows that cross in our sky ;
But the foe who has trampled it down to the ground,
Let him lie in the place where the relics are found.
Up, men of the North ! ye are mighty and strong :
Strike boldly to crush down oppression and wrong ;
Let the boom of the cannon be Slavery's knell ;
Strike, freeman ! for country and honor as well.

Here, men of the North, have brave men been bred !
The pilgrims, your fathers, are honored, though dead ;
And the blood you inherit you will not disgrace :
Wipe the dust, O New England ! from Liberty's face ;
Strike ! the Lord God of battle will hinder you not ;
Leave the page of our history free from a blot ;
Leave the stars on our banner undimmed as our fame ;
O men of New England ! wash out every stain.

Hail, men of New England ! the flag you uphold,
O'er a nation of freemen, oh, let it unfold !
Let the crimson that stripes it foretell, in the sky,
The flush, in the East, of Liberty nigh :
Then white, in the dawn of our Country's release,
Shall the silvery stars light the banner of Peace ;
And the waves of our freedom, as white on the shore
Swelling up into Heaven, be broken no more.

WE ARE THREE.

BEAT, O November rain! to-night I cannot sleep :
Within my throbbing heart is stirred a memory deep ;
I live again those years, when, sharing joy and pain,
We three beneath one roof were listening to the rain ;
But now we are but two, and we two live apart :
Beat, O November rain! to sobbing of my heart.

Beat, O November rain! in youth's seraphic hope,
We only saw the light, where now we blindly grope ;
We only saw the sea in glittering surges swell,
Where now its turbid waves are beating a farewell ;
O youth, for ever dead! I measure back, and see,
By this great sense of pain, how dearly loved we three.

Beat, O November rain! I cannot sleep to-night :
One, weary of the strife, went drifting out of sight ;
On her majestic peace we looked with blinding eyes,
Yet knew in skies afar she saw the white dawn rise.
O bridge that she has crossed! O changing, restless
    sea !
Only us two are left, and yet we number three.

Beat, O November rain! we surely number three ;
For Death is but a strain of minor harmony :
I listen as to hear an echo from that shore
Where Love's celestial song is rising evermore ;
Where neither sea nor change can keep us three apart,
And Heaven shall *more than* still this sobbing of my
    heart.

MY NEIGHBOR.

My neighbor's voice is very sweet,
　My neighbor's words are very true ;
She never seems to have to beat
　Against the tide, as many do.
Her ways are winning as her face ;
　She wears a look of high repose,
As though her soul had conquered space,
　　　　And lost — its woes.

Her eyes are full of softened light,
　Her smiles are gentle and serene ;
And something stately in her height
　Gives certain stateliness of mien.
Her thoughts, I know, are sanctified,
　Like one whose doubtings can but cease,
Because she sees the *other* side,
　　　　And knows its peace.

Her nature is so purely calm,
　I often envy its repose,
Like the perfections of a psalm
　That leaves us holier at its close ;
That, written on the grandest key
　And sung with grandest words and choir,
Inspires us, with its majesty,
　　　　To something higher.

To me, whose changes are as great
   As Summer's sky and Winter's woe,
This calm is a mysterious state
   Past comprehending ; but I know
Her friendship is a steadfast thing,
   Her love an offering as complete
As when the flowers their odors fling,
      Yet still are sweet.

I know, too, that her soul is high ;
   I see it shining on her face,
And, like a halo from the sky,
   Invests her with a tender grace ;
And, waiting, sometime she will touch
   That " other side " we now foretell ;
And so, because she " loved so much,"
      All will be well.

MRS. JULIA VAN NESS WHIPPLE.

—◆—

THE VOICE AMID THE TREES.

AS I sit beside my window,
    On this summer eve so fair,
Oft I hear, amid the stillness,
    Whisperings borne upon the air,
Gently swelling, and then dying
    'Mid the leaves on yonder tree :
Sweet the words, though mostly sad ones,
    That they whisper unto me !

Softly sighing, — now it brings me
    Cherished memories of the past,
Sunny childhood's happy hours,
    Girlhood's joys, — too bright to last.
Dear loved voices, long since silent,
    Seem to speak again to me,
As I listen to the murmuring
    'Mid the leaves of yonder tree.

As it speaks, my tears are falling
    For the dearly loved and gone ;
And the shadows seem to darken,
    That across my path are thrown ;
'Still your whispering ! O sad voices,
    'Mid the leaves of yonder tree,
If you bear with you no healing
    For those memories sad to me.

Hark ! again the voice is speaking ;
    Soft and gently sweet 'tis now ;
And methinks the wings of angels
    Gently fan my burning brow.
Why so grieving, so despairing?
    Why so weary on thy road?
Think, O child ! thy path of sorrow
    Is to bring thee closer God.

Dry thy tears for the departed ;
    Weep not for the living dead ;
Strong and firm be in thy duty ;
    Follow where thy Saviour led.
When sad memories throng around you,
    Meet them not with murmuring sigh ;
Listen to the voice that's with you,
    Saying, — " Fear not : it is I."

Thus it is those gentle voices,
    'Mid the leaves on yonder tree,
On this soft sweet summer evening,
    Have been whispering unto me.

WINTER.

Aha ! Old King with the hoary brow,
You are making yourself right busy now ;
You have shaken your locks o'er mountain and dale,
From the loftiest peak to the lowliest vale.

Old Boreas obeys your kingly call,
And comes from his bleak old northern hall :
He makes himself heard by rich and poor,
At the lowly cot and the palace-door.

But, nevertheless, ye frosty twain
Bring comfort and pleasure in your train :
Hurrah, hurrah, for the gay sleigh-ride,
And the calmer joys of the fireside !

The fair young belle hails with delight
Your drifts of snow so soft and white ;
And joy is seen in her merry glance,
For this is the time for the merry dance.

And the schoolboy shouts aloud with glee,
Oh, the Winter, the Winter's the time for me !
And he builds himself a snowy fort,
Oh ! this is the time for the schoolboy's sport.

But we must not think that *all* is mirth ;
There is many a cold and cheerless hearth :
Oh ! forget not the words once spoken to thee,
" As ye do unto them, so ye do unto Me."

EASTER SUNDAY.

ALL hail! great Queen of days,
  Type of that glorious morn
When death shall at the last yield up
  His captives held so long ;
When, from the grave's cold bed,
  The awakened sleepers rise
To join the rapturous song that bursts
  Triumphant from the skies.

The Lenten Fast is o'er ;
  The Church bids one and all
To hasten to her holy courts,
  To keep High Festival.
Thy call, dear mother Church,
  We joyfully obey,
At Advent, Christmas, Lenten Time,
  And glorious Easter Day.

We dry our falling tears,
  And join, with glad accord,
The song triumphant that proclaims
  The Church's risen Lord :
Christ from the dead is raised,
  And death's dread power is o'er ;
The grave henceforth is but the path
  That leads to heaven's bright shore.

26

And we, his followers here,
  Need dread that path no more ;
Knowing, though dark may seem the way,
  Our Lord has passed before.
Children of his dear Church,
  Bought with his precious blood,
Only our bodies sleep in earth,
  Our spirits rest with God.

Gladly, O blessèd Lord !
  We follow on thy way :
Oh ! tune our hearts to gladsome praise
  On this bright Easter Day.
Be with us while we live,
  Be with us when we die ;
Raise us on Resurrection morn,
  To reign with thee on high !

S. ADAMS WIGGIN.

— ◆ —

L O V E.

 HIS morn I wandered in the wood,
   And asked a wild-bird free,
Where dwells true love, — the highest good ;
   And he carolled thus to me :

Love is thy holy Paraclete,
   To comfort and sustain :
To make thy life with joy replete,
   And Eden bloom again.

Love is the harp of David, sweet,
   To calm your wild despair,
And lay your soul at Jesus' feet,
   An offering pure and fair.

Love is the " Holy of Holies " fane,
   Where burns the sacred flame
That frees the heart from every stain
   Of sorrow, guilt, or shame.

Love is the bearing of the cross,
    Christ's easy yoke to wear,
To count for him all things but dross,
    So you his " crown " may wear.

For Love is God, and God is Love :
    In him find all thy rest :
Centre thy hopes on things above,
    And *Love* shall fill thy breast.

Love wings thy flight to realms of light ;
    Love opes the " gate " for thee ;
Love decks in robes of spotless white.
    With palms of victory.

This is the song the wild-bird free
    Warbled in tuneful strains :
My soul was cheered, bent was the knee ;
    My heart the song retains.

VICTORY.

On to victory ! is the watchword :
    Hear the pæan grand
Throbbing at the hearts of freemen,
    Ringing through the land !

On to victory ! friends and brothers,
    Gird ye for the fight :
Our proud flag shall float for ever
    With its starry light.

On to victory!   Right must triumph
  Over all its foes ;
Freedom's onward march shall usher
  Peace and sweet repose.

Boston: Printed by John Wilson and Son.